A WOMAN'S SCREAM PIERCED THE CITY'S SILENCE

⚜ ⚜ ⚜

Duncan's heart seemed to freeze at the sound, but not his feet. He was running even before the thought could form.

He ran toward the city gates that had been closed and barred against invasion. But no—one side stood open to the road. And in its frame played a scene from the mouth of Hell.

A girl, a creature of love and tenderness, struggled with a man. His upraised hand gripped an odd-shaped sword; even from the distance Duncan could see the blood on the blade. With all the strength of her slender body, the girl was holding against him. Duncan pushed his body to its limit and beyond, but they were so far away—too far away.

The man looked straight at Duncan. An odd smile twisted his face. Suddenly Duncan knew what was to come.

The cry began in the pit of his stomach. The war cry of his clan, a sound as untamed as the hills that gave it birth, poured from Duncan's throat. Two hundred years of civilization fell away with the sound . . .

W9-DHI-406

Also in the Highlander Series:

HIGHLANDER™

THE PATH

A NOVEL BY
REBECCA NEASON

ASPECT®

WARNER BOOKS

A Time Warner Company

WARNER BOOKS EDITION

Warner Books, Inc.
1271 Avenue of the Americas
New York, NY 10020

Visit our Web Site at
http://pathfinder.com/twep

Ⓦ A Time Warner Company

Printed in the United States of America

First Printing: August, 1997

10 9 8 7 6 5 4 3 2 1

Chapter One

Duncan MacLeod smiled as he raised a glass of orange juice toward his lips. Some mornings were better than others, and this had been one of the good ones.

He had begun his day with an hour of *kata,* both sword form and open hand, pushing himself through the stylized movements until his body warmed and his mind focused. For over two hundred years this had been his way of putting the mundane concerns of daily life into perspective; it was his path to the balance he needed to survive his Immortality.

Suddenly, the presence of another Immortal seared through MacLeod like the blare of a trumpet felt in the bones. His hand went to the hilt of his *katana,* the Japanese samurai sword that was never far from his side. His muscles tensed, ready to spring into the action of survival as his eyes swept across his familiar surroundings, automatically checking defensive positions and strategies.

A second later a voice reached him. "Hey, Mac—Mac, you home?"

As quickly as it had come, the tension drained from MacLeod's body and he smiled again, not bothering to answer. By now Richie would have felt MacLeod's presence the same way Duncan felt his, the way one Immortal always sensed another.

The old-fashioned freight elevator connecting the dojo and the apartment started to rattle; Richie was on his way up. From the sound of his voice he was excited about something. But then, MacLeod thought, Richie was always excited about something. That was his age, or rather, that was his youth.

Richie was a young Immortal, new to the Game, and his age still matched his physical appearance. He looked to be, and was, a well-built young man in his early twenties. MacLeod, on the other hand, looked in his thirties, maybe thirty-five, but the reality was quite different.

Duncan MacLeod was four hundred years old.

Whether thirty-five or four hundred, MacLeod looked good for his age. Some of his appearance—the thick dark hair he usually kept pulled back in a ponytail, the heavy-lidded dark eyes that flashed beneath thick lashes, the high cheekbones and strong chin—were genetics, and he could take no credit for them. But the sleek, well-toned body, the broad shoulders, muscular chest, stomach, and thighs, the balance and catlike grace were all things he worked hard to maintain. It was not vanity, it was survival—a sloppy Immortal lost his head.

The elevator stopped. Richie opened the slatted wooden door and stepped out into Duncan's apartment. It was as though a wave of energy crested through the confined space, sparking out of his hazel eyes and the curls of his light reddish brown hair. MacLeod turned to look at the young man who was his student, and his friend.

"Hey, Mac," Richie said, "I've got something you're going to love."

"And what's that?" MacLeod asked, his smile not quite hiding the cynicism in his voice. Richie's idea of fun was sometimes as far removed from MacLeod's as, well, as their generations. Centuries apart.

"You know there's this big rally down at the stadium tomorrow?" Richie walked over to the counter and poured himself a glass of juice from the pitcher MacLeod had left sitting there.

"I've heard about it," Duncan replied.

"Well, I got us tickets."

He looked at MacLeod, full of self-congratulatory smiles, obviously waiting for Duncan's enthusiasm to match his own. But MacLeod just shook his head slightly and turned back to his half-finished breakfast.

"I don't think so, Richie," he said.

"Oh, come on, Mac—I thought this was just the sort of thing you'd love. You know, world peace, brotherhood of man . . ."

"Look, Richie," MacLeod said as he forked up the last piece of egg on his plate. "I think it's great that you want to go, but I don't think it's a good idea for me."

MacLeod stood and carried his plate to the sink, trying to ignore Richie's disappointed expression. Richie's face was always expressive; it could go from one extreme to the other and back again in an instant. MacLeod had ceased letting himself be influenced by it. Most of the time, anyway. Seeing that, Richie changed his tactics.

"I don't get it, Mac," he said. "I mean, the Dalai Lama's the main speaker at this rally, and even *I* know who he is."

"Then you should definitely go hear him, but count me out."

MacLeod headed for the elevator. Downstairs at the back of the dojo was his office and some paperwork he had promised himself he would finish today—and he had a new member due in an hour. It was days like today when he most missed Charlie's deft hand at running the dojo. Duncan knew his friend was doing something he believed in, but in the three weeks since Charlie had left for the Balkans, the rhythm of the dojo had changed—and MacLeod found he missed Charlie's style of in-your-face caring.

Richie followed MacLeod into the elevator. As soon as the door closed, he started in again.

"What am I missing here, Mac? You can't mean it's *because* of the Dalai Lama you won't go to the peace rally?"

"That's right."

"But he's one of the 'Great Men of Our Time,' isn't he? I mean everyone respects him—except, maybe, the Chinese government that exiled him. Even living in exile he keeps working for world peace. I thought you'd want to go hear him. He talks about a lot of the same stuff you do."

"If we talk about the same thing, why do I need to go hear him?" MacLeod countered with a smile as they stepped off the elevator. "Let it go, Richie."

It was a vain hope, and MacLeod knew it even as he said it. Richie never let anything drop until his curiosity was satisfied—or he got his way.

MacLeod walked into his office and took the seat behind the desk. Again Richie followed him. He paced restlessly across the small area and back again. Then he stopped and leaned forward on the desk, looking into his mentor's eyes.

"Talk to me, Mac. So far you haven't given me a single reason that makes sense. Besides"—he straightened and gave MacLeod one of his best "trust-me" smiles—"I had to pull a lot of strings to get these seats—eight rows back, right on center aisle. They're great seats, Mac, and expensive."

Duncan leaned back in his chair and looked up at the young man, pleased in so many ways by what he saw. The Richie of today was very different from the seventeen-year-old petty criminal who had broken into MacLeod's antique shop a few years ago. Oh, he still thought he could charm the bees out of their honey—and sometimes he could—but the old Richie Ryan would never have attended anything more serious than a rock concert, not unless there was a get-rich-quick scheme involved.

But the years with MacLeod had made quite a difference in the young man, and Duncan was proud of the changes. It was more than the martial arts and sword training, though MacLeod was a great advocate of the physical and mental discipline they accorded. By the time Richie "died" the first time and became aware of his own Immortality, he had already seen enough to know the Game was in deadly earnest. He had thrown himself into his training with the single-mindedness felt only by the young. It had paid off; MacLeod no longer worried about Richie meeting another Immortal each time he left the dojo.

While this physical training would help him stay alive, it was the internal changes that would in MacLeod's opinion, make the years, perhaps centuries, ahead of the young man worth living. Under Duncan's sometimes stern, sometimes amused tutelage, the street-wise opportunist that circumstances had forced Richie to become had given way to the man of honor Richie had always been beneath the veneer.

MacLeod knew he could not take all the credit. Much of it went to Tessa, the remarkable mortal woman with whom Duncan had been living when Richie first appeared. She had been a woman of rare beauty, beauty that began with her face and went all the way through to her soul. MacLeod had loved her as he had loved few others.

To Richie she had been a friend and, though perhaps he did not realize it, something of the mother for whom he had always been looking. She had known and accepted the truth about MacLeod. Her example had helped Richie do the same so that, in time, he was able to face his own Immortality without the terror and confusion that MacLeod, and so many others, had experienced.

The same act of random violence that had given birth to Richie's Immortality had ended Tessa's life. For her there was no awakening, no continuance except in the lives of those she had loved. MacLeod would have continued teaching Richie anyway—as Connor MacLeod had taught him; as the Immortal Ramirez had taught Connor; as Graham Ashe had taught Ramirez, on and on back through time—but in Tessa's memory he did so with more understanding and patience than he might otherwise have offered.

Richie was still waiting for an answer. Now MacLeod was ready to give him one.

"You're not going to give up on this, are you?" he asked, already certain of the answer.

Richie's smile broadened. He lifted his hands in the familiar gesture that was half a shrug, half a brag. "Hey, you know me."

"Yeah, I do," MacLeod said.

He waited a moment longer, still studying Richie. Then, mentally, Duncan gave a small sigh; he might as well get this over with, he thought as he gestured toward the chair across from him.

"Have a seat, Richie," he said, "and tell me what you know about the Dalai Lama."

Richie sat in the office's other chair and leaned back. "I know he's some sort of religious leader from Tibet who's been living in exile for, like, thirty years, since the Communists took over his government."

"Thirty-seven now, since 1959. What do you know about how the Dalai Lama is chosen?"

"I suppose he's the most holy dude in the temple or something. Wait a minute—isn't there some sort of reincarnation thing involved?"

"That's right," Duncan answered. "The current Dalai Lama is the fourteenth incarnation in a line that goes back hundreds of years."

"But you don't believe that stuff, do you, Mac? I mean reincarnation—isn't that, like—"

"Impossible? As impossible as, say, Immortality?"

"Good point," Richie conceded with a quick grin. "But that still doesn't explain why you won't go to the peace rally."

"Richie—it's a long story."

"Well, Mac," Richie said with an expansive shrug, "you keep reminding me I have plenty of time."

Duncan looked down at the papers in front of him. Again, he gave a silent sigh; he knew he would have no peace until Richie had his answer.

Still the words did not want to come. With four hundred years of memories, not all of them were pleasant ones. Some were filled with regrets and sorrows that he preferred to keep private. He stared for a moment more out of the windows of the office into the empty interior of the dojo, where everything was orderly and calm. A part of him wished life could be just as serene. But it was not; life was, well, life—full of all the twists and turns that made a man who he was.

Duncan looked at Richie's expectant face and knew he would honor the young man's friendship with honesty. "Richie, I knew the Dalai Lama once, a long time ago, and we didn't part on the best of terms. I don't think it's a good idea for me to attend this rally."

"You knew him? When, Mac—before he left Tibet?"

MacLeod could not help the quick grin that quirked the corners of his mouth. "Yes, before he left Tibet. It wasn't *this* Dalai Lama I knew. It was the eighth, two hundred years ago."

"The eighth Dalai Lama," Richie repeated. "And this guy's like the fourteenth, right? Well then, Mac, where's the problem? I mean, why would he even recognize you?"

"Because one of the ways the Dalai Lama is verified in each new incarnation is the ability to recognize the people and things from his past lives. I don't want to be one of them. Now, I've got work to do. Go find a girl you can impress by your social consciousness and take her to the rally."

"That wasn't what I had in mind when I bought the tickets," Richie said, nodding, "but it might work. See you later, Mac."

"Yeah, later. Now get out of here."

As the young Immortal left, MacLeod shook his head, amused. Richie would, no doubt, find a way to turn a rally for world peace and freedom into a night of romance.

Oh, to be that young again.

The door closed behind Richie, and, in the sudden silence, MacLeod once more stared at the papers in front of him. They were balance statements for the dojo's expenses, minor book-keeping that he had done hundreds of times in different jobs over the centuries, but today the words and numbers passed before his eyes without entering his brain. There were too many memories already there.

Damn Richie for bringing all this up, MacLeod thought a bit savagely, but part of him was grateful, too. It had been too long since he had thought about his time in Tibet two centuries ago—too long since he had thought about *her.*

In four hundred years there had been many women in his life. Some were no more than brief and pleasant encounters, some were passions lasting months or even years. But there was one whose name he rarely spoke. He kept her name and her memory locked away, guarded in his heart like a precious jewel.

Xiao-nan Choi—even now, two hundred years later, her name called up all that was best in him. Her love, given with such tenderness, had brought his heart back to life at a time when he was drowning in weariness.

MacLeod put down his pen, sat back in his chair and closed his eyes. Immediately Xiao-nan's features filled his mind. He smiled in his solitude as he saw again the softness of her skin, shining golden as polished amber washed in the roseate blush of dawn; her eyes, dark with all the mysteries of womanhood yet bright with the light of love and laughter; her lips, her smile, so artless and beguiling . . .

But memories are fickle things, not easily controlled, and with a sudden twist all the pain two centuries had not dulled came crashing in on MacLeod—the loss, the sorrow, the anger. He should have protected her better.

Nor was his own anger the only one he remembered. The eighth Dalai Lama, that gentle young man who for months had been Duncan's teacher and friend, had been angry, too. He had banished Duncan from the holy city and from his company. And Duncan had fled back to Europe, only to find a world about to go mad with the Reign of Terror called the French Revolution.

Now, remembering that day from the safe distance of two

hundred years, Duncan saw in the Dalai Lama's face what he could not see at the time. Anger, yes—but hurt and disappointment as well.

Was there a chance their wounded friendship could be healed, even after so long a time? Duncan wondered. Or perhaps, as Richie had said, it was something for the past, something that would remain forever buried where not even an Immortal could resurrect it.

With that thought, Duncan knew he would go see the Dalai Lama; he did not want to carry this regret forever.

Chapter Two

MacLeod's assessment of Richie's libido might have been correct, but he forgot about the young man's tenaciousness. Like the Airedale terrier his curly hair made him resemble, whose jaws closed upon prey and locked, not letting go until one of them was dead, Richie would not so easily give up his original idea. He had bought these tickets for himself and MacLeod—a gift for the teacher who had given him so much.

And there was still a part of Richie that needed to prove himself to MacLeod, that needed the older man's approval. The need was less obvious than it had once been and manifested less frequently, but it was there. So he returned to the dojo a few hours later determined to persuade MacLeod to come with him to the peace rally.

He arrived at the martial arts school just as one group of members was leaving. The dojo would be empty now for a couple of hours. Plenty of time.

MacLeod was back in his office again. Richie waved at him as he hung his jacket on a peg, then walked over and drew one of the practice *katanas* off the wall. This, he knew, was one sure way to draw MacLeod onto the floor. He would pretend not to watch at first, but soon he would be out here correcting something in Richie's form, showing him how a slight variation in balance or swing could make it more effective—and help him keep his head.

A few stretches to wake up his muscles and get the blood flowing, then Richie began moving through the basic motions he had been taught: guard, slice, thrust, upward cut, downward cut, diagonal left, right, different angles, entries, and parries, keeping his balance on the balls of his feet, imagining an opponent's sword, his body, his head.

Soon Richie was sweating; his taut muscles warmed and

loosened. He almost forgot about MacLeod as he tightened his focus on what he was doing. *Make the sword a part of yourself, an extension of your arm;* in the past few years these words had become as familiar to him as the sound of his own name. *Extend your energy, your ch'i, to the tip of the blade. Let the sword do the work.*

"You dropped your left shoulder on that one," said the familiar voice behind him. "It left your guard open. I could have disarmed you and taken your head."

Richie nearly smiled. MacLeod was just the right kind of predictable. He turned to face his teacher. Duncan stood there with a sword in his hand. It was not his own *katana*—he never drew that lightly—it was the other practice sword from the wall.

Without further discussion, MacLeod saluted Richie, one swordsman to another, then dropped into his favorite stance with the graceful ease of a big cat stretching. His movements were always so precise they inspired, and slightly intimidated, Richie. He did his best to match MacLeod's position.

A few seconds later the dojo rang with the clash of blade upon blade. The sound echoed off the walls, filling the space like a miniature thunderstorm. Richie pressed his advantage every time MacLeod gave him an opening, and each time Duncan forced him back. Whenever Richie dropped his shoulder, MacLeod's blade would come up and slap him. Through it all, the older man kept smiling. It was infuriating.

Finally, shoulders sore and forearm aching, Richie stepped back and saluted, signaling a halt.

"You're improving," MacLeod said, still smiling.

"Yeah, right. Then why do I still come out of these encounters with my shoulders bruised?"

"Because you keep dropping your guard. Don't worry, Richie—another couple centuries of practice and maybe you'll beat me."

"I doubt it."

MacLeod smiled over his shoulder as he walked to the wall and returned the *katana* to its holder. "So how did your search for a date go?"

Richie shook his head. "It seems that listening to the Dalai Lama isn't what most girls think of as a fun way to spend a Friday night. I guess I'll just have to eat the cost of these tickets. Unless—"

MacLeod turned and leaned back against the wall, casually folding his arms across his chest. He was still smiling his same infuriating I-know-what-you're-going-to-do-before-you-do-it smile.

"Unless what?" he said.

"Unless you go with me."

"I already said no."

"I know, Mac, but I've been thinking. I know I said these are good seats—and don't get me wrong, they are—but there'll be hundreds of people there. You'll see the Dalai Lama okay from where you're sitting, clear as a bell, but there's no reason to think he'll see you."

"I don't know, Richie—"

"Think about it, Mac. It's not like he's one of us who'd be able to feel your presence, right? You'll just be a face in the crowd, same as everyone else."

"Okay, Richie."

"What—you mean you'll go?" Richie could hardly believe it. This had gone a lot more easily than he expected.

Then it hit him. He had not talked Duncan into anything. MacLeod had given in this easily only because he had already changed his mind. That made it Duncan MacLeod 2—Richie Ryan 0, all in the space of an hour.

Someday, Richie thought, *someday I'll win one.*

"So what time does this thing start?" MacLeod asked him.

"Eight o'clock."

"Fine. I'll pick you up at seven."

Eight rows back and on the aisle, and just as Richie had promised, they were good seats. The indoor playing field at the Seacouver Municipal Stadium had been transformed into the site of an *Event*. Across the field that usually hosted football, soccer, and baseball games, folding chairs in neat sections and rows and a large wooden stage had been assembled. The quest for victory had, at least for a single day, given way to the quest for world peace. In spite of his earlier reluctance, Duncan found that he was glad Richie had invited him.

The place was filling up fast. Richie turned to MacLeod and smiled at him triumphantly.

"See, Mac, it's like I said—hundreds of people. Nothing—"

"—to worry about, I know. And thanks, Richie."

"Hey, anytime."

Out of the corner of his eye, MacLeod watched the young man's face beam with pleasure and pride and felt a certain gratification at having changed his mind. Richie, the foundling, the child of orphanages and foster homes, had had few people in his life he cared enough about to want to please. MacLeod was glad he was among the few.

Duncan, too, had been a foundling, but he had been lucky enough not to learn of it until after he "died" the first time, as a grown man. Then his father had cast him out and the people of his clan had turned from him in superstitious fear, but they could not take from him the memories of a childhood filled with love and belonging. He was still Duncan MacLeod of the Clan MacLeod—and always would be.

But that first winter alone, bereft of all that he had known and loved, had been one of the worst times of his life: days and nights of cold and loneliness, belonging nowhere. Duncan could only imagine what Richie's early life had been like, when that feeling of never belonging, never being at home, was his constant existence.

Well, Connor MacLeod had eventually found Duncan and given him more than the rules of the Game and the training to stay alive. Connor had given him friendship, a sense of belonging again, and a reason to go on living. It was a gift beyond price that Duncan could only repay by passing the gift on—to Richie.

The room around him quieted, then erupted in applause as a group of men walked onto the wooden stage. Most of them were dressed in business suits, but at their center, dressed in the saffron and maroon robes of his religion, walked the fourteenth Dalai Lama.

He was of unremarkable appearance. Dressed in other clothes he would be easy to pass on the street, merely an oriental man of late middle age, with a balding hairline, a slight paunch, and glasses. But even from where he sat, Duncan could feel a special aura about the man. Others must have felt it, too, for the arena quieted again.

The master of ceremonies stepped up to the single microphone. MacLeod recognized him at once. It was Victor Paulus, a mortal and onetime student of Darius—priest, Immortal, and to Duncan a good friend. Duncan had not seen Paulus in a couple of years, not since he had twice saved him from the Immortal Grayson, who was systematically killing all of Darius's protégés in an attempt to draw the priest off of Holy Ground and into battle. MacLeod had followed Paulus's career, and although he had not yet won the Nobel Peace Prize, there were many, MacLeod among them, who thought he should.

Paulus began to introduce the people behind him. They were civic and religious leaders from the city who, like himself, were known for their advocacy of world peace, human rights, hunger relief, and other social/moral causes. It was an impressive lineup, but Duncan's attention was fixed on the man in the center who sat with his head quietly bowed.

Only once during the long introductions did the Dalai Lama look up. His eyes scanned quickly across the audience until they met and locked with MacLeod's. In that instant Duncan knew he had been recognized.

Up on the stage, the Dalai Lama bowed his head, but his mind was far from silent. He had felt MacLeod's aura from the moment he walked into the arena; its strength and vibrance, so well remembered, had drawn his eyes unerringly to its owner's face.

"Like attracts like," the Dalai Lama knew modern science would say. With his contemporary education and world travels, he had been exposed to the laws of physics in ways his predecessors had never dreamed existed. But in spite of the scientific knowledge he had gained over the years, he knew there was more at work here than one type of immortality recognizing another. He knew it now the same way he had known it two hundred years before when the eighth Dalai Lama, whose spirit he carried, had first met Duncan MacLeod.

Once more, the holy man raised his eyes slightly, looking out through the tops of his glasses over the crowd. So many people. He could feel their collective goodwill, and from some their doubts, swirling around him like warm and living breath. Over them all, the presence of MacLeod shone like a beacon through the fog.

As their eyes met, the Dalai Lama gave a small, internal nod. *You have grown,* the Tibetan leader thought, *but there is still much unfinished between us. Do you feel it, too, Duncan MacLeod? After so long a time, how much of Tibet do you remember?*

Duncan tried to keep his mind on each of the speakers. As interesting as they were, MacLeod's attention continually drifted back to the Dalai Lama. Often he found his gaze returned. But there was no expression, however small, that revealed the religious leader's emotion. Each time their eyes met, the Dalai Lama would bow his head again, leaving Duncan to wonder what he read in those dark eyes, what, if any, signal he was receiving.

At last the Dalai Lama came to the microphone. In spite of his heavy accent and quiet voice, he proved to be a consummate speaker. Like the predecessor MacLeod had known, this Dalai Lama had the gift of drawing his listeners in and making each one of them feel an important part of the whole, as if their personal involvement was the key to ultimate success. It was a gift modern politicians should envy.

Peace through Compassion was the Dalai Lama's theme and, for Duncan, listening to him was like going back in time. These were the same words, just a different voice speaking them, and despite the accented English coming out of the microphone, the slightly uncomfortable seats, and the modern surroundings, MacLeod had only to close his eyes halfway for the man on the stage to transform into the Dalai Lama Duncan had known so well.

A touch on his arm brought Duncan's thoughts back to the present. Standing beside him was one of the stadium's security guards. The sight made his stomach tighten; he was certain he would be asked to leave.

At least he knew now what expression he had read on the Dalai Lama's face. The friendship they had once known was indeed to remain buried in the past. There would be no healing of misunderstandings, no regrets laid to rest.

Well, Duncan would accept the Dalai Lama's wishes now, as he had two hundred years ago. He was about to stand, ready to leave, when the guard handed him a note.

Mr. MacLeod, it said, *His Holiness the Dalai Lama requests that you come to the green room to speak with him. The guard will escort you. I did not realize you and His Holiness were acquainted, but after your help the last time we met I find it does not surprise me. I am glad to know you are in the audience.* It was signed *Victor Paulus.*

Duncan looked up at the stage. He found the Dalai Lama watching him with the same immutable expression he had worn all evening. Duncan nodded once to the Dalai Lama, then slipped the note into the inside pocket of his jacket.

The rally was close to ending, and Duncan had been to enough such events to know exactly what would happen. There would be a summing up by Victor Paulus, again in his role as master of ceremonies, hearty handshakes all around, crowds milling in the outer hallways and lobby where books and fundraising efforts were displayed; Richie would find plenty to occupy him while Duncan was busy. He nudged the young man.

"I'll be back in a while," he said.

Richie looked at him quizzically, but said nothing more as Duncan stood and followed the guard. Like most security personnel, the man was taciturn and offered no conversation as he led the way up into the lobby, then around the building to the back of the stage where the mechanics of such an event took place. MacLeod ignored the milling stagehands, as he stepped around cables and amplifiers, unused lighting racks, folding chairs, and abandoned clutter.

The guard's presence gave MacLeod the passport he needed through the organized chaos. Although people stared as he passed, no one questioned him, and MacLeod was glad of the silence, glad to be left to his own thoughts.

This was an odd moment in his life. Few enough mortals knew the secret of his existence. There were the Watchers, of course—they had been observing Immortals for centuries before he had become aware of them. But other mortals who were still alive from some other *when,* like the members of the French Resistance with whom he had fought in World War II, those he carefully avoided. The few who had seen him thought he was the son of their old companion, whom a twist of fate and genetics had given his father's face.

Now the roles were reversed; he would see not the physical, but the spiritual descendant of the man he had known. *Just what memories will this Dalai Lama carry?* MacLeod wondered. *Am*

I just a name and a face he wants to put in perspective? Will he remember the friendship or only the reason I left Tibet?

Immortality, his thoughts lingered on the word. *Are our lives the same song, just danced to a different tune?* he wondered. Even after four hundred years, Duncan knew his own Immortality was something he did not understand; it was merely a reality he confronted every day.

But the Dalai Lama's life of continuing remembered reincarnation—that was as strange a thought to him now as it had been two hundred years ago. What would it be like, Duncan wondered, to begin each new generation as a child, having to learn to walk and talk and think again, but without the question of moral and spiritual identity that was the strongest thread binding mortal and Immortal together? How did it feel to begin life already knowing who you are and what you are meant to do? Did that make it easier or harder?

Well, he would have an answer soon, he thought, as the guard opened the door to the green room. After a terse "please wait here," the guard turned and walked away.

Duncan stepped into the room, and it was like walking back in time. The floors were covered with Tibetan rugs and scattered cushions took the place of chairs or couches. The lighting in the room was soft with the glow of golden-shaded lamps, and a faint smell of incense clung to the air. Modern artwork had been replaced by tapestries. Scenes from the Buddha's life and depictions of the Compassionate Deities smiled benevolently at him. But one tapestry directly caught and held his eyes in a shock of recognition. He went to stand before it.

The once-vivid colors had faded with age, but it was still the Kalachakra Mandala, the Wheel of Time and Palace of Enlightenment. Looking at it, MacLeod remembered all that Tibet had meant to him.

It had been 1781, a bad time, a time when Immortality seemed too heavy a burden to carry, and Duncan MacLeod felt as if his whole life reeked with the stench of death.

He was not certain he would have survived without the help of the Dalai Lama. . . .

Chapter Three

"You must go to Lhasa." The words were said kindly, with no hint of reproach or sadness over his decision to leave. Duncan MacLeod was grateful, as he was grateful for the many kindnesses he had received from this tribe of Tibetan nomads. He had come over the passes from Mongolia and lived with them for six weeks now. In all of his travels he had never met a people more gentle or more eager to be kind.

"Yes, you must go to Lhasa," the nomadic leader, Zhi-yu, said again. "Soon it will be the time of the Kalachakra ceremony. We cannot leave our herds—calves are being born, and soon we must find better grazing. But you can go for us, Duncan MacLeod. You can spin the prayer wheels in the holy city for us. You can see the great Kalachakra Mandala for us. You can join in the prayers for peace while keeping this people in your heart. It will be an act of great compassion. Will you do this for us, Duncan MacLeod?"

Duncan looked at the faces around him. Their usually merry expressions had turned pensive as they awaited his answer. He did not care where he went; Lhasa or elsewhere, it was all the same anymore. But these people had been kind to him. They had welcomed him into their tents and their lives, shared with him their food and their warmth, and helped him to laugh at a time when his heart ached with the lack of joy. To them it mattered, and for them he would go.

"Yes," he said aloud, "I will go to Lhasa. I will do all that you have asked with this people in my heart."

"You will be blessed by this action, Duncan MacLeod," Zhi-yu added sagely. "Your karma will benefit from your compassion."

"As you say," Duncan answered vaguely.

Karma was something the nomads spoke of a great deal, and

they could not understand either MacLeod's ignorance or indifference. His ignorance they set about to rectify, teaching him as they would a child about *samsara* and its cycles of birth, death, and rebirth, and about the Great Mandala, the Wheel of Time. They used simple words, laughing with him—and helping him to laugh—as he endeavored to master their language, which differed from the Chinese he had learned on his travels a century ago.

But not even their merry temperaments could completely penetrate MacLeod's indifference. It filled him like a dark void, a hole in his soul too many years in the making. After almost two hundred years of life, he was weary. He was tired of the Game. It felt as if his existence was only about death anymore—killing to survive.

So he wandered, as he had wandered here, looking for that word or smile or touch, that one moment that might bring his heart back to life. For the last two years he had been through China, renewing old acquaintances, perhaps looking for the man he had been when he had visited the "mysterious East" a century before.

He had seen Kiem Sun again, only to find that the last hundred years had sadly changed his Immortal friend. Fearful of the Game, Kiem Sun lived on Holy Ground, obsessed with perfecting an ancient formula of herbs that would create an invincible warrior. He thought it would protect him when the time of the Gathering finally arrived, but in his search for the preservation of his life he had ceased to truly *live*.

Kiem Sun had sent him to May-Ling Shen—delicate as a flower, deadly as an Immortal warrior had to be—and for a time he had found comfort in her arms. But the restlessness had come, as it had come to him here on the Tibetan plateau, and he had needed to be on his way again. He left May-Ling with a kiss and a smile, both of them hoping to meet again, and both of them knowing there could be no permanence for Immortals. Death might await on the blade of the next sword.

"You will leave with the sunrise, you say?" Zhi-yu's wife, Ruoyin asked, her voice bringing MacLeod's thoughts back to the present. She handed him a steaming bowl of spiced yak milk, one of the staples of the nomad's diet.

Duncan nodded. "That's right," he said.

Ruoyin gave him a patient smile that seemed to say how foolish she thought he was to be leaving at all. Then she went to sit beside her daughter, a new mother who was nursing her infant son.

Duncan wrapped his fingers around the bowl, enjoying the heat. He had almost said, "as soon as it is warm enough," but he was not certain that time ever came at these altitudes.

That was all relative, he supposed. Back home in Scotland, no one would believe anyone could live at these heights, let alone flourish. Yet these mountain nomads did just that. They lived happily, raising their families and their herds of yak at altitudes of 14,000–17,000 feet.

Here on the Tibetan plateau, the daytime temperatures rose barely above freezing and at night were cold enough to almost stop a man's blood in his veins. This was the "Land of Snows," the "Rooftop of the World."

It was a harsh life, but one lived among breathtaking beauty, where rainbows could appear in a cloudless sky and be reflected back again by the deep crystal of mountain lakes. And the mountains themselves, snowcapped and shining like a jewel-encrusted crown of the earth. Duncan had seen other mountains—the Alps, the Pyrenees—but nowhere had he seen anything like the mountains of Tibet.

In spite of the hardships, the Tibetan nomads were a merry people. They lived communally, relying on their herds for almost all of their needs. They housed themselves in huge tents woven from the animals' thick hair, fed themselves with its milk and meat, and burned its dung for fuel.

The tent in which MacLeod was sitting was one of great comfort by the nomads' standards. The largest in the camp, it was over twenty feet square. The thick yak hair from which it had been woven kept out most of the wind and the night chill. The small, portable brazier in the corner, which had replaced the ancient practice of a central fire pit, heated the air to a moderate temperature, and the double layer of rugs, hand-knotted and also made from dyed yak hair, both insulated and added beauty.

Over in the corner one of the tribal grandmothers was spinning her small prayer wheel and chanting softly to herself. Nearby, two other women were talking and laughing while they combed and spun from the ever-present basket of yak hair at their side. Ruoyin still sat next to her daughter and grandson, crooning a lullaby to the now sleeping infant.

The men in the tent were clustered around MacLeod. They had accepted his decision to leave with the same good humor they had shown on his arrival, and now their conversation had turned to other matters, such as where next to move the herd. As they talked, the men's hands worked ceaselessly, almost mindlessly, with the bowls and pestles in their laps. They were grinding *natag,* a powdery snuff made of cardamom, cloves, to-bacco, and the fine ash of burned juniper.

This grinding went on every evening; Duncan had quickly realized the slow, methodical action was more of a habit than the snuff itself. He had tried the *natag* once, out of good man-ners, when he had first come to live among the nomads. That once had been enough. But he enjoyed sitting among the men, watching the almost hypnotic movement of the pestle in the bowl and smelling the pungent aroma of the crushed spices.

As he sat there, hearing their voices without really listening, it was like being transported back in time, back two hundred years to the Highlands of Scotland when his people had lived much this same way. Had the world really changed so much, he thought, or was it just him? Somewhere in the last two cen-turies, the *wonder* in him had died.

With that thought, restlessness again gripped him. He stood abruptly and headed toward the thick hide-flap that served the tent as a door.

"There is a Yeti-wind blowing, Duncan MacLeod," the tribal leader called after him. "The Demon of the Snows will be prowling tonight. Do not go beyond the smoke of our fires."

"I will be careful, Zhi-yu," Duncan assured him, not quite smiling at the old man's words.

In this, too, the Tibetans reminded Duncan of his own peo-ple. He could almost hear his mother's voice telling him not to go out when the "goblin moon" was high. Goblins, witches, wood sprites, fairies—his childhood had been filled with sto-ries of these creatures stealing human babies from their cradles and human souls from the unwary. The Christian Church had never quite banished the fears of ancient lore.

Tibet, too, had its horde of demons the people feared. Some

were creatures of spirit and fire; others walked the world in physical form, but were demons, nonetheless. The most terrifying of these was the Yeti. It was said to be eight feet tall, with long white fur and with teeth and claws powerful enough to rend man or beast. The nomads burned branches of a special bush to keep the demon at bay. This was "Yeti-wood," their only fuel besides dried yak dung, and at night they did not go beyond the boundaries of their camp's comforting blanket of smoke.

In two hundred years of life and all of his travels, the only demons Duncan had seen were the human kind—and usually they had a sword in their hand.

The night air did little to refresh MacLeod as he walked through the nomads' camp. There was not much to see at this late hour. The large black tents were but deeper shadows rising on the darkened landscape. Prayer flags hung everywhere, squares of brightly colored cloth on which prayers had been printed, and during the day they fluttered gaily in the sun. But now they hung still, silent, and dark. The only light came from the sliver of the waning moon and from the stars, which here on the high Tibetan plateau looked almost near enough to reach out and grab by the handful.

MacLeod pulled his long fur-lined coat more closely around himself and felt the comforting presence of his *katana*. Even here he would not go unarmed, though out of respect for the beliefs of his hosts he tried to make his weapon as unobtrusive as possible.

He walked to a nearby boulder and sat, waiting for the silence of the night to enter and calm him again. But it was not really silent; as he sat there, Duncan could hear the voices of nomads, laughing and talking in their extended families. This was the sweet and gentle sound of communal life. It was a life Duncan knew he could never be a part of, even if he stayed. He could never live and grow old among people he loved. That knowledge kept him moving and fed the restlessness he had lived with for so very long. That—and the Game.

Even here he knew it would eventually find him. It always did. And with the Game came death. Mortals had their wars, their causes and laws; Immortals had their swords and the end was the same. More death. Always death.

Duncan drew in a deep, cleansing breath and let it out again slowly. The cold of the night air was beginning to penetrate even through his thick coat. One more deep breath, then he started back toward the tent. He would stay here tonight and be on his way in the morning—to Lhasa to attend this ceremony that meant so much to his Tibetan friends, a final thank-you for their kindness. After that, Duncan gave a mental shrug. *Who knows?* he thought. *Does it really matter?*

Many miles to the south, on the other side of the massive Himalayas, the kingdom of Nepal was a land of ancient splendors and ancient sorrows. It was a land of warrior-Kings and fierce, bloodthirsty gods, where a man's fate was decided before his birth by the caste into which he was born.

But three hundred years was enough to overcome any stigma of birth, if one was determined and ruthless enough. Nasiradeen Satish was both. No one but himself remembered his origins, the filth and squalor of his earliest years, the pain and soul-numbing poverty of being the only child of outcasts, untouchables.

His parents had died of hunger and disease when he was only eight years old, and he had watched their maggot-ridden corpses decompose because no one cared enough to bury them, and he was too small to do the work himself. Even at that age, something in him had been fierce enough to stand against fate. He vowed that he would not die forgotten and alone. He would find a way out of the caste into which he had been born.

Now, Nasiradeen Satish stood at the pinnacle of power. Over the centuries, from the time of his first death at age twenty-nine, he had fought and clawed and killed relentlessly to get here. He had "died" countless times; with each reawakening, he had renamed himself into a higher caste, gathering the strength and skill, the training and knowledge, and the wealth to back up his claims. He paid homage to the gods only when their will coincided with his own and otherwise ignored them, as he ignored or overrode the will of any who stood in his way.

Nasiradeen was not the king—he was something far, far better. Nasiradeen was the leader of the Gurkhas, the royal army of Nepal. Ten thousand men vowed to fight and die at his command. Only the King had greater power, at least in name, and to Nasiradeen's most elite troops, the five hundred men he had picked and trained himself, even the word of the King was not enough to alter their allegiance.

He would soon use those troops to gain a kingdom.

Tonight he stood alone on the rooftop of his grand home, a dark silhouette against the star-filled sky. At nearly six and a half feet, he would have been tall among any people, and among his own he was a giant. The turban on his head, like the clothes that covered his muscular body, was of the finest silk, with a large ruby burning at the cross-hatch of the wrappings. Other jewels sparkled on his restless hands, and a large brooch of diamond and sapphire pinned the cloak he wore against the cold. Boots of leather and lamb's wool encased his feet like clouds of warmth.

Below him, the whitewashed walls of his many rooms were hung with silk brocades and tapestries. Slaves waited to serve him on gold-washed plates and with jewel-encrusted goblets. Concubines were ready to give themselves for his pleasure. He had only to make a gesture, mention a desire, and it would be fulfilled.

But his mind was on none of these things. In truth, they bored him. Tonight, standing in the cool, crisp air under the light of the waning moon, he faced north toward the mountains and beyond. Toward Tibet.

His plan was already in place, and his spy, his instrument of betrayal, already living among the people in the Tibetan capital of Lhasa. The information he had already sent—maps of the city and of the roads, reports on population, water and food supplies—had helped Nasiradeen firm his plans.

There would be more reports coming, as Nasiradeen readied his troops, and there was one, in particular, for which he was waiting. He must know when the Dalai Lama was again in Lhasa; no conquest of the country could be complete without the Dalai Lama's death.

That was the true purpose his spy served; information, yes, and to open the gates when the army arrived—but above all, to kill the Dalai Lama. It would not be long before together they would strike.

Before the rains come again, Nasiradeen promised the night, the darkness, himself, *Tibet will be mine.*

Chapter Four

The entire tribe turned out to wave Duncan on his way as he prepared to ride off in the morning sunlight. They had provisioned him well, including a bundle of Yeti-wood to burn in his evening fires and a small tent in which to sleep, all loaded onto one of their sturdy mountain ponies. Zhi-yu himself gave Duncan directions on which trails to follow in order to reach Lhasa. Then the tribal leader enfolded him in a bearlike embrace.

"Our farewells are only temporary, Duncan MacLeod," he said, stepping back and smiling his merry smile. "We will meet again, if not in this life, then the next, when the Great Wheel spins."

Taking the reins of the pack pony in one hand, Duncan mounted his horse and rode away. As the sound of the nomads' voices faded in the distance, so did Duncan's smile. He thought of Zhi-yu's parting words, and they brought him no comfort. Did reincarnation exist, as the Tibetans believed, governed by the spinning Wheel of Time? Did lives that touched once keep finding each other again and again? Duncan had no answers, but he knew that there were many people, mortal and Immortal alike, he had no desire to see again in any life.

Perhaps for Immortals there was no returning. All spins of the Wheel gathered into one that could last through the millennia.

What about an afterlife? he asked himself. He had believed in one once, and there were people—parents and friends, teachers, past loves—whom he would like to think of as happy somewhere, eternally beyond the touch of pain or sorrow. He would like to believe he would see them again.

The silence in his heart was the only answer he needed. It seemed that all such simple and comforting beliefs had died with his mortality.

*   *   *

Duncan rode throughout the day in a solitude more profound than he had ever known. The eternal silence of the mountains. It was different than being alone in the hills of his homeland. There the wildlife rustled and twittered and the trees, gorses, and heather were in constant motion from the winds. It was different, too, from the solitude of the ocean, where whales and dolphins danced among the waves and the waters below teemed with life, where seabirds would light upon the sails to rest from their travels and the ship's creaks and groans were overlaid by the voices of crew and passengers.

Here, on the mountain road of Tibet, it was as if those things belonged to another world, a world of grosser needs and appetites. The only relief to his solitude was the sight of an occasional bird soaring high overhead, or even more rare, of a building off in the distance. Constructed on tall stone outcroppings and rising upward like part of the mountains that surrounded them. MacLeod was unsure whether they looked dreadful or wonderful in their isolation.

The silence in which he traveled soon became filled with memories, and his own thoughts turned deafening. By the time to make evening camp, it felt as if his mind would surely burst from the cacophony of voices and the swirling kaleidoscope of faces from the past two hundred years.

He found a sheltered spot that would protect himself and the horses from the worst of the night air. He needed to be busy; he did not want to think or to remember. Not yet. He set up his small tent and made a fire, smiling with the thought of Zhi-yu as he set a few pieces of Yeti-wood on the flames. Then he fed the horses and melted snow for their water.

His own dinner was no more elaborate—dried yak meat and strong, smoky tea. Duncan missed the fruits and vegetables of Europe. The thought brought a strong wave of memories of home. It was late May, and he knew that in Scotland the days were lengthening and turning warm and the nights were sweet with the fragrance of blooming heather.

"It still feels like bloody winter here," he muttered to himself, putting some more fuel on the fire and pulling his coat more tightly around his body. But in spite of the climate, MacLeod knew he did not want to be in Scotland.

With thoughts of home, the floodgates of memories opened and refused to be shut again. If he could not stop the memories, he could at least control them, he thought grimly, fixing with determination on the happier times of his life. He saw again the faces of his mother and father, of the clan in which he had been raised—of Debra Campbell, the girl he had loved and once hoped to marry. It was all so long ago, and they were all dead now. He had seen so much death.

It was true he had been raised to be a warrior, in the Highland clan where fighting was as much a part of life as eating, sleeping, or making love. He'd had a sword in his hand almost from the time he could walk, the wooden ones of childhood soon enough replaced by blades of forged steel. Highland weapons were not weapons of grace or style, but of power, and Duncan MacLeod's strong arms had quickly learned to wield them well.

Like the other Highland clans, the MacLeods were a proud people, fierce in their independence. They fought each other in duels of honor; they fought other clans out of blood-feuds or for the lands and possessions needed to survive; and sometimes, if the cause was great enough, the clans put aside their differences and fought against the common foe—the English.

Though the Scots, as a people, fought most fiercely to keep their dreams alive, Duncan had no such illusions. In truth, he had few illusions anymore. He tried to fight only when he must and to choose his battles carefully, but too few other Immortals lived by the same code. When they came, he had to take their heads to survive. He was nearing his two hundredth birthday, and it felt as if killing and death were all his life held anymore.

That was the Game, and he was tired of it. He was sick of being Immortal. He wanted peace.

Enough, Duncan thought. *Enough—I'll remember no more.* Other names, other faces, a hundred different times and places still clamored for attention.

Mortal man was not meant to have so many memories, Duncan thought, then he shook his head in the darkness. He was not mortal; he was Immortal, and the burden of memories was one of the costs he carried.

It's all this bloody silence, his thoughts continued. *It might serve for monks or hermits, but not for me.*

This thought, too, brought a wave of memories—of Brother

Paul and his monastery, Holy Ground where Immortals could rest. Duncan had stayed there for a time and had quickly realized he would never be called to the religious life.

Even the monastery had not been as silent as the mountains of Tibet. Along with the inevitable noise humans made, there had been music, beautiful, glorious music. Duncan knew that a singing voice was not among his strongest attributes but a song, even from him, would banish the silence for a time and, he hoped, quiet the memories.

He began to sing, lifting his voice in old folk tunes he had learned as a child.

> *"As I gaed doon by Strichen toon,*
> *I heard a fair maid mournin'*
> *And she was making sair complaint*
> *for her true love ne'er returnin'.*
> *Sae fare ye weel, ye Mormond Braes,*
> *where oft-times I've been cheery;*
> *O fare ye weel, ye Mormond Braes,*
> *for it's there I lost my dearie. . . ."*

A few feet away, the horses blew and stomped nervously at the sudden noise. Duncan chuckled.

"It's not as bad as all that," he told them as he rose from his seat by the fire and went to reassure them. The songs had done their trick, however, and Duncan felt once more in control of his thoughts. Still humming, more quietly now, he banked the fire and crawled inside his tent, ready to welcome the mini-oblivion of sleep.

Two more days of riding down mountain trails and Duncan was heartily sick of the sound of his own voice. He talked to the horses as he rode, telling them tales of his homeland and of the mighty victories of his forefathers. He talked to himself, making lists of the places he had been and the places he still wanted to see. He sang through his entire repertoire, bawdy songs to nursery rhymes, but in the end it was as if the mountains gobbled up the sound and spewed more silence back at him.

Silence and cold; cold was his other companion. His fur-lined coat and boots held off the worst of it during the day, as did the fire and his tent at night, but like the silence it was always present, always looking for a vulnerable moment to attack.

On the afternoon of the third day, the narrow path down which Duncan had been riding finally reached a main road. This was the road Zhi-yu had said he would find, and with relief Duncan turned the horses onto its hard-packed surface. Neither muddy nor dusty, it was as if centuries of feet had compacted the top of the soil into stone. The horses picked up their pace, eager for the place of rest and food that might be ahead. Duncan wanted a warm fire and a hot drink to chase the chill from his bones.

He rode for another hour. Finally, as he neared the crest of one of the road's many rises, Duncan began to hear voices. Coming over the rise, he saw in the distance that the road was lined with people as far as he could see. After so many hours of silent solitude, the sight seemed unreal, and MacLeod blinked twice, trying to clear his mind of the mirage. Then he urged the horses into a canter.

Another road merged with the road he was on, and it, too, was lined with people. Duncan saw that many among the crowd held long white strips of cloth in their hands, while others, especially the children, carried bunches of the early wildflowers he had seen growing in sparse clumps among the hills. They all chattered excitedly, speaking far too rapidly and in dialects too diverse for Duncan's limited knowledge of their language.

Suddenly, from down the other road, the noise built, and around him the excitement turned palpable. Two words were repeated often enough for Duncan to finally understand.

"He's coming," the people whispered among themselves, shouted to each other. "He's coming."

Duncan turned his head and strained to see, same as the people around him. Down the long road came a line of Tibetan monks, their robes of maroon and saffron creating a bright undulating stream of color. As they walked, they chanted and rang small hand bells whose sound carried faintly through the still air.

Row upon row they came, walking in pairs. Duncan counted—twenty, thirty, fifty, eighty. Then, in the middle of the procession was a covered litter, its yellow cloth glittering like gold in the sunlight. The people on the road surged toward it, but there was an orderliness even to their enthusiasm.

Moments passed as the litter neared. Duncan sat on his horse, watching the spectacle in fascination. One by one, the people stepped to the litter, bowing and presenting their offerings of flowers and white scarves. From inside the litter two hands reached out. Constantly in motion, they seemed to flutter like a bird's wings as they touched the foreheads of the children in blessing, accepting their gifts or lifting the white cloths from the outstretched hands of the adults, draping them over reverently bowed necks.

With the same orderly chaos, the people who had come forward backed away again, making room for the next. The crowd ebbed and flowed like a great wave slowly rolling down the road toward MacLeod. He stayed seated astride his horse, too entranced to ride on.

The rows of monks were passing now as the golden litter drew near. MacLeod could see that the bright yellow cloth had been intricately embroidered with tiny figures of birds, flowers, trees, rivers, lakes and mountains, all outlined in threads of gold and silver that flashed in the springtime sun.

A few words were spoken, and the monks carrying the litter slowed. Another word and they stopped in front of MacLeod, setting the litter upon the ground. The people around him gasped as the monks quickly moved to help the person inside disembark.

MacLeod was not sure what he expected, but he was surprised as a young man, certainly no more than twenty-five and dressed no differently than the monks around him, emerged from within the bright cloth. He waved any assistance away and sprang swiftly to the roadway. Then, dark eyes twinkling in his smooth, unremarkable face, he looked up at the tall stranger on a horse and smiled. With that smile, the young man's face filled with radiance. Duncan suddenly knew that here was something more than bishop or local prince, as he had assumed. Here was someone quite unique, someone truly holy. Duncan quickly dismounted and bowed.

The young man walked toward him, blessing the people as he passed with his smile and his touch. When he reached MacLeod he stopped and spoke, but too rapidly for Duncan to catch more than a word or two. He shrugged and shook his head. The young man understood the gesture and began again, speaking slowly and carefully.

"Please tell me who you are," he said.

"I am Duncan MacLeod of the Clan MacLeod," Duncan answered.

"Your name is as strange to me as your face. But not too strange. Are you also a missionary, as the others of your kind who live in my city?"

Duncan was startled to hear the Western word on the other man's tongue. "Missionary?" he repeated.

"It is their word. Jesuit and Capuchin also. But no, I do not think you are as these men." The young man stopped and cocked his head to one side, looking deeply into MacLeod's eyes. In a strange sensation, Duncan felt as if his soul were suddenly laid bare and being read.

"You carry a great burden, I think," the young man continued after a moment. "You must come to Lhasa, to the Potala and live among my household. We have something to teach each other, I think."

Duncan bowed again, acknowledging the young man's words and his invitation. But Duncan was not certain he had understood correctly; what could he, whose knowledge was of swords and warfare, of how to stay alive in the Game, possibly teach such a person?

The young man turned away and was walking back to his litter, obviously expecting MacLeod to follow. Before Duncan remounted his horse, he turned and spoke softly to the Tibetan native nearest him.

"Tell me this young man's name so that I may address him correctly," he said as quickly as his limited language would allow. All those who heard his words turned and looked at him in wonder. How could anyone not *know*, their faces seemed to say.

"That is Jam-dpal Rgya-mtsho," one of them answered. "His Holiness, the Dalai Lama."

The Dalai Lama, the Ocean of Wisdom—Duncan had heard that title spoken with reverence among his nomad friends. The Dalai Lama was both temporal and spiritual leader of this land, the Priest-King, an "Enlightened One" who embodied the Path of Peace.

Well, peace—peace of mind, peace in his soul—was what Duncan MacLeod needed right now. He remounted his horse and, gathering up the reins of the pony who carried his possessions, slowly guided them to the back of the procession.

Chapter Five

Duncan rode behind the procession for eight more miles. Everywhere the crowd stared at him as he passed, the great white stranger towering over the litter of their Holy One. Some even drew back in fear. It did not take long before MacLeod was wishing for some other means of travel, some form of anonymity. But despite the number of people he saw, not once did he feel the presence of another Immortal. *Perhaps,* he told himself as he sat a little straighter in his saddle and tried in vain to ignore the staring eyes, *that is anonymity enough.*

Finally, another crest in the road, and Lhasa, the holy city, capital of Tibet, appeared like a city out of a fairy tale, filling the valley before them. The lower city where the people lived, where they worked and loved and played, was enclosed behind a high stone wall. Even from astride his horse, MacLeod could see little of it, but what he glimpsed gave the impression of a pleasure garden, a place cultivated to please the senses and calm the mind.

Rising at the back of this beautiful city stood the great Potala, the home of the Dalai Lama. It was a religious house and royal residence combined, and, like the other Tibetan monasteries MacLeod had seen, it had been built atop a tall stone outcropping. There was to this building a special grace, however, an impression of airiness given by the many windows and archways, as if the stone was trying to melt into the sky, and its whitewashed walls made it gleam like a palace of silver.

The altitude was lower here, a mere twelve thousand feet, and the vegetation, which had been so lacking where the nomads wandered, was rich and lush. The hills leading down to the city were a carpet of green, dotted with the whites, pinks, purples, yellows, and blues of wildflowers.

And there were trees—not just the stunted stands of Alpine

willow and *Glang-ma,* whose long branches the nomads used to weave their intricate basketry, or the twisted bush that provided the Yeti-wood for their fires—but around Lhasa were forests of spruce and fir, pine and spreading yew, black and white birches, oaks and poplar. MacLeod had not realized how hungry his eyes were for the sight of real trees until he saw them. It was as if something inside of him relaxed and felt at home.

More people lined the road in a thick mass; the population of Lhasa had turned out to welcome their spiritual leader home. MacLeod found he was glad of his horse as the people fell into line behind the procession, escorting the Dalai Lama into his city and staying with him all through the winding roads up to the great stone steps of the Potala. Traveling through the city, Duncan saw flowering fruit trees, blooming shrubs, finely painted houses and well-tended gardens, but with the crowd of people all around him, the sights were fleeting. He looked forward to exploring the city later, after the excitement died down.

When they reached the Potala, the Dalai Lama disembarked from his litter. With great patience, he sat on the palace steps and let all those who had not received his blessing approach him now. Not knowing what else to do, Duncan dismounted and stood off to one side. He waited and watched, wondering about a man who, even at so young an age, could inspire an entire nation to such devotion.

An hour passed before the last of the supplicants filed by. Through it all, the Dalai Lama's smile never wavered. Freed from this responsibility at last, he rose with no sign of fatigue and approached. Duncan bowed.

"Now, Duncan MacLeod of the Clan MacLeod," the Dalai Lama said, giving a strange, almost musical pronunciation to the unfamiliar words, "we have a time that we may talk before my duties call me away again. Do not be concerned for your horses. They will be cared for, and your belongings taken to your room. Come with me with an easy mind."

"As you wish, Your Holiness," Duncan replied, bowing again and hoping he had chosen the correct manner of address.

The Dalai Lama again cocked his head to one side and looked up into Duncan's eyes. His face looked almost babyish in its contours, yet his eyes held hints of ancient, even timeless, wisdom. The contrast was startling until he smiled. It was the kindest smile Duncan had ever seen.

After a few seconds, the Dalai Lama gave a little nod and turned away. He began walking up the long staircase that led into the palace. It was one of several such stairways, each having, MacLeod guessed, over a hundred steps. By the time they reached the top, the high altitude had winded Duncan. The Dalai Lama stopped and waited for him to catch his breath, himself unaffected by the climb.

Duncan was a bit embarrassed, but the Dalai Lama merely smiled at him again. "One must be born to our air, I think, to be at ease here," he said. "You have done very well. The first of the missionaries who came to visit me could not climb these stairs without many rests."

His words made Duncan feel a little better, but not good enough. In the last weeks he had become lax in his physical training, excusing himself for being tired in the thin mountain air. Now he vowed silently that such excuses were at an end. Morning and evening, starting tonight, he would again drill himself in the skills that had kept him alive for two centuries.

He followed the Dalai Lama through the great doors. It was as though they stepped into another world, a world that combined the glories of a palace with the harmonious silence of a monastery. At either end of a long hall, giant gold-washed statues of the Buddha glowed in the soft light of hundreds of tiny votive lamps. Along the wall, tiered stands of burning candles alternated with long tapestries, illuminating their strange and glorious images.

In each of these, the Buddha seemed to be the central figure and Duncan guessed the tapestries represented important events in his mortal life. Duncan would have liked to examine them, but the Dalai Lama set a brisk pace down the long hall, and Duncan could do no more than admire the tapestries in passing.

The walked on through numerous twists and turns, through rooms of grace and splendor. MacLeod saw figurines of jade and alabaster, enameled bowls and lamps of gold and silver, intricately carved screens of wood or softly painted silks and bright oriental rugs. After a while he ceased to notice them individually and they became a blur of beauty upon beauty.

Finally they entered a room of more spartan luxuries. There were more rugs on the floor, hand-knotted in the flowing patterns of reds, blues, and yellows that were famous all over the world. On the rugs, instead of chairs, were large pillows of maroon silk. A few small tables were set between the pillows, with legs carved in delicate designs of trees, birds, and flowers, and tops of inlaid wood. Although lamps hung from the ceiling on long chains, most of the light came from the three large windows that filled one wall.

This room, too, had a gold-washed statue of the Buddha with rows of little votive lamps burning at his feet. The Dalai Lama prostrated himself three times before the image, then crossed to one of the pillows and sat down. Duncan stood, uncertain of what to do next; surely he was not expected to bow before the statue as his host had done?

From his cushion, the Dalai Lama laughed. It was a merry sound in the silent room, and Duncan turned instantly toward it. With a sweep of his hand the young man indicated a pillow next to him.

"Come and sit at ease, Duncan MacLeod. Tea will be brought and food to refresh us while we talk."

The glass in the windows kept out the cold and concentrated the heat of the sunlight. As Duncan took a seat on the pillow, he finally felt warm enough to remove the heavy coat he had worn for his travels, realizing that he did feel at ease. What was it about this young man that made one's heart relax? he wondered as he looked at the religious leader whose gentle, beatific smile had not faded.

One look into the Dalai Lama's eyes and Duncan knew there was no simple answer. His eyes, though they, too, smiled and held a look of kindness and peace, were penetrating. Here, as on the road outside the city, Duncan felt as if the young man's gaze held the power to reach in and read his soul.

"Now, Duncan MacLeod of the Clan MacLeod," the Dalai Lama said, "you must tell me of your homeland. It is very far away, I think."

"It is, Your Holiness. Very far away. The land of my home is called Scotland."

"Scotland," the Dalai Lama repeated, trying out the word. "It is a big country?"

"No, Your Holiness, it is not, except in the hearts of its people. It is part of an island far to the west, on the edge of a great ocean."

"Islands I have seen in mountain lakes, where birds nest in the summertime. It is difficult to picture an island large enough to be a country. An ocean, I have never seen. Teach me of the ocean, Duncan MacLeod."

Before Duncan could speak, the tea and food arrived, carried by silent monks, who put the trays within reach of their leader, then bowed and backed away. After they had left, Duncan did his best to describe the ocean to the Dalai Lama, speaking of winds, currents, and waves, of seabirds and great mammals, of ships that rode upon the waters and the life that swam within it.

When he had finished, the Dalai Lama smiled again. "You have seen great wonders, Duncan MacLeod, but I think they have not made you happy."

He stopped and cocked his head to one side, his smile fading as he stared into Duncan's eyes in silence.

"You are a strange man, Duncan MacLeod," he said at last. "Your face is a young man's but your eyes have the look of the very old who have seen too much suffering. Are you then, like they, ready to give up your life?"

The Dalai Lama's words shocked Duncan. They cut through to the one question he had feared to ask himself.

It would be so easy—just stop fighting, not raise his sword at that critical instant, and it would all be over. No more of the Game.

But he did fight, and he did raise his sword.

What then did he want?

A gong sounded off in the distance. An instant later, the doors opened. The Dalai Lama stood; Duncan hurried to do the same.

"I must leave you now, Duncan MacLeod. You will be shown to your rooms, but you need not remain there unless you wish. There are gardens of beauty here at the Potala, or the people of my city would welcome you. Ask and you will be shown the way. We will talk again soon. Go now, Duncan MacLeod of the Clan McLeod, and be at peace."

Duncan bowed. "Thank you, Your Holiness," he said. "I look forward to speaking with you again."

A young monk was waiting at the door. With another bow, Duncan turned and followed him. This time, as he walked down the long corridors of the Dalai Lama's palace, Duncan was oblivious to the loveliness around him. Each footstep seemed to echo the religious leader's question and open the door to others just as difficult to answer. By the time he reached his rooms, they had all melded together until only one question remained.

What was the truth of Duncan MacLeod?

He thought he knew once. His life, his beliefs, had been black and white, like a fairy story in which good will always triumph. But through the centuries he had seen too many good men die, too many just causes fail. Now the hopes and dreams, the ideals that had once formed his soul seemed like shadow figures on a dimly lit wall, fading so soon into nothingness.

Fading so soon . . .

In the void that remained, he was left to wonder how a man lived without hope.

Chapter Six

As Duncan left the room, the Dalai Lama cocked his head to one side and stood for a moment thinking. *What is this burden you carry, Duncan MacLeod of the Clan MacLeod? What is the sorrow that fills your eyes with such weariness, and what has brought you to my city?*

Again the gong sounded in the distance. It was time for meditation and prayer. The Dalai Lama knew that throughout the Potala the monks would be leaving their other occupations to gather in the inner chamber and wait for him to come lead them. This was his joy and his duty. Yet as he walked down the beautiful corridors of the Potala, his mind was not on the Teachings. He could not stop thinking about Duncan MacLeod.

All Westerners are strange, he thought, *but this one is different. He has none of the arrogance of the others in my city, the missionaries. They speak humble words but do not have humble hearts. This one, this Duncan MacLeod, has the humility of a burden carried too long in silence. He is a man who has lost his path.*

How can I help him? the Dalai Lama wondered as he entered the meditation chamber and sat in his accustomed place.

His small brass handbell, the *darja,* and string of prayer beads sat on the floor in front of his cushion. Before him, the monks sat in long rows facing each other, ready to begin chanting the subtle triple tone that was the sound of the universe at harmony with the soul. The expectation on their faces slowly turned to patient puzzlement when he made no move to pick up the handbell.

The Dalai Lama bowed his head and waited for either inspiration or silence to enter his mind. Although in this life he was a young man, only twenty-three, he had lived through seven previous Enlightened incarnations, and he had the memories of those lifetimes to guide him. Suffering was something he thought he knew in all its forms—but never had he seen eyes as haunted as those that looked at him today. It was as if each word spoken brought back memories too painful to be borne.

And what of the age I saw in those eyes? the Dalai Lama wondered, head still bowed in silent contemplation. *How many lifetimes has Duncan MacLeod lived and by what spin of the Great Wheel has he come to this place?*

The Dalai Lama raised his eyes and looked out at the rows of monks still awaiting his signal. Old and young alike, he knew he had only to ask and each one of them would try to lighten his burden with their compassion and advice. But helping MacLeod was something the Dalai Lama knew was his karma alone.

Suddenly, into the expectant silence, came the inspiration he had been seeking. They were teachings so basic to his beliefs he had looked past them, searching for some more esoteric words that would both inspire MacLeod and give answer to the complicated questions he felt surrounding this strange Westerner.

Ah, foolish man, he chided himself. *It is from simplicity that truth arises.*

He picked up the handbell.

Duncan did not visit the Potala gardens, as the Dalai Lama had offered; neither did he go into the city of Lhasa. After his weeks in the nomads' camp and his days on the trail, being inside a building with walls and windows, heat and light was a luxury.

He was given a room of simple elegance, where spaciousness felt like part of the decor. The furnishings were few—a bed, a chest, a small table—but each one was a work of beauty. There was a chimneyed brazier in one corner and two oil lamps, one on a long chain from the ceiling, one on the table, that had been lit and filled the room with warmth. More light came in through the long narrow window. There were rugs upon the floor, two large pillows to sit on, and a privacy screen in the far corner. Above all there was room, space to move, to think with his body.

Alone in his room, Duncan removed his shirt, his fur-lined boots, and stockings. The warm air on his bare skin was a sensual pleasure. He felt his body *breathe*. Going to the center of the room, he began to stretch, muscle by muscle: feet, ankles, knees on up through his arms, shoulders, neck. He stretched out the stiffness of his long ride and the weeks of inattention.

From the stretches, Duncan moved into *kata*, the precise series of movements used to train the body, focus the mind, and control the breath. They flowed together like a ritual dance. This was a practice he had begun in Japan under the tutelage of Hideo Koto—a mortal and one of Duncan's greatest teachers.

Was it really only three years ago? Duncan thought, wondering at the twists of time that made some things, especially actions of his youth, feel as if they happened only an instant before while other events felt distant, belonging to another person or a different life.

Perhaps it was not time, but pain that kept them separate, Duncan realized as his body warmed. Memory is stored in the muscles, Kiem Sun had once told him and as Duncan kicked and lunged, struck, turned, and parried, images of the months he had spent in Japan emerged. He saw again Hideo Koto's face as he had first seen it; eyes shining, sword in hand—every inch the proud and fierce warrior MacLeod came to know and respect.

His death had been a hard blow. Harder still was the knowledge that his death had come for MacLeod's sake. The samurai had known about the law forbidding the harboring of Westerners, of "barbarians," yet when MacLeod had found himself alive once more on the shores of Japan, still surrounded by the flotsam of his destroyed ship, Koto had taken him in as the honorable thing to do for the stranger who had saved his life.

Honor governed every moment of Hideo Koto's life—and it had governed his death. To save his family's name and honor, he had chosen *seppuku*, the ritual suicide, rather than execution for his disobedience of the law. It had been one of the most difficult acts of MacLeod's long life to stand as Koto's second; one of the hardest blows he had ever had to strike, to use Koto's own *katana* to sever his head and end the ritual.

At that moment, and at this, MacLeod hated death.

He'd had enough of memories. Too much. He pushed away the image of Koto's lifeless body, pushed his own body harder, until all he could think of was controlling his breath in the thin

Tibetan air. Soon his blood was pounding in his ears, his body bathed in sweat. He did not want to remember; he had come here to forget.

Forget.

That single word became a mantra of his own making. He breathed it in and held it deeply. It fed his soul like the oxygen that sustained his body.

Forget.

He pushed the memories out with his breath, exhaling them like poison. He struck at them with his hands, kicked at them with his legs.

Forget.

The past is a darkness filled with ghosts. Put them to rest.

The future is a chasm, a void unseen.

Forget.

Forget.

He continued through all the multiple *kata*, changing from the karate forms he had learned from Hideo Koto to the *kata* of the Way of the White Crane he had been taught by May-Ling. Light from the window moved toward shadow, and finally he sank to his knees, too exhausted to push his body further. His muscles burned, and he welcomed the pain. It gave him focus. For a moment the voices were silent, the faces withdrawn. For this instant there was nothing more than here and now.

A gong sounded somewhere in the Potala. Duncan tried to ignore it, but it shattered the delicate silence in which he was existing. Reality crashed back in upon him.

Duncan sighed and reached for his shirt. *I wonder how they feel about baths in this place,* he thought as he began to wipe the sweat from his torso. Frequent bathing was also a habit he had picked up in Japan. It was difficult to maintain during his travels and had been close to impossible while living with his nomad friends. Maybe here in this great palace there would be the chance of hot water.

I'll ask, he told himself. *All they can do is think I'm as crazy as I probably am.*

With a wry grin, he stood and looked around for where they had put his bag with his change of clothes. He would like to wash before he put on clean things, but he could not run half-naked through the palace trying to find a tub.

It took him a few minutes to find his possessions, neatly folded and stacked behind the privacy screen. He left the small tent and blankets, the water pouch and the sack of food, and carried the long, narrow bag that held his few traveling clothes to the bed. Unlacing it quickly, he lifted and shook out each of the three silk shirts he had brought with him from China, the extra pair of wool pants, and, finally, the long robe that he had carried from Japan. In the bag were a pair of soft-soled sandals, also from Japan, and a lighter pair of boots.

His favorite of the shirts was a deep, almost iridescent blue. He picked it up and fingered the soft cloth, wondering again about the chance to wash before putting it on, when there was a faint knock on his door. A young monk entered and bowed.

"The Dalai Lama wishes for you to join him at his evening meal. If you are willing, someone will guide you in one hour."

"Aye," Duncan agreed. "I'll have dinner with His Holiness."

The monk bowed again and started to turn away.

"Wait," Duncan called. "Is there a place where I can wash first? I'd like to bathe."

"You wish to go to the lake?" the monk asked, his voice cracking with youth and incredulity.

"No," Duncan answered quickly. He'd had more than enough of cold lakes and mountain streams. "I'm talking about a bath, in a tub of hot water, with soap. Have you such a thing?"

"We have," the monk answered hesitantly, "for His Holiness. I will ask about your use. You will wait, please."

"Aye, I'll wait."

The monk left and Duncan laid the clean shirt aside. He might not have to put it on while he was dirty after all—and the prospect of a hot bath was worth waiting for.

Chapter Seven

An hour later, the Dalai Lama sat in the room where he and Duncan had met before. He knew that MacLeod was being conducted toward him and he did not mind waiting. He never minded; there was always so much to contemplate.

He sat on his cushion, legs crossed and his hands folded in the pattern of Mandala offering. His downcast eyes no longer saw his intricately folded fingers. He was hardly aware of the room in which he sat. His sight was turned deeply inward, focusing on the-Jewel-that-is-Compassion.

The certainty that had come to him during the afternoon's meditation had not left him. It was his karma to teach MacLeod the four Noble Truths and the Way of the Eightfold Path. These he knew would help MacLeod find peace, but how receptive would he be to instruction? The other Westerners who had come to Tibet, the missionaries who lived in the city, had no desire to hear any words but their own. Would the same be true of MacLeod? *If so,* the Dalai Lama wondered, *what then is my karma?*

The sound of the door opening seemed to come from far away, but the Dalai Lama recognized the sound and began to pull his thoughts back into the present. He changed the tone of his breathing, brought his focus back outward and his sight back to the room in which he sat. Then he looked up and smiled. MacLeod stood in the doorway, looking slightly less weary but hesitant to approach.

"I did not mean to disturb your thoughts," he said. "I can come back another time."

"Come in, come in," the Dalai Lama replied. "I was waiting for you."

MacLeod walked quickly into the room. He was wearing his blue silk shirt. His long pants were tucked into the tops of high leather boots and his hair was loose about his shoulders. As he neared, the Dalai Lama could smell the clean scent that surrounded him.

"You have then enjoyed your bath?" the young man asked as Duncan sat on the cushion next to him.

"Oh, aye—though I think I shocked a few of your people by asking for one."

The Dalai Lama chuckled. "It is their way to wash themselves in the lake behind the Potala or go to the warm spring in the hills. I do not care for the cold water of the lake, and each time I leave this place a great procession forms. My people love me, as I do them, but I do not need to be escorted merely to wash the dust from this poor body. And so, the tub. Please make use of it whenever you wish."

"Thank you, Your Holiness."

The Dalai Lama inclined his head graciously, but his eyes were hooded as he considered how best to break down the barriers he sensed MacLeod had drawn around himself. Permanent barriers, he was sure, and not easily broached.

"Tell me," the young man said into the uneasy silence that had fallen, "what does it mean 'Duncan MacLeod of the Clan MacLeod'?"

"In my country, Scotland, clan is the word we use for family," Duncan explained. "It means I belong to the family of the MacLeods. Duncan was my great-grandfather's name, and it was given to me in his memory."

"Ah, then your family, your clan," the Dalai Lama pronounced the new word carefully, "believe that in you the spirit of your ancestor is reborn."

"No, Your Holiness. My people do not believe that the spirits of the dead return."

"You believe then in this heaven of which the missionaries teach?"

"Those are the beliefs of my people," Duncan said.

So carefully answered, the Dalai Lama thought. *What do you believe, Duncan MacLeod? Do you know?*

"Tell me about your people," he said aloud as their dinner arrived. "Tell me of this Scotland from which you come."

"Ach, it is a beautiful land, Your Holiness," Duncan replied, his gentle brogue deepening as he thought of home. "It is a land of green forests and deep rivers, of whole hillsides covered with the purple blooms of heather . . ."

Duncan continued talking as they ate their meal, and the Dalai Lama watched him, noting how his face glowed with love and pride while he spoke of his homeland. Yet neither did the young man miss the shadow that filled MacLeod's eyes.

Why did you leave this land of yours? the Dalai Lama wondered, *and what is it that you fear? Perhaps soon you will tell me—but not today. Today we will speak only of pleasant things. This we will do until you see that you can trust me.*

Over the next days, Duncan and the Dalai Lama fell into a pattern. Each morning and evening the young monk would come to Duncan's room and escort him to the religious leader's presence. Then Duncan and the Dalai Lama would share a meal and conversation. Usually these consisted of Duncan answering questions about someplace he had seen and people he had known. The Dalai Lama's curiosity about such things appeared to be insatiable.

At first Duncan was wary, with the guarded watchfulness that had become the habit of two hundred years. Surely, Duncan thought time and again, the Dalai Lama wanted more than a guided tour through his memories. But with each hour in the young man's presence, the wariness was breaking down.

There was a freshness about him, as if he held each moment as a gift, an excuse for laughter. Duncan thought it must be a product of the Dalai Lama's youth, of years as yet untouched by pain or suffering, heart-wrenching decisions and bitter loss. Yet, there was also something ancient, something that stood outside the realm of time, about the young man. It shone from his eyes and from the look of utter compassion that so often graced his features. Slowly, it was setting MacLeod's heart at rest.

During his first few days, Duncan spent his afternoons exploring the Potala and its grounds. Despite its beauty and its fifteen hundred rooms, it was more of a monastery than a palace, filled with countless prayer wheels of every size, from a few inches tall to twice the height of a man. Set in individual niches, they lined the walls in corridors and stairwells or outside walkways. They were the central figures in gardens and meditation rooms. Some were plain and made of brass. Others were brightly painted in reds, yellows, and blues; all were filled with thousands of invocations that when spun were believed to ascend to the Compassionate Heart of Buddha. MacLeod often spun them as he passed, each time remembering his nomad friends and the promises he had made to them.

The gardens behind the Potala contained a sight Duncan had not thought to see at this high an elevation. Here several fruit trees, stands of peach and walnut, apple, pear, and apricot grew in happy cultivation along with poppies and tiger lilies, marigolds, hydrangea, hollyhocks, and carnations, all carefully tended by the monks as part of their contemplative duties. The gardens were places of serene beauty enhanced by the presence of the lake created by excavating the materials to build the massive structure of the Potala. The lake was fed by underground springs and runoff from the mountains. Out of curiosity, Duncan put his hand in the lake and came away shaking his head, wondering how anyone, even a Tibetan monk, could bring himself to bathe in such frigid water.

On the afternoon of his fifth day at the Potala, MacLeod decided to venture down into the city of Lhasa. The day was bright with sunshine and the air about forty-five degrees; a warm spring day for Tibet. Duncan left the Potala with no more destination than a pleasant walk in mind.

The streets of the city were not laid out with the orderly progression of a European city. They curved and meandered like a strolling path in a woodland park. The entire city had a parklike air with small, brightly painted houses bordered by flowering shrubs and well-tended gardens. Everywhere they could be hung, prayer flags fluttered in the breeze, gay as banners on a parade ground.

The people, too, wore colorful clothing, predominately shades of blues and greens, white, pink, and coral, with black bands and trims that made the lighter colors appear all the more vibrant. Here, as among the nomads, men's clothing was darker and married women wore the five-colored aprons that denoted their status. Occasionally Duncan saw someone wearing yellow, orange, or red. These, he knew, were religious colors marking someone who had taken a vow. He was careful to respectfully bow to any such person who passed him.

The people of Lhasa showed no fear of the tall white stranger walking their streets. Children ran to him, calling out their greetings and squealing with delight when he answered them. Adults paused in their work to smile at him. It was like walking through the garden of paradise, and Duncan found himself more warmed by the people than by the sun.

Following the curve of the streets, Duncan came suddenly upon one of the city wells. Clustered around it, a group of six young women sat chatting and laughing. Wrapped in the soft sunlight, it was such a scene of feminine beauty that Duncan stopped, not wanting to move and shatter the moment.

The young women were all of an age when the full bloom of adulthood had ripened their bodies but the ravages of worries and weather had not yet touched them. Lovely as they were, there was one among them who seemed to sparkle with an inner light. Duncan could not take his eyes from her.

"The Tibetans are comely people, aren't they?" said a voice by his side.

Duncan quickly turned to find a man in clerical garb standing next to him. His long black cassock looked out of place among the brightly colored houses, and the English he spoke was both welcome for its familiarity and an intrusion, a reminder of the life Duncan wanted to forget.

Though his words were English, his voice cultured and educated, his face was Nepalese. Here was one of the missionaries of whom the Dalai Lama had spoken. From the manner of his attire—the black cassock that did not button down the front but fastened at the neck and was tied by a sash at the waist, the knee-length black cape and the black biretta he wore—Duncan knew this one was Jesuit. It did not surprise him, for the Jesuits, knowing there is no one so zealous as a convert, frequently ordained from within the native population.

But at least he's not an Immortal, Duncan thought. The Game had still not found him.

Still, Duncan narrowed his eyes and looked at the man suspiciously; two hundred years of experience had left him with little love for the members of the Society of Jesus.

"I am Father Edward," the priest said, offering his hand.

Duncan hesitated the briefest moment before shaking it. "Duncan MacLeod of the Clan MacLeod," he answered formally.

"I had heard there was a European in Lhasa. The people regard you with a bit of awe, you know."

"Me?" Duncan could not keep the surprise out of his voice.

"Oh, yes. You're the special guest of their Dalai Lama. They think of him as the incarnation of their god, and that makes you a person of importance—and of speculation. Father Jacques, the other of my Order who lives here, and the three Brothers of the Capuchin Order of St. Francis are the only Europeans most of these people have ever seen, and we do not live at the Potala. Indeed we would not, even had we been invited. All those heathen images." The priest shuddered expressively. "Don't you find them offensive, Mr. MacLeod?"

Duncan was beginning to find *the priest's* presence offensive; he spoke with a pomposity Duncan did find irritating. "No," MacLeod answered quickly. "Many of them are quite beautiful."

"Of themselves, perhaps," Father Edward agreed, "but not of what they represent. Indeed, it is their heathen beliefs and practices that keeps this place from being a true paradise and these people from being among the most sanctified."

"And you're here to change all that, I suppose," Duncan said, irritation turning to anger.

"Should God grant me that grace," Father Edward replied, but his tone was fierce not meek.

"Well, you'll get no help from me." Duncan turned on his heel and strode off, leaving the priest staring after him.

Duncan walked quickly, letting the movement vent his anger. His own religious feelings were ambiguous at best, but intolerance was the one thing that even as an Immortal he did not have *time* to practice.

MacLeod, intent upon distancing himself from the priest, had not seen the change that came over the man's face when MacLeod left him standing on the street of Lhasa. Black eyes narrowed, following Duncan's movements, calculating stance, balance, and strength. Here, he thought to MacLeod's retreating back, is a threat to plans so carefully laid.

I must watch this one, he thought. *When the time comes, he must not be allowed to interfere.*

Chapter Eight

═══════

Thoughts of Father Edward stayed with Duncan for the rest of the afternoon, casting a shadow over the brightness of the day. Did the Dalai Lama know anything about these priests living in his city, Duncan wondered, about the type of men they were and the opinions they held? Did he know of their plans to convert and control the people?

Duncan shook his head. *How can he, young as he is? He's never really seen anyone from the world away from Tibet. He needs to be told that not all men have generous hearts, no matter what they profess.*

Aye, Duncan thought, accepting the responsibility and age experience laid upon him. *I'll tell him this very evening. His Holiness must learn the truth about these* Jesuits.

Even his thoughts spat the word. He had seen too many atrocities for it to be otherwise—the Inquisition, the witch-hunts and burnings, all in the name of their religion. *They may call themselves missionaries, but I call them fanatics and murderers.* It was the Jesuit activities in Japan that had led to the law forbidding the harboring of Westerners, and that in turn had led to the death of Hideo Koto.

Duncan MacLeod had little cause to love men like Father Edward.

The priest's presence and his words worked like a slow poison in Duncan's mind as he sat in the Potala garden and watched the afternoon slowly pass toward evening. They ate away at the fragile peace of mind that MacLeod had felt slowly descending upon him. Once more, wariness surfaced. The missionaries had not been invited to live here in the Dalai Lama's palace, Father Edward had said, so why had he? Duncan wondered. What was it the young man wanted from him?

Duncan knew he needed to have his answer—and, if possible, he meant to have it tonight. He hurried back to his room to await the Dalai Lama's summons.

It was not long coming. Duncan had barely had time to remove his coat when the young monk appeared at his door. With a silent bow, he turned and Duncan followed him. As they walked down the long corridors MacLeod tried for a conversation, hoping to gain some insight into the Dalai Lama's feelings about the missionaries before he reached the young man's presence. The Dalai Lama was, after all, a ruler, and in Duncan's experience rulers tended to keep their true feelings hidden behind the veil of necessity.

"I went down into Lhasa today," Duncan said pleasantly. " 'Tis a beautiful city. Do you go there often?"

"When my duties allow," the monk answered.

"Have you met the other Westerners then, the priests who live in the city?" Out of the corner of his eye, MacLeod watched the monk's face, looking for any subtle change of expression that might reveal the young man's feelings.

The monk's face remained impassive as he gave a barely perceivable shrug. "I've met them," he said. "They are just men like any other, and so in need of compassion."

"In need of—" MacLeod swallowed back the retort that nearly sprang from his lips. "Do many people in the city visit the priests?" he asked instead.

"Everyone visits them."

MacLeod was surprised by the answer, and immediately anxious for the welfare of this gentle people.

"Does His Holiness know?" he asked.

The monk smiled faintly. "The Dalai Lama knows everything," he said in a tone that ended the conversation.

Aye, Duncan thought, *I'm sure he does at that. He has his spies everywhere, no doubt. Are you one, my young monk? Is that why you're the one who comes for me each day?*

MacLeod found the thought of royal spies was, in an odd way, comforting. He had been in courts around the world, been friend, advisor—and sometimes lover—to all manner of nobility. All of them had an intelligence system, a means of keeping their ears and eyes on the actions of their people. How else could they rule effectively?

It seemed the Dalai Lama, at least in this respect, was no different. It made Duncan feel that he had a better idea of what he was dealing with now and how to act accordingly.

They reached the room Duncan had come to think of as the audience chamber. Without another word, the young monk bowed and turned away. Duncan watched him go. Their conversation had only firmed his resolve to make certain the Dalai Lama was told the truth about the Jesuits. He might know his people visited them, but that did not mean he understood their zeal for conversion or the havoc their condemnation could incur.

Duncan knocked once on the door and then entered. As always, the Dalai Lama sat on his cushion, smiling serenely.

"Come in, Duncan MacLeod," he called his customary greeting. "Come and sit so we may talk."

As Duncan moved to obey, he wondered how to keep the conversation off his past travels and bring up the subject of the missionaries. For once, however, the Dalai Lama had no questions about foreign lands.

"You went down into my city today, I hear," the young man said. "Was your visit enjoyable?"

"Much of it was, Your Holiness," Duncan replied. "But not all."

"Tell me, Duncan MacLeod, what troubled you. Were my people unkind?"

"Oh, no, Your Holiness, it was not your people." Duncan stopped and took a deep breath, then plunged ahead. "I met Father Edward today."

"Ah, one of the missionaries," the Dalai Lama said with a nod. "But why does he trouble you, Duncan MacLeod?"

"Because I have known others like him and have seen what their presence can do. You should banish them from your city, Your Holiness."

"No, Duncan MacLeod."

"But do you know what their purpose is?" Duncan could hear his voice becoming gruff, his tone curt as he tried to find the words that would make this young man listen to what experience had taught him. The price of those lessons was something MacLeod did not want to see the Tibetan people have to pay.

"Do you know that your people visit the priests?" he asked more softly.

"Of course my people visit them," the Dalai Lama replied with a smile, his eyes calm and unperturbed. "How else may compassion be shown? I know that these missionaries have come here to speak the words of their God to my people. We do not fear their words. The Compassionate Buddha taught that all words of truth, whoever speaks them, are the words of Buddha. Let your mind be at peace about these missionaries, Duncan MacLeod. They will bring no harm to my people."

Duncan wished he could believe it. There was more, much more, he wanted to say, but he recognized the tone of royal command. Father Edward and his intentions were a closed subject. Since he was a visitor to this city, Duncan would accept the Dalai Lama's wishes, but he would also watch carefully. If his fears were indeed groundless, he would say nothing more—but if Father Edward or the others did anything that might harm the people of Lhasa, Duncan would not be so easily silenced again.

MacLeod cleared his throat. There was another question he still wished to pursue.

"Your Holiness," he began, keeping his tone respectful, even humble, as past experience with royalty had taught him to do. "Why did you invite me to stay here?"

The Dalai Lama put down the bowl from which he had been drinking and turned toward Duncan, looking at him in silence. As on the occasion of their first meeting, Duncan felt as in the young man's gaze plumbed the depths of his soul, both reading the secrets hidden there and inviting Duncan to freely speak of them. It was an unsettling feeling, but odder still to see eyes suddenly filled with such ancient awareness in such an inexperienced, unmarked face.

"Are you unhappy here, Duncan MacLeod?" the Dalai Lama asked. "Is there something more needed for your comfort?"

"No, Your Holiness. I am most happy here, and you have been very kind, but I know that you did not invite the missionaries to live in the Potala when they were strangers in your city."

"That is true." The Dalai Lama again nodded, his voice remaining patient and undisturbed. "When they came to the

Potala and asked if they could live in my city, their eyes said they found no beauty here. They have room in their hearts for no words but their own. So why waste the words of invitation? Your eyes said you needed to be here, and so you are. The Wheel spins and brings all to where it should be."

Duncan felt the conversation slipping away from him. It was not a sensation he particularly enjoyed. There were things he needed to understand—perhaps for his own peace of mind, perhaps only to impose the familiarity of Western logic on the evasive explanations of Eastern thought. In an effort to once more gain control, he tried another question.

"On the road outside Lhasa, why did you stop to talk to me?"

The young man seated next to him, cocked his head to one side, and smiled. "Every soul, Duncan MacLeod, has its own aura and yours is very strong. I felt it reaching out to me as we approached, so I stopped. I found that your aura is also wounded and in need of rest. You are here to rest and, I think, to heal.

"Now, Duncan MacLeod, what part of your travels shall we speak of today?"

There was no mistaking the tone of finality in the young man's voice. Once again, MacLeod was reminded that in spite of the Dalai Lama's apparent youth, he was the leader of his country. MacLeod knew he would receive no more information, and no explanation of the meaning behind the Dalai Lama's words. They raised more questions than they answered and perhaps, Duncan realized, that was exactly what was intended.

Aye, he thought, *he's a crafty young fox. He knows that sooner or later I'll have to ask him to explain.*

Two hours later, Duncan took his leave of the Dalai Lama. After the door had shut behind him, the young man folded his hands and closed his eyes. He let the silence of the room envelop him with its peace.

I said you have a strong aura, Duncan MacLeod of the Clan MacLeod, he thought into the silence, *and today in your agitation, it boiled around you, filling this room like a fire. I know you were angry that I would not let you speak your words against the missionaries. You fear for my people—but I fear for you. You carry so much pain. I could not let you speak and give it more strength, more power over your soul. You must let go of your pain and your anger. They are passing. They are insubstantial.*

The Dalai Lama opened his eyes and stared at the tapestry on the wall across from him. There was no Buddha figure in this one, no figures of fierce or compassionate deities, no saints or monks or Bodhi tree; no obvious symbols of Enlightenment. But this tapestry was Enlightenment itself. It was of the Kalachakra Mandala, the Wheel that is Time. During his fifth incarnation, the Dalai Lama had it hung in this room where so many came to him for counsel, to remind himself that all existence is fleeting; it was one of his most clear memories from that life. The reminder was often indispensable to his peace, for it helped ease the burden he too often felt as he opened his heart to compassion for those who came to him. And somehow the Dalai Lama felt that helping Duncan MacLeod was going to be both his greatest challenge and greatest necessity.

As the Dalai Lama stared at the tapestry, at the brightly colored designs flowing clockwise, his thoughts again returned to the *age* he felt surrounding MacLeod. It puzzled him. An old soul that had seen many other lifetimes, perhaps, but that was not the only answer. It was too simple—and the Dalai Lama knew there was nothing simple about Duncan MacLeod.

Tomorrow, my friend, the Dalai Lama thought, *tomorrow, I think, we will cease this game we have been playing. Tomorrow we begin to walk the path of deeper truth. Are you ready? The only way to walk that path is to release your secrets and the pain they cause you.*

But what is a man except his secrets—and his pain?

Down in the city of Lhasa, the man known as Father Edward was also thinking about Duncan MacLeod. The other Europeans in the city—his companion, Father Jacques, the three Capuchin Brothers—posed no threat, but MacLeod worried him.

The way he carries himself he must be a soldier, maybe a mercenary, Father Edward thought as he wandered through the rooms of the house that served as both home and church, tugging with irritation at the stiff white collar around his throat. He hated it, just as he hated the European clothes and the long black cassock he was forced to wear.

He wanted to be back in uniform again, riding beside the invincible Nasiradeen, leader of the Gurkhas; he wanted to be sword in hand against the foe, any foe. Instead he was stuck here, pretending to be a priest because he had been educated by European missionaries. He spoke their language and knew the things they said about their God.

He had hated the missionaries and their school when he was a child, and he hated them now. He smiled into the silence as he remembered the real Father Edward. How easy it had been to walk up to him, speaking a greeting in his own language. How the priest had smiled a welcome—a smile that turned to a scream when the sword pierced his heart.

That sword, the one that had killed the priest, the spy had had to leave behind when he assumed Father Edward's identity. He missed his weapon, but its discovery would have been a threat to his mission. Soon he would find another one, or something that would serve, and he would use this identity he had assumed to get within striking distance of the Dalai Lama. He, too, would soon fall by Edward's hand.

Nasiradeen, himself, had been pleased by this plan. The Gurkah leader wanted Tibet; he wanted to rule this city as he wanted few other things, and if it could be delivered to him, the rewards would be well worth the current discomfort.

This thought brought the false priest's mind back to MacLeod. What was he doing here? *Are you a scout for some advancing army?* he wondered, *Or a fortune hunter on your own? What is your secret, Duncan MacLeod? Whoever you are, I will not let you stop me.*

The other Jesuit, Father Jacques, was already in bed. He would be up before dawn, full of energy and ready for the day ahead. But the Nepalese man he knew as Father Edward preferred the night. The darkness and the silence set his mind free and gave him solitude for his real work.

He walked out into the little courtyard behind the house where rows of birdcages had been built. The Tibetans who visited here thought this was an amusing hobby, but it was much, much more. It was communication and contact with his real people and purpose. It had been an easy communication line to establish, effective in its simplicity.

The cages contained pigeons. They had traveled here amid Father Edward's belongings, but were trained to return to their cages in Nepal, to the great temple in Kathmandu. Their counterparts had been bought here in Tibet, trained to these cages in Lhasa, then sent to Nepal with a traveling merchant. The birds gave Nasiradeen the eye into Tibet he craved and gave Edward a way to please his master; he took very good care of them.

The pigeons cooed a gentle greeting as Edward reached behind for the paper and writing stylus he kept hidden there. A few quick lines and he was ready. He carefully folded the scrap of paper and placed it inside a metal ring that would soon grace a pigeon's leg. Then he opened one of the cages.

The bird he chose was a fine black male with a silver ruff around his neck. Father Edward put the ring on his leg, then stroked his back gently.

"Fly well, my beauty," he whispered, "and when you reach your destination there will be a special treat. Before long we'll both have our rewards."

Chapter Nine

The next morning Duncan rose early, before the first light of dawn appeared in the narrow window of his room. He had not slept well, and his mind was even more restless than his body, still filled with foreboding about the priests' presence in Lhasa.

Duncan had seen too much. He had lived through the Reformation and Counter-Reformation movements in Europe; he had seen the anger, hatred and betrayal they caused. He had both seen and heard tales of the Church's ventures into other lands, other cultures; and where the Church went, fortune hunters and soldiers were never far behind.

His thoughts flew back to his nomad friends and the way they had welcomed him into their tents and their lives. These were true innocents—and if the greed of the West came here, innocence would not survive.

Perhaps the warlords were right in banning Westerners from Japan, Duncan thought for the first time. He still could not forgive the law for causing the death of Hideo Koto, but in the stillness of the Tibetan dawn, he could for the first time understand it.

Perhaps, his thoughts continued, *the Dalai Lama should pass such a law here.*

Yet the Dalai Lama had made it clear he would not listen to Duncan's warnings. Despite being the ruler of his country, the Dalai Lama was an innocent as well. It was a nation of innocents, and Duncan wondered, a bit sadly, if there was truly anything that could be done to protect them.

The feeling of sadness and fatalism did not leave him as he waited for the Dalai Lama's messenger to come escort him to the young man's company. When the monk arrived, however, he stood in the doorway and bowed formally to MacLeod.

"His Holiness, the Dalai Lama, sends a message to Duncan MacLeod," he said. "His Holiness begs your understanding, but he cannot meet with you this morning. Other matters have come to him that demand his presence and attendance. He says that he will see you at the evening meal."

As the young monk spoke, MacLeod's brow furrowed with concern fed by the dark foreboding that had filled his night. Perhaps danger was closer than he realized. The Dalai Lama might, even now, be trying to deal with matters whose full consequence he could not possibly understand. Duncan almost rose to push past the monk and go to the Tibetan's leader's side.

His past dealings with royalty stopped him. Undesired interference often caused more harm than it prevented. Once more Duncan reminded himself that he was only a visitor in Tibet.

"Is His Holiness all right? he asked, carefully watching the monk's face for any signs of worry or confusion. "I would happily lend my aid, if he has any need for my services."

The only emotions the young monk showed were peaceful confidence overlaid with a touch of hauteur. "The Dalai Lama has no need of your help," he said. "He is the Ocean of Wisdom and needs no advice from the unEnlightened." The monk bowed and turned away.

Well, Duncan thought, slightly amused, *I've been put in my place. If I'm to have my day free, I think I'll go into the hills. Perhaps I'll find those hot springs His Holiness once mentioned.* He quickly changed his soft-soled boots for his stout fur-lined pair, grabbed his coat, and headed for the outdoors. The prospect of wandering alone in the hills was suddenly extremely appealing.

Duncan exited the Potala through the palace gardens, stopping to sit for a while beside the lake. The peace of the setting helped him lay to rest, at least for the moment, the fears that had kept him awake all night, and he was able to set off for the hills with a lighter step.

Not many minutes had passed before he realized how much he needed this day of freedom. He'd had enough of indoor hours and occupations. He needed *movement,* and even doing *kata* twice a day was no substitute for the feel of his own feet under him. This had always been his way, even as a child.

Whenever he was confused or troubled, he had gone off alone to wander the Highlands until his thoughts cleared again.

The trail into the hills was a good one, and MacLeod soon fell into a steady rhythm. He began to notice that the hills were not as barren as they had looked from a distance. Lichens and cresses spread intricate patterns of greens, grays, and muted reds across the rocks while stands of tiny wildflowers provided splashes of unexpected color. The silence of the mountains closed in on him again, but for the moment he welcomed it.

As he walked, Duncan felt the remainder of his worries drain away. Instead of feeding his loneliness, as the silence had done on the trip into Lhasa, today it was as if the mountains absorbed all troubles of the heart and mind and by their massive existence made human concerns insignificant.

Here, in the bright sunlight, he nearly laughed at himself. *Two hundred years has turned you into a clucking old hen,* he thought, *seeing predators where none, perhaps, exist.*

But that has kept you alive, another part of him whispered.

He continued walking, slowing his pace as the trail steepened, letting the combination of movement and fresh air soothe him. It took a few minutes for him to become aware of the sound he heard growing in the distance. It was a gentle sound— the sound of women's laughter.

Duncan slowed his pace again. Whoever the women were, whatever they were doing, he did not want to frighten them away. In all his long life, he had never seen anything more miraculous than a woman. Old or young, women were, in his opinion, the true glory of creation.

The vegetation was thicker here, indicating the presence of water, and the chatting, laughing voices were louder. Coming around a bend in the trail, he was met by a sight that filled him with wonder.

Whatever he expected from the hot springs, it was not what he saw now. The pool was surrounded by wild flowering shrubs, tall enough to provide a sense of privacy but not so tall as to block the sun. The rocks provided ledges and gentle steps down into the water that was deep and wide enough for the women in it to splash and swim with ease.

And the women themselves—MacLeod realized he was staring and quickly backed away, but not before the sight of two naked bodies, shining with water and sunlight, imprinted itself on his memory. He stood for a moment, fighting the desire to steal into the bushes and quietly watch them at their ablutions. Perhaps it was only good manners that kept him from the impulse, perhaps a sense of chivalry and honor, but it was enough.

He wondered what to do. Should he return to the Potala or find some place to wait until he saw the women coming back down the trail? Looking around for a place to sit comfortably, he noticed the bell hanging from a tree limb. It was old, and the mosses that covered it made it blend with its surroundings, but MacLeod could guess its use. He crossed to it and rang it once, its deep gong filling the silence.

He heard the sound of the women's voices change. Their laughter stilled and there was a moment of purposeful splashing, then all was silent. A few minutes later they appeared, properly attired in long wrapped skirts, boots, and short jackets. As they neared, Duncan saw that one of them was the young woman he had noticed yesterday at the well.

The women passed by him, hardly sparing him a glance. On impulse, he stepped out onto the trail after them.

"Wait," he called. Both women turned to look at him, but he could hardly tear his eyes from the one. She was even more beautiful here in a natural setting than she had seemed yesterday. Duncan stepped toward her.

"Please," he said, "who are you? What is your name?"

She glanced at her companion, then lowered her eyes. "I am Xiao-nan Choi," she said softly.

Her voice was low and had a breathless quality, like an intimate whisper. Duncan was at once entranced by it.

"Xiao-nan Choi," he repeated. "Please don't go. I do not know the area around here. I would be glad of some company."

Xiao-nan looked up at him, her dark eyes wide with surprise. "Did you not come here for the water?" she asked.

Duncan smiled. "I can bathe another time. I would rather have your conversation."

Behind her the other woman giggled. Xiao-nan quickly turned and hushed her.

"I meant you and your companion," MacLeod added, not wanting to violate any cultural taboos.

"No," Xiao-nan answered. "My sister must return home. Our

mother will be waiting. I will stay and talk with you for a time." She stopped and smiled at him. "But you must tell me *your* name."

Duncan found that when she smiled she was among the most beautiful women he had ever seen. Her large dark eyes sparkled like polished jet and yet were gentle even in her laughter. Her skin shone like the golden sky when still touched by the first blooming light of dawn. Even, white teeth stood like petals of a flower behind flowerbud lips so red Duncan found himself wanting to kiss them, to see if they were indeed as soft as they must be.

She was looking at him expectantly now, still waiting for him to speak. "I am Duncan MacLeod of the Clan MacLeod," he said almost automatically, still dazed by her beauty. "Your sister may assure your mother you are safe. I mean you no harm or disrespect."

Xiao-nan laughed gently. Duncan found he was as delighted by the sound as by everything else about her.

"She already knows this, Duncan MacLeod," she said his name slowly, as if embracing it with her lips and tongue. "You are the friend of the Dalai Lama, and he would not have one with him whose heart could not be trusted."

This simple statement of faith, in the Dalai Lama and in himself, touched Duncan. He bowed deeply and formally to Xiao-nan Choi. She acknowledged his bow with one of her own, then turned and said a few rapid words to her sister. As the young girl started off down the trail, Xiao-nan turned again to MacLeod.

"If you have not come to this place for the waters, have you another place you wish to see? There are many beautiful places in the mountains."

Duncan smiled at her. "Lead the way wherever you wish, Xiao-nan Choi," he said, "and I will surely follow."

Chapter Ten

Xiao-nan led the way farther into the hills, up to a glen where the wild marmots played in the sunlight. It was a quiet place where she often came when she wanted to sit and feel the world in balance.

She did not know why she had chosen this place to bring MacLeod; there were many others just as beautiful and less personal she could have shown him. But somehow, she thought as they settled on the stone outcropping where she habitually sat and waited for the marmots to lose their fear of intruders, it felt right that he should be here.

Soon, a small white-and-brown face peeked out from the bushes across the glen. Xiao-nan saw it and gently touched MacLeod's arm. Slowly, using no swift motions that might again frighten the creature, she pointed. MacLeod saw the marmot and smiled.

It is a good smile, Xiao-nan thought, *a smile of the heart as well as the face.* It warmed Xiao-nan to see it.

Why should it matter if he smiles? she asked herself, knowing only that it did. What was there about this man that so instinctively drew her. She felt as if somewhere inside, far beyond the realm of conscious thought, a spark of recognition flared, touching soul to soul.

They stayed in the glen, speaking only occasionally and in muted voices. But the silences between the words were not empty. Unlike many people whom Xiao-nan knew, even the most quiet moments seemed to ring with his calm, unfrenzied strength.

The marmots soon accepted their presence. MacLeod watched them as they scampered in the sunlight, and Xiao-nan continued to watch him out of the corner of her eye. She would not be so impolite as to stare, but she liked the way his white teeth shone against the weathered tan of his skin when he smiled; of the soft waves in his dark hair, so unlike her own, which fell in a straight black cascade to her waist, and she liked the look of his strong fingers as he absently twirled a leaf he had found on the stone next to where he sat.

His look pleased her, but it was his company that affected her most deeply. She felt comfortable and safe, and again she asked herself why? Had they known each other in some previous life? she wondered. Or had they always been searching for each other, wandering through the circles of existence until the Great Wheel should bring them together?

It was something only time could answer.

When Duncan returned to the Potala several hours later, he felt better than he had for many weeks. Xiao-nan's company had worked on him like a patent medicine "guaranteed to lighten the heart and brighten the eyes."

It was not anything she said that so affected MacLeod. Her conversation had, in fact, been limited. But her smile had been eloquent, and her gentle laugh of delight had said more than words ever could.

Laughter came easily to Xiao-nan. It was the laughter of true innocence, like a child at play unafraid of adult censure. Nor did that laughter come at anyone's expense. Instead it was the feel of the breeze lifting her long hair from the back of her neck, the sight of the marmots they had watched and the birds flying their intricate mating ritual that brought joy to her lips.

From her lips to Duncan's heart; she fascinated him and even as he left her at her parents' door he knew that he must see her again.

Duncan had barely reached his room in the Potala when the familiar young monk appeared at his door.

"His Holiness has sent for you," he said solemnly.

"Then let's not keep him waiting, m'lad," MacLeod answered, his voice loud and full of life. He walked over and gave the monk a good-natured slap on the shoulder, nearly laughing aloud at the wide-eyed look of surprise that spread over the young man's face.

Duncan stepped past him, this time leading the way to the

audience chamber himself. His companion had to rush to keep up.

"What are you called, boy?" MacLeod asked. "What's your name?"

"Gaikho," the monk answered hesitantly. MacLeod could see him wondering what mood had taken hold of the strange Westerner. MacLeod did not care; he felt too good to care how odd others might think him. He knew the elation would not last, and he was intent upon enjoying it.

MacLeod no longer needed a guide to reach the audience chamber, but the monk stayed with him, doing his duty to the Dalai Lama by delivering Duncan. When they reached the outer door of the chamber, MacLeod turned and bowed with a flourish to his companion.

"Thank you, Gaikho, for your fine company," he said.

The monk again looked startled as he returned MacLeod's bow. Once more Duncan clapped him on the shoulder then turned away, knocking once on the chamber door before entering.

From the moment he stepped into the room, he could see that the Dalai Lama was weary. The young man's shoulders were slumped, and although he greeted Duncan with his usual smile, the merriment was lacking from his eyes. MacLeod felt some of his own joviality fade in response.

With a small wave, the Dalai Lama gestured toward Duncan's habitual seat. "Come and sit," he said. "Tell me of your day while we wait for the meal to arrive. I am sorry I could not speak with you this morning, but other matters arose."

"Aye, so Gaikho said," Duncan answered.

He tried to keep himself from frowning as he crossed the room and sat upon the cushion, but the feeling of sadness and worry that emanated from the Dalai Lama made Duncan immediately want to offer his sword in the young man's defense.

Other courts in other lands, however, had taught Duncan that such offers had to be made carefully. He was not certain his knowledge of the language was up to the challenge of fancy phrases such as he might use in France or Spain, Italy or England, where he would know how to strike the proper blend of flattery and deference.

But for all his travels, he was still a Scotsman, a Highlander, direct and plainspoken. With the Dalai Lama, he would just have to speak his mind and hope the young man understood the intent without taking offense.

Duncan drew a deep breath. "Your Holiness," he began, "I can tell you've something on your mind. I know I'm not one of your people, but I've a strong arm and a good sword. Both are yours if you've need of them."

The Dalai Lama looked at him with an expression of infinite gentleness, as a parent might gaze upon a child struggling to shoulder a burden too heavy for tender years. Again, Duncan was struck by the dichotomy of youth and age.

The Dalai Lama said nothing while his look seeped down, deeper and deeper into MacLeod's soul. For a moment, Duncan thought he could see other faces overlaying the young man's, each with the same tender look in their eyes.

Immortality, the word sprang quickly through his mind. Immortality was something Duncan knew down to the very sinews of his body; it was the reality of every breath he took. And yet—as he looked at the young man before him, Duncan could not help but think how much akin and how very different their types of immortality must be.

Duncan had not chosen his long life, though he did choose survival. If his head came away from his body, he was through. The Dalai Lama's immortality was based on rebirth, continuing remembered cycles of life. So different, yes, but they both witnessed the fleeting nature of mortal existence. They both saw time, that unstoppable river, carry away loves and hopes and dreams, changing forever the landscape of the soul. They both lived with the lessons only the centuries could teach.

This was the connection between them; it was as slender—and as strong—as a silken thread.

The Dalai Lama smiled and the vision faded. "Thank you, Duncan MacLeod," he said gently. "I know your words are well meant, but the answer for my people is not found on the point of a sword."

"Is there something else I can do then?" Duncan asked. "I want to help you if I can."

"I want to help you," the Dalai Lama repeated softly. "These are good words, Duncan MacLeod. Words of Wisdom, and it lightens my heart to hear them. All through this day I have listened to those who came to me for answers but did not want the words I would give them. They came seeking only their own way and brought with them the suffering such selfish thoughts always carry. They left with their burdens no lighter."

The Dalai Lama stopped and sighed. He ran a weary hand across his eyes. "Oh, Duncan MacLeod," he said, "it is true that all unEnlightened life is *dukkah.*"

It was a word Duncan had never heard before. "I'm sorry, Your Holiness, I don't understand."

"It is the first Noble Truth taught by the Compassionate Buddha. Each year of my many lives has shown me the reality of it. *Dukkah* means suffering, but it is the suffering of a wheel out of balance constantly grinding against itself as it tries to find the center it does not have. So it is with the life that is not bound in compassion. The unEnlightened life is truly a life of pain. Do you not find it so, Duncan MacLeod?"

Duncan thought for a moment, still not quite certain what the Dalai Lama meant. Surely there were times of pure joy; today in Xiao-nan's company he had experienced such times—hadn't he?

"What about love, Your Holiness?" Duncan asked. "If life is suffering, what about love?"

The Dalai Lama cocked his head to one side and looked at Duncan for a long, silent moment. "Love that is pure, free of self," he said, "perhaps. But how many of us can claim such feeling? And for the rest, is there truly no suffering in love, Duncan MacLeod?"

Duncan thought about the past loves he had known. They had filled his life with joy, yet amid the joy was pain—the uncertainties and misunderstandings, the needs of heart and soul that love alone awakened, the union that no matter how perfect only accentuated separateness, the separation that is death— yes, love also contained suffering.

The Dalai Lama was still awaiting his answer. All Duncan could do was bow his head.

The Dalai Lama nodded. "You see, Duncan MacLeod," he said, "all life is *dukkah.* We are out of joint, dislocated from the truth."

"What is the truth, then?" Duncan asked.

"Ah, a good question. It begins with the acknowledgment

that all is suffering. That is the first Truth. The second Truth teaches that suffering comes from within ourselves, from the selfishness of our desires, from *Tanha*. Always we must ask ourselves what is it we truly desire. Do you know, Duncan MacLeod?"

MacLeod felt his mind reeling. Of course he had desires—what man did not? But he was no Religious or mystic to have put such things into words. He was a man of action, a warrior who for two centuries had lived by the strength of his arm, his wits, and his sword. Soldier or mercenary, scout or bodyguard, that had been enough for him.

Until recently. Until now.

Looking into the Dalai Lama's eyes, Duncan saw an elusive *something* for which he knew he was seeking. It was more than acceptance or resignation to the human condition. It was more than peace or humor or compassion. The word used by his nomadic friends when they spoke of their Dalai Lama had been *Enlightened*. Perhaps that was the only word that fit.

The young man was watching him now with his gentle, aged smile. "You are impatient, yes?" he said. "But also you are young. The questions you ask yourself are often many lifetimes in the making—and many more in answering. But to those who seek, Enlightenment does come."

Duncan opened his mouth, then closed it again without speaking. How was it that this man who was barely more than a boy, should call MacLeod *young* with such authority? And how long is a lifetime? Duncan almost asked. Is it twenty years, fifty, one hundred?

How would you answer if you knew my *truth?*

Chapter Eleven

The black homing pigeon flew fast and true, not caring about the message it carried or the lives it might change. It only knew that at the end of the flight was the safety of a cage, was food, water, and rest. It flew through the mountain passes, riding the wind currents that added speed to its wings, avoiding the talons of the hawk and eagle, on into the heart of Nepal. It flew to Kathmandu.

On the roof of the sacred temple of Pashupatinatha, home of the servants of Shiva, its cage waited. When it set its feet upon the perch, a bell rang within the temple, alerting the Hindu priest who served there of the bird's return. The priest had neither concern nor curiosity about the message the bird carried; their dutiful care was for the bird itself. A sacred duty.

Nasiradeen Satish, leader of the Gurkha army, did not care about the bird; it was only a tool. He wanted the words on the paper banded to its leg. He wanted the power the words would bring him. He wanted Tibet.

It was he who had chosen the temple for the bird's cage, and he came every day to see if it had arrived. No one questioned his daily attendance at the temple. It was assumed he was as devout in his service to the gods as to the King. In truth, he was neither, but it served his purpose that the people—and the court—thought it so.

He had no love for the boy-King who occupied the throne or for the council of regents who actually ruled. The late King, Pathvi Narayan Shah, had been of another kind. He had been a warrior who let nothing stand in the way of what he wanted. He had conquered the other two principalities and created a united kingdom of Nepal, then moved his capital to the fertile valley of Kathmandu. Nasiradeen had been proud to serve him; they had understood each other, recognized their kindred spirits despite the separation of mortality.

But he had died, as even the best mortals do, and for the last six years Nasiradeen Satish had found no one else worthy of his respect. He had returned to the practice that had brought him out of the filth of his childhood, that had given him power and kept him alive. Nasiradeen supported no one but himself.

Oh, he did it carefully, mouthing phrases of flattery to the young King, who cared about nothing but his own amusement. All the while the leader of the Gurkhas made certain his men stayed loyal to him first and all else, including the throne, second.

And he made his plans, here on Holy Ground where no one could touch him. In this small antechamber built for the meditation of priests, he kept his maps, his lists and tallies of men and supplies, and here he received the messages from his spy. While he was here, mortals would respect his solitude and other Immortals that chanced to come to Kathmandu would honor the rules of the Game.

In the 312 years Nasiradeen had been alive he had learned to play all the games well.

He received the latest message, still tightly folded, from the hands of the priest, who then turned away, glad to leave Nasiradeen to the solitude he demanded. The Gurkha Immortal quickly unfolded the paper and scanned the words. As he read, a scowl darkened his visage and suspicions began to crowd his mind.

A Westerner in Lhasa, the message said. *Not a missionary. Befriended by Dalai Lama. Scout or mercenary?*

Or maybe something more, Nasiradeen's thoughts finished what the message could not say. *Whoever you are, you're too late. Lhasa is mine—Tibet is mine, and I'll soon be there to take it.*

Nasiradeen strode across the room and pulled the bell rope to summon a priest. He stood tapping his foot impatiently while he waited. It took only a few moments for the priest to arrive but to Nasiradeen it felt much, much longer.

"A pen and paper," the Gurkha Immortal ordered before the priest had entered the room. "Bring them quickly."

The priest bowed and left as silently as he had arrived. Nasiradeen paced around the small chamber. His long robes swirled around his ankles, and the sandals he wore made slapping noises upon the mosaic floor, reminding him with each step these were court clothes, good for nothing but idleness.

His hand went to the hilt of his sword, the long, curved saber not even court life could strip from his side. *Soon,* he thought, *I'll be back in proper clothes, a warrior's clothes.*

That day could not come swiftly enough for Nasiradeen. The only impediment was the King's regents; they had not yet agreed either to support the invasion of Tibet or release Nasiradeen from court service so he could lead the army on his own.

But the Gurkha leader had almost convinced the young King of the need for the venture. Nasiradeen played to the boy's vanity—it was such an easy thing to do—filling his head with tales of glory, making him think he could be the great leader his father had been.

Soon, Nasiradeen thought again. *A few weeks at most, and I'll take my army to the north.*

The Hindu priest returned with paper and pen. Nasiradeen snatched them from his hand.

"Wait," he ordered as he quickly scribbled a return message to his spy. *Watch carefully,* it said. *Report often. Invasion soon.*

Folding the paper, he turned and handed it to the priest. "This must go out at once," he said.

The priest sighed and bowed, then turned away. Nasiradeen could tell he was not happy with his charge—but he would obey. The Gurkha paid this temple enough gold to make certain of their obedience.

After the priest was gone, Nasiradeen left the small antechamber and went into the main temple. On the raised dais at the far end, the statue of the god Shiva sat behind a cloud of incense. The white stone from which it had been carved was changed to ash-colored from the years of smoke encircling it and the blue on its throat faded now to an indistinct gray.

Nasiradeen hardly noticed as he took his place among the worshipers. His eyes went instead to the bone held in one of the god's many hands, to the necklace of skulls around its neck and finally to the three eyes in the statue's face.

It was the third eye on which Nasiradeen fixed his attention. It bestowed inward vision, yet when turned outward brought burning destruction on those toward whom it was focused. Shiva was the great god, the Auspicious One, but he was also the Destroyer. It was to this aspect Nasiradeen prayed.

He bowed and touched his forehead to the floor, seeking the words that would win the god's power to his side.

I will build you a great temple in the hert of Lhasa itself, he told the god. *The holy city will become your city. I will destroy all who will not worship you, and you will drink the blood of their sacrifice. Be my aid and my strength, great Shiva, and nothing will stand before us.*

Duncan MacLeod left the Potala early, when the sun had barely risen. He left before the monk Gaikho could summon him to his usual morning meal with the Dalai Lama.

MacLeod meant no disrespect to the spiritual leader and hoped his absence would not be taken as such. But for the last two days they had spent most of their time together, student and teacher, while Duncan learned of the four Noble Truths that made up the basis of Tibetan Buddhism.

Although Duncan was grateful for the many hours the Dalai Lama was giving up from his other duties, today he needed to get away. He needed time to think, to absorb what he had already heard, to let his mind *breathe.*

His first thought was to go to the mountains, to the beauty and the quiet. Yet he found himself heading down into the city of Lhasa, where another beauty awaited him. The living beauty that was Xiao-nan. He knew it was early to be calling at her door but maybe, just maybe, he could persuade her to take a walk with him. Her company—the light of her eyes, the gentle sound that was her laughter—would help him put everything in perspective.

He found her house easily, remembering the route from the day he had walked her home. But when he arrived he stood uncertainly at her door, feeling like a schoolboy come courting instead of a two-hundred-year-old Immortal. *What,* his sudden doubts said, *if she did not want to see him, if her pleasant company the other day had been nothing more than the compassion to a stranger that seemed to be the unwritten law of this land?*

He did not know that Xiao-nan had watched for him each

day and was just on the other side of the door waiting for his knock.

Seconds ticked by as he stood there, battling his fears and chiding himself for his foolishness. If she said no—well, it was not the first time in his long life a beautiful woman had turned him down. *Ye'll never know by standing here, ye daft fool,* he told himself, his mind slipping into the brogue of his childhood. He raised his hand and knocked.

The door opened so quickly he nearly fell through the sudden space. And Xiao-nan was there, smiling up at him, even more beautiful than he remembered her.

"I . . . I know it's early," MacLeod stammered, groaning silently as he stated the obvious. Truth be told, something about her left him feeling awkward, even tongue-tied. It had to be more than her beauty; he had known beautiful women all over the world, and he had two centuries practice of how to talk to them, charm them, win their favor. But something about Xiao-nan said she was different, and the difference disconcerted him.

"Will you take a walk with me?" he asked her. "We won't go far."

"I would like very much to walk with you, Duncan MacLeod," she answered, her voice making music of his name. Duncan knew he wanted to hear her say it again and again.

A voice called from within the house. Xiao-nan turned and answered it quickly. Then she stepped out beside MacLeod and gently closed the door.

"I have told my mother we are going, so now we may walk together. Where would you like to go?" she asked.

"Anywhere you want," Duncan answered.

MacLeod was delighted to stand and watch her as she thought about a destination. As a little frown creased a line between her eyebrows, he fought the urge to bend and kiss it away. Then, suddenly, her face lightened.

"I know where we will go," she said. "There is a place where the blue orchid blooms on the hill. It is very beautiful in the early light."

As are you, Xiao-nan, Duncan thought. "I don't think I've ever seen a *blue* orchid," he said aloud as they started toward the city gate. "Is it truly blue?"

"Oh, yes," Xiao-nan replied. "Blue as the summer sky, with

little black flecks at its heart and a sweet scent that is like no other flower."

She picked up the pace, eager to show it to him. "Hurry, Duncan MacLeod," she said. "We must be there before the light passes."

He laughed and walked faster. He wanted to take her hand and run together like happy children, but he knew that in Tibet men and women did not touch casually in public. All he could do was stay by her side, delighting in each moment. Somehow that was enough. In her company, Duncan felt as if the weight of his years vanished and his heart was freer than it had been for a century gone.

Up in the Potala, the monk Gaikho reported Duncan's absence to the Dalai Lama. The spiritual leader nodded and dismissed him. He suspected whom Duncan had gone to see, and he approved; it would be a good match—for both of them.

The Dalai Lama took a deep breath, folded his hands in a pattern of serenity, and closed his eyes. He chose no direction for his meditation, but let his thoughts overlap like gentle waves upon a shore. Soon, it was as if he floated in a golden ocean of bliss, where all striving had ceased, all hopes had been realized, all was peace.

Here was the gateway of Nirvana. On one side, only a breath away, was the final state of liberation he would enter only after his work upon this earth was done and all beings had attained Enlightenment. On the other side was *samsara,* the cycles of birth, death, and rebirth he willed to enter again and again.

But here was timelessness. Here was clear and perfect thought, perfect truth, perfect compassion. It was here he came to refresh his mind and see how best to guide his people—all his people; he counted Duncan MacLeod among them.

He knew it was difficult for a man of MacLeod's nature to spend his days in inactivity, no matter how important the lessons or whom the teacher. The restlessness was there in the constant shifting of his eyes, in fingers that were never quite still, even when he was deep in thought. The strength of MacLeod's aura filled whatever room he occupied like the radiant energy of the noontime sun.

It was a good aura, of a man who strove to do what was right, what was best, but it was not the aura of a man at peace, either with himself or the world around him. The Dalai Lama knew the Eightfold Path was the way to that peace. He knew it through the centuries of his own experience.

In the quiet of his mind, the Dalai Lama smiled, knowing that to Duncan MacLeod he appeared only as a young man of twenty-three. But how else could it be? What could a man of the West, whose culture was blind to the truth of reincarnation, know about immortality?

Chapter Twelve

MacLeod and Xiao-nan wandered together into the hills. With each passing moment he found himself more charmed by her. She was like candlelight in a darkened room, warm and soft and golden.

She led him to where the blue orchid grew and, as she promised, it was the most exquisite flower MacLeod had ever seen. By comparison, his memories of the gardens of Europe, with their mazes and topiaries—even the roses of France and England and the heather-covered hills of his native Scotland—seemed overblown.

The ground was spongy and damp, so Duncan spread out his heavy coat and they sat on it, surrounded by the heady fragrance of the orchids and listening to the woodland symphony of breeze and birdsong. Xiao-nan laughed when Duncan wove a chain from some of the flowers and placed it on her head, but he could only think how even these orchids paled by comparison to the beauty of her eyes. Dark as a moonless night, they hinted at mysteries a man could gladly spend his lifetime trying to understand—even an Immortal.

"How old are you, Xiao-nan?" he asked her suddenly.

"I am nineteen," she replied, giving him a sidelong smile that nearly made his breath catch in his throat.

"Nineteen," he repeated softly with a hint of wonder in his voice. He was two centuries and she not yet two decades. He knew that nineteen years was nothing, the slightest wink of time, but Xiao-nan seemed timeless, ageless, a creature of both youth and eternity.

He knew, too, that in the life of mortality Xiao-nan lived nineteen was the age and past when young women thought to marry. He had to know if she was free.

"Is there some young man in your life, Xiao-nan?" he asked. "Should I stay away?"

She turned and looked him full in the face, saying nothing for a long moment as her eyes stared deeply into his own. Duncan wanted to curse himself for being three kinds of a fool. He should have gone more slowly, felt his way through their conversation more gently—but somehow he thought Xiao-nan would want nothing less than honesty from him.

She was still looking at him in silence. As with the Dalai Lama, Xiao-nan seemed to possess the same ability to reach deep into Duncan's soul with her eyes. Whatever she saw pleased her, for a slow smile lightened her features.

"There is no one else, Duncan MacLeod," she answered his honesty with her own. "None has brought light to my heart—until now."

Duncan reached out and drew a finger gently down the softness of her cheek. For this culture, it was a boldly intimate move to make when they had known each other so short a time, but Xiao-nan made no move to shift away. She seemed, rather, to welcome his touch.

Slowly, giving her time to turn her head or in any way indicate his kiss was unwanted, Duncan leaned forward. She made no move, but waited in perfect stillness until his lips brushed hers. The touch was brief, the softest of kisses, and yet in that instant Duncan was filled with the urge to protect her, to keep her forever safe from anything that might rob Xiao-nan of joy or peace.

Yet even as he thought it, another voice nagged inside his mind. *And what of your Immortality?* it whispered. *Do you dare hope for her love once she knows the truth?*

Duncan had no answer; he did not want an answer yet. He wanted this day free of anything but Xiao-nan's smile. He stood and held out his hand to her. When she took it and rose to her feet, it was only to flow against him, graceful as a cat, warm and soft as living water. Once more he kissed her, and she returned it without fear or hesitation.

She kept her eyes open as they kissed and MacLeod felt that if he could look into them long enough, he would find the answers wise men had sought throughout the ages. Perhaps here, at last, was the woman to whom he could truly open his heart.

* * *

Hunger drew them back to the city. Duncan would have left Xiao-nan at her door and gone back to the Potala to find a meal, but she insisted he come inside with her.

"My parents will be honored by your presence," she told him. "Please, Duncan MacLeod."

How could anyone tell her no, he wondered, knowing he could not. He went with her into the little yellow house that was her home. Both her parents came to greet them, their kind words of welcome quickly setting to rest any uncertainties Duncan had about how they would respond to the stranger who had spent all morning with the daughter.

The house, though small by Western standards, was elegant and furnished with the deceptive simplicity of the oriental mind. Duncan saw a single flower floating in a crystal bowl that was somehow more lovely than a full vase would have been. There was a sculptured screen inlaid with ivory and placed where the soft light of the window would sweep across it to highlight the carving of cranes in flight. The house smelled of ginger and jasmine.

Duncan was taken through to the courtyard out back, where the garden was just beginning to bloom. Stone benches had been set beside a small fountain. Water trickled slowly over stone in the sound of serenity, to gather in a pool where white water lilies blossomed.

Xiao-nan made sure Duncan was comfortably seated, then disappeared back into the house. She returned a few minutes later with a tray of food, sitting on the stone bench and putting the tray between them.

"You must eat now, Duncan MacLeod," she said, giving him a smile sweeter than the fruits and cakes she had brought. Some things on the tray Duncan recognized and others he did not, but it did not matter what he ate. Sitting here with Xiao-nan, MacLeod knew he was happy.

They say the love of a good woman can heal a man's heart of many things, Duncan thought. Yet the burdens his heart carried were very different from those of ordinary men, men whose lives lasted a few score years—if they were lucky. Would even the love of someone as precious and rare as Xiao-nan be enough to heal his heart for long? he wondered.

What is happiness or joy? the Dalai Lama had said to him more than once in the last few days. *And what also is sorrow? What is suffering? They are nothing, passing as the wind that blows in one direction, then another. It matters only what is done with these emotions. It matters only if by them compassion grows. In compassion only is found peace for the weary heart.*

"You are frowning, Duncan MacLeod," Xiao-nan's gentle voice broke across his thoughts. "You are displeased by something?"

"Oh no, Xiao-nan. Everything is wonderful. I was just thinking about something His Holiness said. Sometimes his words are difficult."

"But you must try to understand, Duncan MacLeod," she said, looking at him with her serenely serious eyes. "He is *bodhisattva*. Always he speaks the highest truth."

"*Bodhisattva?*" Duncan repeated the word slowly. "I don't understand."

"*Bodhisattva* is one whose inner being is perfected in wisdom. Nirvana awaits him, but he chooses rebirth that he may teach others the Path. Our Dalai Lama is such a one. He is the Ocean of Wisdom. My people will travel many days to see him, to hear him, sometimes to ask him a single question. That he teaches you is a great gift. You must listen to him, Duncan MacLeod."

"I will listen, Xiao-nan," he assured her.

"And you must hear not only with your ears, but with your heart."

"I will try."

Just then, Xiao-nan's sister came bounding into the garden, erupting into the small space like a personal volcano. She threw herself onto the ground by their feet and snatched a plum cake off the tray.

"Mingxia," Xiao-nan said sternly, "we have a guest. Behave with respect."

"He's your guest, not mine," she replied. "Besides, he's not a stranger—we met the other day on the trail from the warm pool."

She turned and smiled at Duncan, and he saw at once that though she looked much like Xiao-nan in facial structure, she was as different from her sister as the sun and the moon. She was also younger than Duncan had supposed when he met her on the trail—maybe thirteen or fourteen; the time when childhood and womanhood are mixed in both mind and body.

"Where were you?" Xiao-nan asked her. "And what have you been doing? Your hands are filthy."

Mingxia shrugged, indifferent as only a teenager can be. "Old Huilan needed some help with her garden. You know her daughter-in-law is worthless with such things."

"Mingxia," Xiao-nan said sharply, "that was unkind. Someday, when you are eight months pregnant, you will probably be 'worthless' in the garden, too."

Mingxia stood, snatching another treat from the tray on her way up. "I'll never be eight months pregnant," she said. "I don't intend to marry."

With that, she turned and hurried from the garden, throwing them one more smile over her shoulder as she went. When her absence finally settled back over the place, it seemed twice as quiet as before.

Duncan burst out laughing, and Xiao-nan turned to him with an embarrassed expression.

"I am sorry, Duncan MacLeod," she said. "My sister is young. She often speaks without thinking and still has much to learn about respect and compassion."

"Oh, don't apologize," Duncan said. "I think your sister is delightful, and certainly not—" He searched for a word in Tibetan, but finally had to resort to his native tongue "—boring."

It was Xiao-nan's turn to look perplexed. "Boring?" she asked. "What is that?"

"Boring is, well, it's everything Mingxia is *not*," he replied.

Xiao-nan still looked a bit confused, but she smiled anyway. "You are very kind, Duncan MacLeod," she said, "to forgive my sister her poor manners."

Duncan did not want to talk about Mingxia anymore; just wanted Xiao-nan to go on smiling at him.

"Xiao-nan," he said, "among my people it is not necessary to say a person's full name each time. Once you know them, one name only is used. Please call me Duncan."

"Duncan," she repeated, her smile turning gently pleased. "What does it mean, this Duncan?"

Duncan shrugged. "It means 'dark chieftain,' " he said, "but that's not why we give names among my people, or not the only reason."

She reached out and softly touched his hair. "Still," she said, "it suits you. Are you truly a chieftain?"

"I was the son of a chieftain," he answered. "But another leads my clan now."

"Your eyes say this makes you sad. Why do you not lead your people, Duncan?"

"It is a long story, Xiao-nan. Perhaps someday I will tell you."

"Someday," she agreed. "There is much time ahead for us."

"I hope so, Xiao-nan," Duncan said. He took her hand and gently kissed her palm. "I truly hope so."

Chapter Thirteen

Duncan left Xiao-nan and walked back through Lhasa, whistling softly under his breath. He smiled at every person he saw, stopping often to bow at them and happily receiving their bow in return. In his current state of mind, the whole city, with its brightly painted houses, fluttering prayer flags, and well-tended gardens, seemed a place of transcendent beauty.

MacLeod was unaware that his every movement was being watched with unfriendly eyes.

Father Edward, the Gurkha spy posing as a priest, had seen MacLeod and Xiao-nan return to the city. He had seen them go together into the woman's family home and noted how long it took MacLeod to emerge again.

So, the Westerner has taken a lover, he thought to himself. *How fortuitous. It will keep his mind off invasions while the great Nasiradeen, my master, prepares. He will want to have this information.*

It would also keep MacLeod from giving the Dalai Lama his full attention and protection, the spy's thoughts continued almost gleefully. The impediment he feared MacLeod might present to his plans was fast becoming nothing more than a crumbling wall, easily broached.

I will go visit the Choi household, Edward thought, *and find out the depths of Xiao-nan's involvement with MacLeod.* That would certainly be in keeping with his role as priest. He knew the girls well—they had been among the first to visit and to welcome him and Father Jacques to the city. The family trusted him, and what would be more fitting than a priest expressing concern over Xiao-nan's welfare?

It truth, it was not the older sister who interested him. Beautiful though she was, she seemed to him too serene, too remote. But Mingxia—she was *alive*. She had a fire to her that he wanted to claim as his own. It was often difficult to remind himself of the role he was playing and keep his distance.

That would change as soon as Nasiradeen invaded. Then, Father Edward told himself, he would have her. Girls of Mingxia's age were often wed in his country, and he would take her—not to wife, for she would be of a conquered people, and it would not then be fitting, but as concubine. What a reward for his work that would be.

Father Edward stopped outside the Choi house and composed himself before he knocked, smoothing down his black cassock as he cleared his thoughts of Mingxia's young body.

Old Yao-hui Choi, the father, answered the door. He bowed at the priest, gesturing for him to enter.

"Peace be to this house," Father Edward said, using the greeting he had so often heard from Father Tierney, the missionary he had known as a child. Much of what he said and did, in fact, was modeled after the old Irish priest.

"Come in, Father Edward," Yao-hui said, again gesturing for the priest to enter. "Come in and have tea with us. You have just missed our guest."

"I know," Father Edward replied. "I saw him leave. I also saw him with your daughter earlier. That is why I am here."

Yao-hui led the way into the main room of the house. His wife rose when they entered and also bowed to the priest, then she hurried from the room. Father Edward glanced around, but the daughters were nowhere in sight.

Unfortunate, Father Edward thought, *but perhaps temporary.* Usually the entire family gathered to greet a guest—and Father Edward wanted to see Mingxia.

Father Edward took a seat on one of the cushions and politely waited while tea was brought and served. As he hoped, Xiao-nan and Mingxia joined them. Now, Father Edward thought, to play his part.

"Yao-hui," he said, addressing the head of the household formally, with seeming respect. "I know you care for your family and want the best for your daughters. You and your family have been very kind to myself and Father Jacques since we arrived in Lhasa. I also care that no harm come to this family, to your daughters. Therefore, I respectfully ask you what you know of this Duncan MacLeod?"

"He is a good man, Father Edward," Yao-hui replied.

"How do you know this, Yao-hui?"

"My daughter has told me, and I have no reason to doubt her."

"Young girl's hearts are often fooled."

"That is true, Father Edward," Yao-hui nodded gravely, sipping from his bowl of tea. "But the heart of the Dalai Lama is not. His heart and mind always see clearly, and he teaches Duncan MacLeod. Therefore, Duncan MacLeod is a good man, and I can trust him with my daughter's care."

Now came the important question. The Gurkha spy took care to phrase it well.

"It is unusual for a man of the West to come to the holy city," he said. "Has Xiao-nan told you why he is here?"

Although Xiao-nan was sitting only a few feet away, Father Edward asked the question of her father, showing respect to his status; this was a polite discussion between men.

Yao-hui turned and looked at his daughter. She answered quickly and quietly. Father Edward could hear her words, but he waited for the father to relay them.

"Xiao-nan says that Duncan MacLeod has not spoken of his reason for being here, but she knows that his heart is sad. She believes he is here to find the Path to Enlightenment. This, the Dalai Lama will teach him."

Their conversation always comes back to that pathetic young man, the spy thought. *He cannot hold a sword or ride a horse, but is carried everywhere in a covered litter like some feeble old woman—yet these people speak of him as if he can do all things. When the great Nasiradeen comes, he will show the people what a true leader is. The people will tremble before him, and the Dalai Lama will be returned to the dust from which he was made.*

The thought gave Father Edward pleasure, and he smiled. He covered the expression by taking a sip from the bowl of tea in his hands.

"I'm sure that if your Dalai Lama accepts this Duncan MacLeod, you are right to do likewise," he said pleasantly. "It is only my concern for this family that has caused my questions."

Yao-hui bowed to the priest-impostor. "You bless my house with your compassion," he said.

Father Edward stood. He bowed to Yao-hui and to each of the family, letting his eyes linger ever so slightly on Mingxia. Then he turned and took his leave; he had a message to send. As he walked back to the house he shared with Father Jacques, his thoughts turned again to the invasion and the prizes he would claim after its success.

Gold—yes, he wanted gold—and wine and fine foods to make up for the life he was now being forced to live, and he wanted silks to wear instead of this black cassock. Mostly he wanted women, starting with Mingxia.

I'll take Xiao-nan, too, he thought. *They'll both be my concubines, fire and ice for my pleasure. And if they please me, I'll let their parents live—as my servants.*

The threat to her parents' lives was, he knew, the only way he would bring Xiao-nan to his bed. Not that he cared about her willingness, only her obedience. *That* he would have, that and her fear.

Mingxia he would woo more carefully, but not so much as to quench her fire. The thought of her excited him anew. The only thought sweeter was of the battle that would come and the part he would play in it.

He would kill Father Jacques himself; he would kill all missionaries if he could, but Father Jacques would do. If he was lucky and Shiva favored him, he would take MacLeod's life as well. Then, with the smell of blood around him and the song of battle filling his heart, he would have the women on whom to satiate his desire.

Xiao-nan was glad when the priest left. She did not like him. She tried to see him with the eyes of compassion, to think of him with kind thoughts, but she knew that often she failed. She did not trust him. She did not like the look that came into his eyes whenever they rested on her sister.

Xiao-nan carried the tea things back into the kitchen for her mother, then she returned to the garden, back to the place where she and MacLeod had sat together a short time ago. It made him seem closer—and it was a nearness Xiao-nan wanted.

She was glad she had not needed to lie to her father's question earlier; she truly did not know what reason had brought MacLeod to Tibet. *It was his karma to come here,* she thought. *That is enough.* But she would have lied if she needed—not to her father, but to Father Edward.

He is like a cat who waits at the mouse hole, she thought, sitting on the little stone bench where MacLeod had sat, *and we are the mice. Someday soon he will bare his teeth and show us his fangs.*

Xiao-nan bent forward and trailed her fingers in the water, softly stirring up the fountain's pool. The white lilies bobbed on the gentle waves, serene and untroubled, riding on top of the disturbance. Xiao-nan told herself that she should likewise rise above the turbulent thoughts Father Edward caused her.

Father Jacques, the other priest, created no such misgivings. He was a kind, soft-spoken man with eyes as gentle as a doe's. Father Jacques did not walk the Path of Enlightenment as her people did, and that made Xiao-nan sad for his sake. But his wit was sharp and Xiao-nan often enjoyed stopping to talk with him—if Father Edward was not nearby.

It seems he is always somewhere near, Xiao-nan thought with irritation. *Like today. What right did he have to come here and question my father, question me, about Duncan?*

She smiled as she thought his name. "Duncan," she said it aloud, enjoying the sound of it, the feel of it. "Dark Chieftain."

She had been right when she said it suited him. It did not matter that another led his tribe, he was the type of man people always followed. He would create his own tribe wherever he went.

She knew that she would follow him; already her heart was won. But why? she wondered. Why did he touch her heart in a way all others had failed to do? She was not given to quick passions, like Mingxia. At fourteen, her sister had already imagined herself in love three times. Young boys danced around her like otters in a waterfall.

Xiao-nan was different. Through the years young men had

come into her life and gone again, disappointed that she could feel for them nothing more than a distant compassion. She had even entertained the thought of leaving the world and withdrawing into the life of seclusion, of *samgha,* and to seek Enlightenment as a Buddhist nun.

But now there was MacLeod and her heart was alive, truly alive for the first time. She felt as if all of her years she had been holding her breath and now, suddenly, the air flowed through her, sweet and fragrant and free.

"Duncan MacLeod," she said his name again, enjoying the slight tremble of joy that shot through her. "Duncan MacLeod."

For her, it was the name of love.

Chapter Fourteen

Nasiradeen Satish stood amid the opulence of the royal court of Nepal, but he held himself distant, watching the people around him through slightly narrowed eyes. He looked with disdain at the soft bodies swathed in fine linens, silks, and brocades, and at the jewels worn by men and women alike.

Two hundred years ago, when he was but a century old, he would have looked at these people with envy. He would have seen their wealth, their status, and the power he assumed it brought to them. But in those years, the memory of his beginnings was still fresh.

Now, as he stood among the court, he felt only contempt. There was not a warrior here; the men were as soft and spoiled as the women. From the boy-King and his regents through the lowest courtesan, Nasiradeen had no use for any of them.

Nasiradeen saw the men eyeing him warily from time to time, as they might a caged beast. He knew he was the object of their speculation—and their fear. He did not care; he reveled in it. Love, loyalty; these could be won or lost. They could, for the right price, be bought and sold like commodities. But fear—that fed upon itself. It was a seed that once planted grew like an incipient weed, sending out its tendrils into every thought, every feeling. To win someone's fear was to win true power, true control.

He drew his lips back in the barest of smiles. His teeth showed in startling whiteness against the tawny darkness of his skin. Those nearest him turned quickly away, sidling cautiously farther out of reach. Though he was dressed as sumptuously as any of them, they knew he was not tamed.

The women, too, watched him carefully, but it was not fear he saw in their eyes. They looked at his lean, muscular body, his height, his obvious wealth, and they whispered to one another behind their hands. *Trading stories, perhaps,* he thought wryly, knowing his skills in the bedroom were almost as legendary as his prowess on the battlefield.

And why not? he thought, pleased with himself. *I'm no eunuch—and I've had a long time to learn the ways of pleasure.*

He had no trouble finding companions for his bed, either. Oh, he took care never to deflower a virgin unless he was going to add her to his household, but that did not mean other women were not available—and not temple whores or women of the streets. He preferred other men's wives. As an Immortal, Nasiradeen knew he would father no children, and if a man could not keep his wife content enough to stay at home . . .

He was a hunter and they the prey, and their conquest was as sweet as a blood-kill.

A slow smile crept across his face as he thought of the night just passed. Last night the wife of Sandep Kumar, the King's third regent, had warmed his bed. That had been especially pleasant; Nasiradeen hated Kumar.

The old fool's no doubt too fat to please any woman, the Gurkha leader thought. But Nasiradeen knew he had pleased Kumar's wife—her squeals of delight had told him so, as had her increasingly eager participation. She had pleased him as well. She was young, but not a child, and well fleshed. Yes, she was a pleasant diversion while he waited to invade Tibet.

"You smile like a wolf who has found a lamb," the King's immature voice sliced through his thoughts. Amused by the image, the King laughed. The sound was high and fluting as a girl's. Nasiradeen silently ground his teeth together.

The King beckoned to him with a plump, bejeweled hand. "Come over here and tell Us what has made you smile such a smile," he called out.

Nasiradeen left the wall against which he had been leaning and strode across the room, pleased by the way the people of the court scampered to clear a path before him. Their eyes betrayed their nervousness as he walked past them, hand on the hilt of his ever-present sword. *Little sheep,* he thought to them. *Yes, I am a wolf in your fold.*

When he reached the King, he bowed with an elegant flourish, then went down on one knee before the throne.

"I smiled to be in your presence, my King," he flattered the young man, "and to see you in a state of such obvious health and happiness. Indeed, what else could bring a smile to a face such as mine? Warriors do not smile easily, my King."

"Then what a dreary life warriors must have," the King replied somewhat dryly.

"Not so, my King," Nasiradeen said.

The others have been at him again, the Gurkha thought quickly, *trying to undo all my work. I almost had him convinced of the glory and wanting to be a warrior.* Nasiradeen knew he had to find a way to recapture the young King's imagination.

"A warrior's life is far from dreary, Sire," he said. "It is just that our pleasures differ from those of ordinary men. Like your father, Your Majesty is far from ordinary. Surely, you of all men know what it is to be bored."

"Yes, that is so," the young King said with a sigh.

Nasiradeen dared to lean closer, as if inviting the King into a personal conspiracy. "There is no boredom on the battlefield, my King," he said softly, pulling the King's attention in with his eyes. "On the battlefield the heart pounds, the blood races with life, all the senses are sharp. And *victory*—ah, nothing is more sweet than to see the enemy kneeling at your feet, to taste their fear in the air and to know that their fate hangs by your word.

"This is a warrior's pleasure, and I can give it to you, my King," he continued. "It is a pleasure more intoxicating than honeyed wine."

The young King licked his lips, as if tasting the words. There was a slight flush high on his down-covered cheeks.

I have him, Nasiradeen thought. *He's mine.*

"The esteemed Nasiradeen, your general, speaks well of a warrior's *pleasures,*" Sandep Kumar, the King's regent, said as he stepped forward from where he had stood listening behind the throne. "But he does not mention a warrior's *life.* He does not tell you of the long hours in the saddle or days of wearing filthy, uncomfortable clothes. He does not mention the discomfort of camp life, of inclement weather, cold nights, and poor food."

Nasiradeen shot a look of loathing at the regent. "There speaks an *ordinary* man, my King," he said, "concerned only with ordinary comfort and ordinary pleasure. What can *he* know of glory?

"But you, my King," once more Nasiradeen lowered his voice to a conspiratorial whisper, "you are not an ordinary man. In you the blood of Pathvi Narayan Shah runs true. Like your father, you are called to greater things than *ordinary* men."

But Kumar's words had done their work. Although the boy still listened to Nasiradeen, his attention wandered, and his eyes scanned the room as if looking for the next diversion.

Nasiradeen was furious with Kumar, though a part of him acknowledged a strategy well played. The Immortal let his voice trail off, then bowed himself out of the King's presence. The boy looked slightly relieved to see him go.

I will not wait on your whims much longer, Nasiradeen thought as he returned to his place by the wall where he could watch the court without having to participate. *Soon I will invade Tibet whether or not I have your support—and the army will follow* me. *If you refuse to be my ally in this, then when I have conquered Tibet you will learn what it means to have Nasiradeen as an enemy.*

As for Kumar . . . The Immortal's gaze shifted to the corpulent regent still standing by the King's side, gloating at his victory over the Gurkha. *I will enjoy exacting my revenge. I already have his young wife in my bed. After I win Tibet, I will find a way to claim his fortune as well.*

With that thought, Nasiradeen smiled again—and those nearest him backed farther away at the sight.

The Dalai Lama and Duncan MacLeod were at that moment sitting in the Potala gardens discussing that day's lesson. The sun was shining through the trees, and they sat in a pool of dappled light. The Dalai Lama watched Duncan fondly as he pulled bits of the grass on which he sat, twirling them between his fingers as he concentrated on what he was hearing. The Dalai Lama knew he felt a deepening affection for this man and marveled that this feeling had developed so quickly.

"No, Duncan MacLeod," he was saying in answer to MacLeod's last question. "Nirvana is not like the heaven of which the missionaries speak. It is not a *place* one enters upon death, although for the Enlightened there is the final liberation from *samsara*. But Nirvana is a *state*—of the soul, yes, but also of the mind. And it is not only for certain people. Anyone can achieve Nirvana."

"If it is a *state,* as you say, then can it be attained here on Earth, by those still living?"

The young man smiled; rarely, in all of his incarnations, had he been blessed with a student so astute or so challenging.

"The answer to your question is both yes and no," he said. "Nirvana is both an emptying and a filling, where nothing exists and all exists. It is for the present, and it is for the eternal."

"Your Holiness, you talk in riddles," Duncan said, throwing down the blades of grass between his fingers. "How can an ordinary man ever hope to understand such things?"

"By laying aside old thoughts and teaching the mind a new way. It takes training, yes. It is not easy, the Path to Enlightenment. But you have trained your body in the use of your sword, have you not?"

The young man laughed at the look on Duncan's face. "Oh yes, Duncan MacLeod," he said. "I know of the sword you keep among your belongings. I know also about the movements you do each morning and evening. You do these to keep your body strong and supple, do you not?"

"Yes, Your Holiness," Duncan answered.

"So it is that we train our minds to follow the Eightfold Path. The lessons take only a short time to say, perhaps a few hours, but the training, the mastery—ah, that can take many lifetimes."

"Your Holiness," Duncan said, "the other day Xiao-nan said something I did not understand. She said that you are—how did she put it?—'perfected in wisdom.' Does this mean you no longer know the suffering of human life, or *dukkah,* to use your word?"

The young man sighed. "Again, Duncan MacLeod, the answer to your question is both yes and no. Let us consider the three types of suffering. First there is the suffering called misery, which is the physical or mental pain such as illness or injury. None of us while living can escape such burdens. But they are passing, insubstantial."

The Dalai Lama stopped, and a look of tender sadness crossed his face. "There are some," he said, "who choose to remain in this state of suffering. They will not free their thoughts or remember the truth of impermanence. Instead they see only *this* moment, *this* pain, until even when the pain is gone the weight of it continues to rule their minds with fear of its return. For these, Enlightenment is still many lifetimes away. But such is not my Path, nor do I think, Duncan MacLeod, that it is yours."

As the Dalai Lama watched, a look of weary acceptance came into Duncan's eyes, as if the passage of physical illness and pain was a thing he knew beyond knowing. As was so often the case, it left the young man wondering about the secrets in MacLeod's life.

"The second branch of *dukkah,*" the Dalai Lama continued, "is the suffering of change. Those who were young grow old or die; that which was new wears out, becomes worn, tattered, withers away. What began as happiness gives way to loneliness, disappointment, loss, grief. This, too, is life, and in this do some also become trapped. But the knowledge of impermanence frees the mind from this as well. Change comes and goes. It is insubstantial."

Again, a look came into MacLeod's eyes that made the Dalai Lama pause in what he was saying. *So, this, too, then, is a suffering you have known very well,* the young man thought as he saw the shadows of memories crowd Duncan's face. *You have, I think, known all the faces of change until now impermanence has become your reality. But has it freed you, Duncan MacLeod, or trapped you?*

"The third suffering," the Dalai Lama said before Duncan could go on too long in the silence of his memories, "is the suffering, the dislocation from peace and compassion, that comes through afflicted emotions. Negative thoughts and actions create this suffering—anger, greed, ignorance, aversion, pride, lust, envy; the list continues. These emotions afflict all who are still traveling *samsara,* the cycles of birth, death and rebirth."

"Xiao-nan said you are freed from this cycle, but *choose* to be reborn," Duncan said.

The Dalai Lama nodded. "Eight times have I chosen not to enter the final liberation. I return to teach my people for their own Enlightenment. For myself, I no longer suffer with anger or pride or greed. No longer does change cause me unhappiness or the weakness of my body rob me of peace. But for my people," he stopped and shook his head. "My people come to me, and their pain is great. Then I must share their suffering, take their suffering and ease it. For my people, I suffer—and not my people only, but any who comes to me in need."

The young man looked up at the sky. "Remember, Duncan MacLeod, that as suffering can be identified, so can it be overcome. But that is for another day. Let us talk now of pleasant things, like the warmth of the sun and the beauty of this garden. They, too, are passing, but they are pleasures for now."

Chapter Fifteen

Father Jacques Beauchamps was kneeling in the dirt, tending the little garden he had planted behind the house. He had left off the cape and biretta so distinctive to his order, preferring the simplicity of a plain cassock for his work.

He often went about dressed as simply as possible, much to the disgust of Father Edward. *He* was always fully attired and immaculate—and he would never consider kneeling in the dirt.

But Father Jacques knew he was happiest here, planting seeds or pulling weeds, and watching as the neat little rows he had turned went from bare soil to thick growths of vegetables and flowers. The study of botany had been his work, and his joy, in France, and he was delighted to continue his labors here, where there were so many new varieties to catalog.

The only thing that made him as happy was playing with the children of the city. They called him Bo-Bo, derived he supposed form the word "boo," with which he would surprise them from behind a tree or bush when they were playing games together. Whatever the origin of the name, he was pleased with it.

Behind him, he heard one of Father Edward's birds enter the row of cages built next to the house. Father Jacques often thought it was an odd hobby his brother priest had, keeping pigeons only to set them free and watch them return. *But then,* he thought as he stood and dusted the dirt from the front of his black cassock, noticing how much of it refused to come out, *he doesn't understand why I like to spend my time in the garden. We are each of us different, unique, as God made us.*

He left his hand spade in the dirt and hurried toward the cages to close the door and shut the newly arrived bird inside. *Edward will want to know of the bird's return,* he thought, *and I could use a walk.* Not stopping to change into a clean cassock or add the cape and biretta, he headed out through the side gate in the garden wall.

As he walked down the city streets, people called out greetings, and he waved to them as he passed, occasionally stopping to ask if anyone had seen Father Edward. Before long a group of children, all about six or eight years old, had gathered around him.

"Come and play, Bo-Bo," they said, their happy voices chattering like the squirrels that filled the trees in his native France.

"No, not now," he told them. "Later. I'm looking for someone now."

"Who, Bo-Bo?" they asked, skipping and running round and around him. He often thought that children of this age were like spinning tops, either madly active or utterly at rest.

"I am looking for Father Edward," he told them. Then he patted the pockets of the trousers under his cassock and felt the lumps of candy he habitually kept there.

"Run and find Father Edward for me," he said, "and when you come tell me where he is, each of you will get a sweet."

Delighted, the children ran off, leaving Father Jacques in a sudden pool of silence. He watched them until they were out of sight. Then, with a smile, he resumed his walk, shaking his head at the wonderment of childhood, when every activity is a game and an excuse for happiness.

He had only taken a few steps when he saw MacLeod turn onto the street a few yards ahead. Father Jacques had heard talk of another European in Lhasa. He was, they said, a friend and student of the Dalai Lama himself. Father Jacques was glad this sudden opportunity had presented itself; he was eager to meet this other man of the West.

He began to walk faster, hoping to catch up to MacLeod, but it soon became evident that he was no match for the youth and vigor of the man ahead of him.

"Wait," he called out in French, panting slightly in the thin Tibetan air. "You, sir, please wait."

MacLeod turned at the sound of the French words behind him. Father Jacques saw the slightly startled expression on his face, the way MacLeod's eyes looked up and down the front of his cassock, and he grinned sheepishly. He knew he was a disheveled sight.

Father Jacques harbored no vanity about the type of figure he cut, even at the best of times. He knew that his wispy hair, once the color of straw, had faded to an indeterminate gray, and that he was thin as an old dog with narrow shoulders that were permanently hunched from years of bending over a shovel or a book. He sometimes thought the Vicar General had sent him to the mission field just so he would no longer have to look at him.

I should have joined another Order, he thought, not for the first time as he hurried to catch up to MacLeod. *I think the Franciscans would have found me easier to accept.*

But his father had wanted him to be a Jesuit and Jesuit he was—if one of unusual sensibilities for the elite Order.

"Bonjour, Monsieur," he greeted MacLeod, enjoying the treat of speaking his native French again and hoping this obviously well-traveled European understood. Other than Tibetan, and Latin of course, it was the only language Father Jacques knew. "I am pleased to finally meet you. I am Father Jacques Beauchamps."

"How do you do, Father. I am Duncan MacLeod of the Clan MacLeod."

Father Jacques was relieved to hear him speaking such good French, even if some of the words were spoken with a trace of a Scottish brogue. MacLeod was still looking at the priest with an amused expression, and Father Jacques made another swipe at the dirt encrusting his cassock where he had knelt on it.

"Yes, I know your name," he said. "I think everyone in Lhasa does by now. I heard it from my brother priest, Father Edward, whom I believe you've already met—and from Xiao-nan, of course."

Father Jacques saw MacLeod's back stiffen slightly at the mention of Father Edward, and he inwardly sighed. His fellow priest was not an easy man to like even for himself, though out of duty and Christian charity he tried.

"You're another Jesuit, then?" MacLeod was saying. "From your habit, I wasn't sure."

Father Jacques laughed. "No, I don't suppose you were. Yes, I am a member of the Society of Jesus, though not, I'm afraid, a very pristine representative."

"Bo-Bo," the children came running back in a crowd, dancing like miniwhirlwinds around him. "Bo-Bo, we've found him. Come and see."

"You've found him already?" Father Jacques at once turned his attention from MacLeod to the children, switching easily to the language of Tibet. "Then you shall each have the sweet I promised you. Let's see," he quickly counted the children, "eight of you. Yes, I'm sure I have that many."

He reached into his pocket and brought out his horde of candy. The children again squealed with delight as he handed them around. Father Jacques found he had two pieces left over and he offered one to MacLeod. When the Scotsman shook his head, Father Jacques shrugged, popped one candy into his mouth, and returned the other to his pocket.

"Come, Bo-Bo," the children resumed their calls, now speaking around the hard sweets in their mouths. They pulled on his hands and cassock with sticky fingers. "Come with us to Father Edward. Then come play with us."

Father Jacques smiled at them. "You lead the way, and I'll follow. Go on now, I'm right behind."

That satisfied the children, and they ran off again. The priest turned back to his adult companion and the pleasantries of his native tongue.

"Will you walk with me a little, Monsieur MacLeod?" he asked, once more in French. "I don't often get to speak my own language, and you would be doing me a kindness."

"Certainly, Father, for as long as we go in the same direction," MacLeod answered. "I have to say," he continued as they resumed their walk, "you seem little like the other Jesuits I have known."

Father Jacques laughed. "No doubt they would be pleased to hear that. Have you known many of my Order?"

"A few," MacLeod answered, his expression turning shut and hard.

And you did not like them, Father Jacques thought. *Ah, well, there have been many I did not like, either.*

"Have you traveled much, Monsieur MacLeod?" he asked, thinking it best to change the subject.

"Aye, Father," Duncan answered, but his expression remained shut, as if this too was a subject he preferred not to discuss.

Are you running from something, Monsieur MacLeod? Father Jacques wondered, *or from yourself, perhaps?*

"You said Xiao-nan had spoken of me," MacLeod said as if offering a safe subject. "Do you know her well?"

"Oh, yes," the priest answered quickly. He understood the offering and was grateful for it. "She comes frequently to see me. She is truly one of God's sweetest children. They all are in this land. It is a haven of innocence, trust, and kindness."

"Aye, Father, that it is—and I would not like to see anything, or anyone, try to change it."

Father Jacques did not miss the edge in MacLeod's voice. "Do you think that is why we are here, Monsieur MacLeod?" he asked softly.

"Isn't that what your kind do?" MacLeod answered. "Don't you come to foreign lands to convert the people, to change them from their own culture and beliefs into your own?"

"We come to tell them of God's love for them, that is true, Monsieur MacLeod. But I would never force others into a belief they cannot share or try to change them from who they are."

"Then, Father Jacques, you are indeed different than the others of your Order I have met."

As their paths continued in the same direction, with MacLeod making no move to turn down a different street, Father Jacques could guess where he was going; the Choi house was only a quarter mile up the road. How much farther he was going he did not know, but he would be sorry to lose the Scotsman's company.

"You must come by our mission house sometimes, Monsieur MacLeod," he said, watching as up ahead the band of children rounded a bend in the meandering street. "Do you like gardens?"

"Aye, Father, I do. I enjoy the look and the smell of them, though life has not granted me much time in them, and I'm not much of a hand at their care."

"Well, you must come by then. We'll sit in my garden, share a glass of wine, and, perhaps, talk of France. The wine is quite *vin ordinaire,* but I should like to talk of my homeland with one who has been there."

Before MacLeod could answer, they followed the children's

footsteps around the bend in the road. Up ahead was the Choi household.

And in front of the house stood Father Edward—with Mingxia.

There was nothing religious in his pose. She stood leaning her back to the house and he with his hands on either side of her, like a lover about to claim a kiss. Both Father Jacques and MacLeod stopped, shocked into stillness. As they watched, Father Edward reached up and took a strand of Mingxia's hair. He began twirling it between his fingers as he spoke to her, bending his face close in an intimate whisper.

Whatever he said pleased Mingxia. Her eyes sparkled, and she shifted her stance slightly into a pose as old as Eve and provocative as Lilith. Her back arched, so that her young breasts pushed upward and her body preened invitingly.

Father Jacques quickly glanced up at his companion. The words "face like thunder" popped into his head when he saw MacLeod's expression. The Scotsman suddenly strode forward, quickly covering the distance between himself and the couple. Father Jacques hurried along behind.

MacLeod spoke no word to Father Edward, and Father Jacques found he admired MacLeod's control. Another man might have struck the young priest. Father Jacques could see that MacLeod was tempted, but instead he grabbed Mingxia by the hand and, without stopping to knock, pulled her into the house. Then he slammed the door, leaving the two priests standing together outside.

Father Jacques waited while Father Edward turned toward him, wondering what explanation the other priest would offer. He found himself taking a step backward from the look of anger and hatred on Father Edward's face.

"One of your birds has arrived," Father Jacques said coldly. "Perhaps that is a better place for your attention than this house."

"Oh, it is," Father Edward replied. The words held such an odd tone that as he turned away and began walking home, Father Jacques could not help but think they contained a hidden meaning.

What are those birds of his? the French priest wondered. *Perhaps I should take a closer interest in them.*

Ahead on the street the children were chasing each other, playing the universal game of tag. "Come play with us, Bo-Bo," they called to him again, oblivious of the scene that had just passed.

He waved at them. "I'm coming," he called back, glad to put thoughts of Father Edward from his mind.

At least for now.

Chapter Sixteen

━━━

"I tell you, Mingxia, that is not the way a priest should act," Duncan MacLeod's voice was loud. He was not shouting, not quite, but he was angry. It was more than the presence of Father Jacques, a man whose honor MacLeod felt instinctively to be true, that had kept Duncan's temper in check and his fist out of Father Edward's face. It was the years of childhood training. It surprised MacLeod that after two hundred years, the conditioning should still be so strong.

One did not hit, or do any violence, upon the person of a holy man. Although Father Edward's actions seemed to rob him of that accolade, he still wore the cloth, the collar and habit of the office. It was this which had stayed Duncan's hand.

The whole family had come running into the main room when he had pulled Mingxia into the house, and now they were gathered around, flinching at his anger. Except Xiao-nan; she sat with her arm wrapped protectively around her little sister, staring up at MacLeod with dark and serene eyes, watching as his hands clenched and unclenched almost rhythmically by his side.

"My sister is young, Duncan," she said, her voice creating a pool of calm in a charged atmosphere.

"She was not *acting* young," Duncan snapped. "I've seen tarts on the streets of London and Paris with the same looks on their faces as the one she was giving that . . . that priest." He spat the word.

Mingxia began to cry quietly. She turned her head into her sister's shoulder, and Xiao-nan's arm tightened around her. The gesture touched MacLeod, reaching through his anger. He took a deep breath and then another, each time concentrating on exhaling his anger with the air. Then he sat down next to the girl.

"Listen to me, Mingxia," he said, his voice quieter now.

"Priests of Father Edward's church take vows, sacred vows, never to be, well, as a man is with a woman. Think of Father Jacques. He would not act as Father Edward did."

Still sniffling, Mingxia turned to him. "Father Jacques is *old.*" she said a little defiantly.

"That does not matter, Mingxia," Duncan continued. "Father Edward's actions today were wrong. If he does not keep the vows he has taken, then he is a false priest and a man without honor. Either way, you must not encourage him. Do you understand?"

Mingxia turned her head back into her sister's shoulder, but she nodded.

"She understands, Duncan," Xiao-nan said. "She will stay away from the priest."

"I'm only trying to protect you, Mingxia," MacLeod told the young girl. "I know more about such men than you do. Please trust me."

When Duncan sat down, Xiao-nan's mother had slipped silently from the room, sensing the worst of his anger was spent. She returned now carrying a tray with tea and drinking bowls. As she set it on the table in the center of the room, Yao-hui Choi came and sat near his daughters. He looked at Duncan with the same calm expression Xiao-nan wore.

"The matter is over, Duncan MacLeod," he said. "My daughter will obey your words, and mine."

"Thank you, Yao-hui," Duncan replied. "And I ask your pardon for disrupting the peace of this household."

"You sought only my daughter's well-being, and you have blessed us by your act," Yao-hui said, his hand waving a dismissive gesture into the air.

Xiao-nan looked at her father in a silent request to speak, to continue the subject he had all but closed. He gave a barely perceptible nod, and she then turned to MacLeod.

"As you have said, Duncan, we know little of these men and their ways, so I must ask you, what about the other men of the Western faith in our city? Are we not to trust them or to show them compassion through our friendship? Must we punish all because of one false action?"

MacLeod smiled tenderly at her, his own heart gentled by the beauty of hers. "No, Xiao-nan," he said. "I met Father Jacques this day, and although I bear no love for the Religious Order he follows, I believe he is a kind and honorable man. I have not met the Brothers in the city, but if you think they are also honorable, then I'm sure they are. You have a mind and a heart that sees clearly."

Xiao-nan's mother passed the tea around and, as they drank, the silence put a seal on the conversation. MacLeod's own unnamed suspicion of the priest had notched a bit higher, but for now all that needed to be said had been said; Mingxia and her family had been warned. MacLeod felt a sense of relief settle over him. He knew, however, that he had best not see Father Edward, at least for a few days, or he could not promise to hold his anger in check a second time.

With the resiliency of youth, Mingxia had already recovered from her tears. She finished her tea first and started to rise.

"Mingxia," her mother said, "you will remain at home today."

"But—"

"No, there has been enough trouble. You will remain at home."

Mingxia turned and fled into the garden. As he stared after her, MacLeod was sorry to see the young girl so unhappy. It showed on his face, and Xiao-nan gently laid her hand over his.

"Do not worry," she said. "By tomorrow she will have forgotten all about her feelings today. Some new activity will capture her attention and she will be fine. My sister is truly proof that all things are impermanent and insubstantial."

"Not all things, Xiao-nan," MacLeod said softly as he intertwined his fingers into hers. With his other hand, he put his small drinking bowl back on the tray. Then he stood, and Xiao-nan came to her feet beside him.

"I think I should go now," he said to her parents, "and let this house return to its usual quiet."

"I will come, too," Xiao-nan said.

MacLeod looked at her, staring deeply into her eyes. The serenity in them seemed to flow from her to him. It warmed him, embraced him until he did not know if a second or an hour passed while he looked at her—nor did he care.

"I have something I would show you," she continued, smiling a little smile that was for him alone and held just a hint of mischief.

He returned it, not knowing what her plans were, but caring only that they would be together. He reached up and drew a finger softly down her cheek.

"All right," he said. He turned toward her parents in time to see them exchange a knowing glance. Were his growing feelings for Xiao-nan so obvious? he wondered. Well, perhaps they were.

They took their leave quickly and stepped out into the afternoon sun. Tibet seemed a timeless place, and somehow, without his noticing, spring had given way to summer. The sun's rays were almost hot on Duncan's shoulders. They felt wonderful; he felt wonderful as he walked down the street with Xiao-nan.

She said no word about where they were going, and he was content to follow her lead. But as they neared a house with a wooden cross nailed above the door, his steps faltered.

"You said you had not met the Brothers who live in the city," she said to him. "It is time you did. Kindness and compassion can only be shown in person, Duncan MacLeod."

Duncan recognized in her voice the same tone her mother had used to Mingxia. Like the young girl, he knew that an argument was useless. He could only say what he had told her once before.

"Lead the way, Xiao-nan," he said, "and I will surely follow."

Her smile was all he needed to know she recognized the words and all of his heart that was in them. She went and knocked on the door.

Duncan and Xiao-nan spent over an hour with the Capuchin Brothers, and Duncan had to admit he liked them. They were quiet, gentle men who radiated the spirit of kindness and of devotion. He understood why Xiao-nan had brought him here.

Of the three of them—Brother Thomas, Brother Peter, and Brother Michael—MacLeod felt he had the most in common with the latter. He was older than the other two, perhaps in his late fifties, Duncan thought, and he had seen much of life before becoming a monastic. It showed in the tolerance he had toward human foibles and in his wry sense of humor.

All three Brothers saw them off at the door with an invitation to return soon. After the door had closed, MacLeod slipped an arm around Xiao-nan's waist and hugged her.

"Thank you," he said, "for your patience with my anger—and for how gently you remind me of the good people in the world."

She looked up at him and smiled. "You are welcome, Duncan," she said.

He kissed the top of her head, smiling into her hair. Honesty was one of the things he loved about her. No demurrings or prevarications; she knew what she had done and why, and she acknowledged it.

"Xiao-nan," Duncan said on sudden impulse. "Have you ever been to the Potala—inside, I mean?"

She shook her head. "I've been to the steps of course, with the rest of my people to greet the Dalai Lama, and twice I have delivered a gift at the great doors. But I have never entered."

"Then come with me now," Duncan said. "There is a beautiful garden with a lake where we can sit and watch the afternoon pass. Will you come, Xiao-nan?"

She laughed, delighted by the eagerness in his voice. "Yes, Duncan MacLeod," she said. "This time you will lead, and I will follow."

Duncan's usual wont when he walked down the streets of Lhasa was to go slowly, savoring the happy sights and sounds of the city. But now his stride was purposeful as he and Xiao-nan headed for the Potala. It was, at least for the present, his home—and he wanted to share with her the beauty of the monastic palace. He wanted to share all things he found beautiful with her.

He was beginning to realize he wanted to share the rest of her life with her.

When they entered the Potala, Xiao-nan became very quiet, but the look of joy on her face was eloquent. MacLeod did not hurry her, and she stared with awe at the huge gold-washed Buddhas and beautiful tapestries that lined the long front hall.

He led the way through the maze of corridors. Xiao-nan spun each prayer wheel that they passed, her long fingers often pausing to trace the delicate etchings or brightly colored designs before they turned.

Duncan stopped briefly at his room to get a blanket to spread on the grass so Xiao-nan could sit at ease. As with everything else, she was delighted to see where he slept.

"It is a place of wondrous beauty, Duncan," she said to him, her arms held out wide as if she wanted to embrace the entire building. "It surely must be easy to fill one's mind with compassionate thoughts in such a place."

"Compassionate thoughts come from a compassionate heart," he told her. "A heart such as yours."

She came to him and hugged him then, resting her head in the hollow of his shoulder. "I am glad you live in such a place," she said.

Duncan took her into the Potala garden. He expected to see the various monks who tended to the care of the trees and flowers, but he was surprised to find the Dalai Lama still sitting where they had spent the morning. The young man sat in an attitude of meditation. His head was slightly bent and his eyes were closed, but the fingers of his right hand were busily counting through the long strand of prayer beads he so often wore wrapped around his wrist.

He looked up when Duncan approached. "Ah, Duncan MacLeod, my friend," he said, his eyes twinkling merrily, "you have returned quickly today—and you are not alone, I see." His glance shifted to Xiao-nan.

"This, Your Holiness, is Xiao-nan Choi," Duncan said.

Xiao-nan stepped forward and bowed very low. She was about to kneel and prostrate her bow in a sign of ultimate respect, but the Dalai Lama stopped her with a gesture.

"Xiao-nan Choi," he repeated her name as if searching for its place in his memory. "Have you not been here twice before with a gift of incense for the temple?"

"Yes, Your Holiness," Xiao-nan answered softly, obviously surprised that the Dalai Lama should personally know of her actions. For a moment Duncan was surprised, too. Then, grinning slightly, he realized that nothing should surprise him about this young man.

The Dalai Lama held out his hand to Xiao-nan. "Come sit beside me and tell me about yourself," he said to her. "A few minutes only, then I will go inside and leave you two to each other's company."

"Oh, please, Your Holiness," Duncan said quickly. "We did not mean to disturb your thoughts. We can go to another part of the garden."

"No, Duncan MacLeod," he said. "I have been too long here already. In the pleasure of the sunshine I have neglected other duties. And, I think," he added, patting Xiao-nan's hand, "there are times when people are best left alone. Is this not so, Duncan MacLeod?"

Duncan smiled openly at the look of merriment on the young man's face. "Aye, Your Holiness," he said. "Perhaps it is."

Chapter Seventeen

Father Jacques spent a happy hour playing with the children, but finally he knew he had to return to the mission house and the unfortunate duty that awaited him. He found Father Edward sitting in the garden staring at his birdcages. The older man knew that though he was loath to do it, there were words that must pass between them. He hated to enforce discipline; it should, he had always thought, be a matter of personal conscience. But they were far from home, far from an ordered life and the Community of their Brothers, and it seemed someone needed to remind Father Edward of his vows.

Temptation can be very strong, Father Jacques thought with a sigh, remembering his own youth. There had been one young woman—*Annabelle,* Father Jacques thought, smiling gently at her memory—toward whom he had felt a very unpriestly attraction. Well, nothing unseemly had happened then, and he was going to make certain nothing happened here, now.

He took a deep breath and stepped out into the garden. The younger man did not bother to look at him as he approached.

"Edward," Father Jacques said, "we need to talk."

"No, we don't," Father Edward replied, still staring at his birds.

"I'm afraid we do."

Father Edward started to rise from the garden bench on which he was sitting, but Father Jacques went and stood before him, blocking his departure. The older priest put on a stern expression that was usually foreign to his features.

"I know I am not the Vicar General," he said, "but I am senior priest here and in charge of this mission. You will listen to me."

The Nepalese man sat back down and resumed staring straight ahead. Father Jacques sat next to him. He sighed again as he looked at the stony profile. Then he gentled his voice and continued.

"Edward," he said more softly, "please believe me when I say I do understand what you're feeling. You are a young man, and Mingxia is very charming. I know you are fairly new to the Church and that you did not grow up in a country where the life of other priests was an example you saw every day. For that reason your discipline will not be as harsh as it might be. You are not to talk to anyone from the Choi household, especially Mingxia, for the next month, and you will make a retreat here in the mission house. Your fast during this retreat need only be moderate—sunrise to sundown—and I think you do not need to make the full forty-day penance. The short retreat will be enough while you contemplate again the meaning of your vows."

Father Edward's head slowly turned and Father Jacques found himself staring into eyes as cold and angry as any he had ever seen. Then, without a word, the younger man rose and walked toward the house. Father Jacques had no choice but to follow him.

"Edward," he called, hurrying to catch up. "I must insist on your obedience in this matter. Otherwise, I will have no recourse but to write to the Vicar General to have you replaced and sent home. The discipline there will not be so simple."

Father Edward stopped and turned toward him. Again, Father Jacques was shocked by the coldness in his eyes.

"I'll make a retreat, if that's what you want," he said, "and I'll not speak again to anyone of the Choi house—but you understand *nothing.*"

"Come now, Edward," Father Jacques said, once more speaking gently, conciliatorily. "I, too, am a man, and, like all men, I have known temptation. Even Our Lord knew temptation. Think on that during your retreat. It may bring you comfort, as it did me many years ago."

The Nepalese man stared at him a moment longer. A little grin twisted one corner of his mouth and a cruel light flashed in his eyes.

"You know nothing," he said again. Then he turned and walked out of the house, letting the door slam behind him and leaving Father Jacques uncertain of what he had just witnessed.

*   *   *

Despite his words to Father Jacques, the Gurkha spy known to Lhasa as Father Edward could not bear to remain in the mission house—not at that moment. Soon he would go back to the game he was playing. He would lock himself away like the good little priest he was supposed to be and pretend to think the pitiful thoughts these men had—if you could call them *men*. But right now, he strode down the city streets trying to walk off his anger and the frustration he felt. Oh, how he hated this place and hated the life he was living here.

The message he received today had only fed his frustration. *Leaving in one week,* it had said. *Do nothing to jeopardize your position in city. You must open the gates. While we attack, you must strike.*

That meant the army was even now preparing. It was gathering arms and provisions, choosing the best horses, sharpening the swords—and he was stuck in this role, pretending to be a man with no blood in his veins.

But *his* blood ran hot and full, he thought as he reached the city gates still open to the day, and looked down the road on which the army would arrive. He'd almost had her. Mingxia had been ready, eager for his kiss. He had seen it in her eyes. Another few minutes and he would have known the feel of her young body pressed against him.

Then he *came*—MacLeod, the Nepalese man thought, no longer even trying to keep the anger from his face. *He ruined it—but not for long. I swear by mighty Shiva, I'll kill MacLeod for his interference.*

That thought made him smile, the same cruel smile Father Jacques had seen in the garden, as he pictured MacLeod on his knees, beaten, begging for his life. *After I have killed the Dalai Lama, I will kill MacLeod—and then the priest,* he thought with anticipation. *Nasiradeen can have the rest of Lhasa, the rest of Tibet, but these two are mine. They think I'm as weak as they are. They think they can control me—but they'll soon learn.*

The priest says he understands. His thoughts simpered with contempt on the word. *Well, before he dies I'll show him how little he understands of anything. I'll have Mingxia right in front of him. I'll take her as I would any warrior's prize, and I'll send him to his God with her screams still in his ears.*

He laughed out loud; a cruel, bitter sound. Then he turned back into the city. For a few more weeks—three, maybe four— he still had a part to play. He was ready now to resume it, but it would be these thoughts he carried with him, these thoughts that filled the hours of retreat the old man was demanding.

When Nasiradeen and the army arrived, he would be ready to act.

Nasiradeen stretched lazily on his cushioned bed. Beside him, Anuja Kumar, wife of the King's third regent, had fallen into a contented doze, worn out by their afternoon of pleasure. He smiled, remembered how enticingly she had protested when he told her he would no longer have time for such activities. He was glad that at least for today, he had relented. Tomorrow he would have to be firm with her. Then he laughed under his breath; being firm was exactly what she wanted from him.

Still, tomorrow he needed to be with his men as the final stages of preparations began. It gave them confidence to know that Nasiradeen was personally overseeing everything—and the loyalty of his men was of first importance to him, certainly more important than any woman, however pleasurable she might be.

And pleasurable she had been, once he had taught her a few things—which was more than old Kumar had ever done. *Well,* Nasiradeen thought as he ran a hand across Anuja's well-rounded hip, *I return her to him a better wife. I hope he appreciates it.*

Anuja stirred under his touch. She opened her eyes and smiled at him, moving her body into a tempting pose. He leaned over and kissed her, his hands lingering along the rich curves of her body. She made a throaty sound of pleasure.

"It is time to be gone now, my little peach," he said a moment later. "Time to return to your husband's household before you are missed too much."

"Sandep is with the King," she replied lazily, making no move to rise. "He will not be home for many hours yet."

"Still, I have work to do."

"Off to your soldiers?" she asked, knowing the answer. "Is this really the last time I will see you for so long?"

Nasiradeen's face grew stern, his voice hard. "Would you

have me call off the invasion, stay at home like some woman? Would you have me be less of a man?"

"Oh, no," she said, moving her body provocatively. "But would you have me be less of a woman not to crave a lover's touch?"

Her answer surprised him. She did not pout or cry or carry on as he expected, as other women would have done. Her answer showed an intelligence he had not assumed she possessed.

Never in his three centuries of life had Nasiradeen taken a wife. Mortal women had never seemed to him worthy of anything more than passing pleasure and Immortal women were few. In his experience, they did not last long in the Game. But this one—he looked at her with new appreciation.

She stretched languidly upon the bed, not flinching under his stare. The thin gauze sheet that covered her did nothing to hide the richness of her body: the breasts, large and firm as melons with nipples as round and red as pomegranates, the full curves of her waist, hips, thighs, the dark triangle between her legs where he knew the sweet nectar of pleasure awaited him. His eyes traveled down her body slowly while she lay there, inviting his stare.

Yes, he thought, *perhaps this one is worthy after all. Perhaps, after I have taken Tibet I will return to Nepal and claim her.*

Of course, he would have to kill her husband and, perhaps, the King as well, Nasiradeen's thoughts continued. But that, too, would be a pleasure. And to gain such a reward for it . . .

He lay back down beside her. "Tell my, my little peach," he said, "when I am victorious, would you be willing to leave all this and come to Tibet?"

Her smile broadened. "Yes," she said, eyes shining, lips lingering on the word.

"It would mean leaving your household behind. I'll not be encumbered by cartloads of women's trinkets."

She gave a shrug that caused her breasts to move enticingly beneath the sheet. "The servants are loyal to my husband, not to me," she said, "and besides a few clothes, what can Tibet not provide once I am there? When you are victorious, you will be ruler, and all her wealth will be for your taking. I have no fear you will be miserly with me."

So far, she had said nothing to change his mind. She was, in fact, showing herself possessed of a spirit wasted in a woman, Nasiradeen thought.

"What of your husband?" he asked. "Are you willing to leave him, to accept the scandal? Your family will disown you. You will never be able to return. Think well, Anuja."

"Pah," she said with disgust. "This marriage was arranged with my father. It has never been *my* desire. I did not know what desire was until you taught me. You showed me how it could fill every hour."

She turned on her side and looked him full in the face. Her eyes were calm and serious. She knew the full meaning of her next words.

"Sandep will not let me go without a fight," she said. "I am his possession, and he is very . . . greedy. He does not love me, but that will not matter."

"And if I kill him?" Nasiradeen asked.

"Then I won't be leaving him," Anuja replied evenly. "I will be a widow and free in my choices. I do *not* choose *suttee*. I will not throw myself on my husband's funeral pyre."

Yes, Nasiradeen thought, *she will do. A woman who can understand a warrior's heart is a rare thing. One who thinks with a warrior's heart is rarer still. This one has the body of a goddess and the mind worthy of a man. Yes, she will do.*

Nasiradeen reached out and pulled her on top of him. Immediately she began to move her body in a way that she knew gave him pleasure. Nasiradeen closed his eyes and smiled at the sensations mounting in his body.

Yes, he thought again, *this woman will do.*

Chapter Eighteen

The week passed swiftly for Duncan MacLeod, swiftly and pleasantly. More than pleasantly; he could not remember when he had last been so happy.

Hours with the Dalai Lama filled his mornings. The doubts MacLeod had felt during his first days at the Potala, when he wondered about the motives behind the Dalai Lama's kindness, seemed like foolishness now. Duncan could only attribute them to his deep weariness when he arrived in Tibet.

The weariness was passing; the memories were healing. Peace and patience, taught by the Dalai Lama and enhanced by Xiao-nan's living example, had slowly, gently, begun to replace the pain that had filled him.

He and the Dalai Lama sat in the Potala garden, as they did most days now that the weather was fine. Duncan was content to sit on the grass in a patch of morning sunlight while the young man sat on a bench a couple of feet away, speaking in his quiet, singsong voice.

"To follow the Eightfold Path: right thought, right action, right intention, right speech, right livelihood, right effort, mindfulness, and meditation," he was saying, running through the list with long-practiced ease, "one must be willing to give up their opposite. The giving up and the embracing are two separate and conscious actions. It is not enough to wish for right thoughts or to welcome them when they come, or even to seek them. There must be the willing and active abandonment of all unwholesome thoughts—and of the actions they generate. Do you understand this, Duncan MacLeod?"

"I understand the words," Duncan answered, "and their intent. But how can a man govern his every thought? Life has a way of interfering with even the best intentions."

The Dalai Lama smiled at him, eyes dancing merrily in his

unlined face. "That is so, Duncan MacLeod, and it is well said. Although Buddha himself set out the steps anyone many follow, the Path to Enlightenment is not easy. We govern our thoughts by *training*, by *meditations*, and by *consciousness*. Yes, that is the key."

"Then you're saying that a man, a *conscious* man, does choose his thoughts."

"The answer is both yes and no," the young man said, and Duncan had to smile. That was so often the answer.

The Dalai Lama saw his expression. "Ah, you smile," he said.

"I'm sorry, Your Holiness," Duncan replied quickly.

"No, no, no," The Dalai Lama held up his hands to stop Duncan's words. "It is good that you smile. Humor, pleasantness, delight—these are good thoughts, right thinking. But, to your question—what, Duncan MacLeod, does consciousness mean?"

Duncan paused, unsure of his answer. "It means he is awake," he said at last.

"Awake, yes," the Dalai Lama nodded, "but what is awake? For a man it is more. The tree here"—he gestured—"it, in its own way, is awake. Its sap flows, it seeks the sun. So, too, the grass and flowers. Also the birds and animals. All are awake with the day, the season, the sun.

"A human being," he continued, "is more. He or she is awake but also *aware*. Of what? Of surroundings, of day or night? Yes, but so are the animals. It is *choices* of which we are aware, choices of thoughts of actions, of *karma*. We can change our situation because we can change ourselves."

"But situations can arrive over which there is no control, no choice," Duncan said. "Sometimes all you can do is respond."

"No, Duncan MacLeod," the Dalai Lama replied. "Always there is a choice. Always."

Duncan became very silent, very still, looking down at the grass beneath him. What could this holy man know of the situations he faced all too often? A choice, yes—live or die, and he chose *life*. Was it wrong to want to go on living?

Duncan stood and began to pace restlessly, searching for an answer to the question he had posed himself. He knew the Dalai Lama was waiting for him to speak, but this was something he could not ask aloud without revealing all of who he was and what a life such as his entailed.

Finally he turned and looked at the young man. As was so often the case, MacLeod was struck by the dichotomy of the Dalai Lama's gaze. The eyes that met his were pools of endless compassion, of understanding that was at odds with his mortal years. Seeing them, Duncan was tempted to reveal his long-kept secret. But habit, and perhaps a touch of fear, stayed his tongue; he did not want to lose this young man's friendship.

Still silent, he sat back down and waited for the Dalai Lama's next words.

The young man sighed, knowing a moment, a choice, had passed.

"So what then is right thinking, Duncan MacLeod?" he said, resuming their discussion. "It is *Compassion*. When Compassion fills us, there is no room for negative thinking, negative actions. If someone is angry at me, what are my choices? To return anger for anger, yes—or to return compassion for anger. I can choose to think he is my enemy or not my enemy. He is a man, like me—with choices, like me. Each time I choose compassion, I am training my mind so that next time the choice becomes easier."

"Are there then no just battles, no causes worthy enough to fight for?" Duncan asked him.

"No man may answer that for another," the Dalai Lama said. "For me, there is never a reason for violence, and that is what I teach my people. Another man? He must ask himself his own questions, he must look at his own thinking, his actions, his intentions. Is compassion served by what is being done? he must ask. Choices, always choices."

"What about justice?" Duncan said.

"There is always justice," the Dalai Lama replied evenly. "There is *karma*. Positive out creates positive returning; negative out creates negative back in. The Great Wheel spins, and it is perfect justice."

Duncan shook his head slightly. It sounded so reasonable, and yet in the world outside this graced kingdom, he doubted it was possible to live only by the laws of compassion and karma. At least for him. Holy men, perhaps, like the Dalai Lama, like saints and martyrs—but he was none of these. For all his Immortality, he was just a man.

And there was the Game.

Duncan sighed. The Dalai Lama smiled at him.

"It is a journey, Duncan MacLeod," he said, "not traveled in a day or a year or even a single lifetime. You have become aware that the journey exists, and that alone is progress. Yes?"

Duncan nodded, trying to find encouragement in the young man's words. "If you say so, Your Holiness," he answered.

Xiao-nan was watching for him. She ran out to meet him while he was still several doors away. The joy of her greeting cleared the last of thought-induced fog from Duncan's mind. Her arms slid around his waist and nothing else mattered. When he looked into her eyes, the only journey that existed was the one to bring her joy.

Duncan MacLeod knew, for well and certain, that he was in love.

They walked arm in arm down the city streets. People smiled at them as they passed, perhaps sensing that here love was still fresh and new. Or perhaps, in a place like Lhasa, where everyone knew and cared for each other, they were as pleased as MacLeod to see Xiao-nan happy.

Duncan did not ask where they were going as they left the city and began to walk down the long road. Over the last weeks Xiao-nan had shown him many places he would never have found on his own; beautiful places—not just the blue orchids, but hidden stands of silver birch and wild cherry, sudden meadows carpeted with wildflowers, eagle aeries and marmot dens; all places of life and wonder.

Today they returned to the river, to a place where the rocks were flat and warm in the sunshine and the gentle sound of the water was soothing to both mind and spirit. Xiao-nan had told him once that this was a favorite thinking spot of hers, and Duncan understood the attraction.

They sat on the rocks, content to hold each other in silence while they watched the birds dip and dive through the air, feeding on a fresh hatch of aquatic insects. Being in Xiao-nan's company was like sitting in a pool of calm. It radiated from her, blessing everything around her with peace. Duncan realized

how much he had come to need that peace as part of his life—
to need Xiao-nan.

He turned to kiss her and she lifted her face to his. As their
lips touched and hers parted gently beneath his, Duncan felt
again the need to protect her, to keep her warm and safe and
happy; it was a feeling that few other women had awakened to
such depths in him. He wanted to hold her forever, in his heart
and in his arms.

The kiss went on for a long, timeless moment. When it
ended, Duncan pulled away slightly to look into her face. He
reached up with one hand and ran a finger gently down her
cheek and across her lips. He desired her, yes, but most of all
he loved her and wanted to go on loving her for however long
her life allowed.

"Xiao-nan," he said softly, "I do not know the customs of
your country, so forgive me if I am speaking in the wrong way
or breaking any traditions—but I want us to be together. Husband and wife. I love you. Will you marry me?"

The look on Xiao-nan's face as she smiled at him was so
filled with love and tenderness that Duncan's breath caught in
his throat.

"Yes, Duncan," she said. "I will be your wife. I, too, want us
to be together." She moved away and sat a little straighter.
"There are customs to be observed," she continued. "The blessing of my parents must be given. You must bring a gift for both
my father and my mother, to give them respect and to show
them that this marriage will not create want or loss in the family."

"What sort of gifts, Xiao-nan?" Duncan asked. "You must
guide me in this."

"For my mother it is easy. Spices for her kitchen, perhaps. A
pound of good tea and a new set of drinking bowls. There are
many choices. My father, however, is not so easy."

Xiao-nan stopped and thought for a moment. Duncan was
content to watch her, amused as always by the little frown she
wore when she concentrated. He ran a hand down her long,
thick hair; it felt like strands of silk beneath his fingertips, and
he found himself wanting to bury his face in it, to inhale the
scent of it, the scent of *her*.

"My father is a good man," Xiao-nan said, her low, breathless voice breaking into MacLeod's thoughts—and it was not of her *father* he had been thinking. He quickly pulled his mind back to the subject at hand.

"He is not a man who seeks after many passing pleasures," she was saying, "but there is one thing I know will please him. My father enjoys *natag*, and his grinding bowl is now very old. A new one would be a good gift."

"Then a new one it is," Duncan replied, feeling pleased with anything and everything she wanted. "We'll go to the merchants tomorrow and see what we can find. Perhaps there will be something for Mingxia, too."

"That is not necessary."

"Maybe not, but I don't want her to feel left out. Besides," Duncan added with a grin, "I think she's still mad at me, and this might get me back in her good graces."

"Well, she should not be mad at you," Xiao-nan said sternly. "She should be grateful you were there to watch over her. All this week she has been acting like a spoiled child, hardly speaking and looking with anger at anyone who speaks to her. I try to be patient with her, but sometimes I think Father should send her to live among the nuns until she again remembers the way of respect and compassion."

"As you told me once," Duncan said, "she is young, very young. At her age little things can take on great importance—until the next thing comes along. It will pass."

Xiao-nan leaned back, settling herself again into his arms. "You are very kind, ..iy Duncan," she said, "to think so well of my sister."

"How can I not think well of your sister, when *her* sister owns my heart. What you love, I must also love."

Duncan had had enough of talking about families, for now anyway. His arms closed around Xiao-nan, holding her close to him, feeling the way their bodies melded together in perfect harmony. As he kissed her, he could only marvel that she had truly agreed to be his wife. The years ahead suddenly offered a realm of sweetness he had never hoped to see, and for the rest of Xiao-nan's life, for whatever time they would have together, Duncan knew that his greatest joy would be to make her happy.

One kiss became another and with it, his desire for Xiao-nan mounted. He wanted their joining to be complete. But for her sake, he held himself back. The life of an Immortal, lived along such a different time line, could not help but be free of many of the cultural taboos that governed mortal lives. But Xiao-nan was not free of such rules, and he would do nothing to shame her. When at last they did come together, he wanted there to be only freedom between them—no reluctance, and, afterward, no feelings of guilt to mar their union. He could wait; he had time.

Chapter Nineteen

Xiao-nan could not sleep. Her mind and her heart were too busy tumbling over themselves, thinking the thoughts universal to lovers. She could hardly believe that today had happened. She would soon be the wife of Duncan MacLeod.

She had no doubt that her parents would give their blessing to the match, and that day could not come soon enough for her. Each time she was with Duncan, she wanted the hours to go on forever—and each moment they were apart felt like an eternity. Xiao-nan could not keep herself from laughing aloud that she, who had never thought to be in love, should be feeling this way.

On the sleeping mat next to hers, Mingxia stirred in the darkness. Xiao-nan immediately became silent, scolding herself; even in her happiness she must not lose sight of the feelings of others nor allow her present joy to disturb their peace.

But Mingxia was not sleeping. "Xiao-nan," she whispered, "what happened to you today? You've been very quiet since you came home, even for you."

"You'll find out soon enough," Xiao-nan answered, not sure she wanted to share her news yet. The joy of it was so deep, so personal.

"Tomorrow," she said.

She could hear Mingxia turning toward her and Xiao-nan did the same, though nothing could be seen in the darkness.

"The night's half-gone," Mingxia replied, insisting. "It is tomorrow."

Xiao-nan still hesitated—and yet, over the years she and her sister had shared many confidences here in the dark. Now that she was to be married, not many such moments between them remained.

"All right," she said finally, "but you have to promise you'll say nothing."

"I promise. Now tell me."

"Your most solemn word?"

"Yes—what is it?" Mingxia's voice rose slightly with excitement.

"Shh," Xiao-nan quieted her. "You'll wake Mother and Father, and they mustn't know yet. Not until later, when Duncan and I return from the merchants."

"The merchants?"

"Duncan is going to buy marriage-gifts for our parents, to give them when he seeks their blessing. He has asked me to be his wife."

There, it was said. Xiao-nan felt a little thrill speaking the words outloud. She was going to be a *wife*; Duncan MacLeod's wife. In her joy, she almost failed to notice how silent her sister had become.

"Mingxia?" she said. "You aren't upset, are you?"

"No," she answered, though her voice was a little hesitant. "Not truly. I like Duncan MacLeod, and he is good to you."

"He'll be glad to hear you like him. He thought you were angry with him."

"You mean because of Father Edward?" Mingxia asked. "I was at first, with both of you. But, well, I don't really like Father Edward."

"Then why—"

"Because of you and Duncan and the way he looks at you. Everything he feels shines out of his eyes. When Father Edward looked at me that day, his eyes were shining, too. *He* wanted *me*—and I liked the feeling. I know all of the boys here. I've grown up with them. Father Edward is like your Duncan. He's different—there's something mysterious about him."

"Father Edward is nothing like Duncan," Xiao-nan said sharply. "Duncan is a man of honor. Father Edward is—" she stopped herself. She would not speak unkindly about anyone, even Father Edward. "Well, he's nothing like my Duncan," she said more quietly.

"And, oh Mingxia," she continued, wanting to hug and scold her sister at the same time. "Wanting isn't enough—not without the love. When that comes, you will find that everything has been worth the waiting. It will come for you, in the right time."

Xiao-nan heard her sister sigh into the darkness. "Sometimes I don't think so," she said.

Xiao-nan found herself smiling at her sister's words, a smile of compassion and understanding. How well she remembered being Mingxia's age, when the feelings of womanhood were so new, when hopes and desires were as changeable as quicksilver; one moment wanting to be fiercely independent and the next, wanting only to be loved, to be held, to be cared for.

Well, she would find her path and her peace, this Xiao-nan knew.

"The right one will come for you, Mingxia," she said. "I promise."

Duncan MacLeod was also lying awake upon his bed, staring into the darkness. His thoughts were not nearly so pleasant as Xiao-nan's.

Now that he was alone in the silence, a hundred doubts filled his mind. Not about loving Xiao-nan; that was the most *right* thing he had ever done. But he wondered if it was fair to *her* to have proposed marriage.

He was *Immortal*. That one word, that one difference, contained a world of potential problems. She would age and he would not; could she live with that or would it bring her only sorrow and pain? Duncan ground his teeth in the darkness; he could not stand the thought of causing Xiao-nan pain.

Children were another issue, the children she would not have if she married him—children which, as a mortal woman, she had the right to bear, to hold, to raise into adulthood. Would his love be enough to fill the void?

And there was the Game.

In all his time in Tibet, first in the higher elevations with his nomad friends and now all these weeks in Lhasa, he had not encountered another Immortal. But that did not mean there were none in this land. How long before they found him and challenged him? How would his gentle Xiao-nan feel knowing she had wed a man who must kill to stay alive?

Duncan turned on his narrow bed, filled with a sudden bitter restlessness. *Perhaps I should leave,* he thought, *go now before I can harm her goodness.*

But he knew it was an idle thought. He would tell her the

truth of who he was, all of it, before they wed. He would give her the chance to send him away. But if she still wanted him once she knew, he would stay. He loved her—heart, body, and soul.

In spite of the two hundred years of life, or perhaps because of it, Duncan MacLeod still believed that love could conquer anything.

When dawn finally came Duncan sent his apologies to the Dalai Lama, saying he would return later in the day, and headed down into Lhasa. The night had left him filled with a restless energy.

He walked down the winding streets that had become so familiar to him, listening to the sounds of the city awakening and trying to picture how his life would be. Soft voices drifted out from the houses, as if carried on the smoke of cooking fires, birds twittered and sang in the trees, dogs barked; they were comforting sounds, sounds of home.

Home—it had been a long time since he'd had a true home.

MacLeod kept walking. The movement came easily now. His Immortal lungs had long since healed the strain of breathing in the thin Tibetan air. As always, movement freed his mind and it, too, began to travel familiar pathways, walking the streets of memory.

MacLeod thought of his early life, his years in Glenfinnan and of all his travels since, trying to catalog the places he had been: Weeks, months, sometimes years spent in hundreds of places, but always as a traveler, a visitor, at least within his own heart. Even returning to Scotland for Bonnie Prince Charlie's cause had not been a homecoming. The people he had known were long dead, and the places had changed with the centuries.

But here on the other side of the world from where he was born, here he had found a home. Here he had found love.

MacLeod paid no mind to where his feet were taking him until he stood outside the Capuchin mission house just as Brother Michael opened the door.

"Mr. MacLeod," the monk said pleasantly. "What a nice surprise."

"Good morning, Brother Michael," Duncan returned.

"Have you come to see one of us? Is there something we can do for you?"

Duncan shook his head. "I was just walking and happened to pass."

"Well, come in," the monk gestured, waving him inside. "Come and have a cup of tea with us."

Duncan found himself smiling. He nodded and stepped toward the door.

"It is a glorious morning, is it not, Mr. MacLeod?" Brother Michael said as he stood aside to let Duncan pass. "I like to open the door on mornings such as this and let the air sweep in. It does more than clear the staleness from the house—fresh air clears the mind. Don't you think, Mr. MacLeod?"

"Aye, Brother, that I do."

Brother Michael led the way to the back of the house where the other monks were already seated at a table with a pot of tea before them.

"We have a visitor, Brothers," the eldest monk announced as they entered the room. "Get him a chair so he may be comfortable."

The youngest of the three, Brother Peter, was quickly on his feet. "Here, he may have mine," he said as he hurried to get himself a stool. MacLeod soon found himself seated and being served tea from the steaming pot as if he had been visiting royalty and not someone who chanced by.

"Were you on the way to call on Xiao-nan, Mr., MacLeod?" Brother Thomas, the third monk, spoke for the first time.

Duncan shook his head. "As I told Brother Michael, I was just out for a walk. 'Tis early to do much visiting."

"But you do plan to see her later?"

Next to him, Brother Michael laughed. "Please excuse Thomas, Mr. MacLeod. He is known within our Order for his blunt tongue. Peter and I are used to it, but it sometimes takes others by surprise. I will admit," he stopped and sipped his tea, "we are all curious about your . . . intentions . . . toward Xiao-nan. She is such a dear girl."

"You need have no fears, then," MacLeod told them. "I've asked Xiao-nan to be my wife."

"Splendid," Brother Michael beamed. "Splendid. When will the wedding take place?"

"I only asked her yesterday," MacLeod replied. "Nothing has been settled."

"A more important question," Brother Thomas spoke again, "is *how* will the wedding take place. Has she converted to your faith, Mr. MacLeod, or have you become Buddhist?"

"Softly, Thomas," Brother Michael admonished. "Softly. Where love is present, the way for such things can always be found."

"I would never ask Xiao-nan to change who she is or what she believes," MacLeod answered Brother Thomas's question. "Nor would I ask her to participate in a ceremony that for her has no meaning. For myself—I am neither Buddhist nor Catholic. Whatever Xiao-nan wants for her wedding will be fine with me."

"But surely you will want a marriage your family will recognize as valid when you return home?" Brother Peter, the youngest monk asked.

"I've no intention of taking Xiao-nan away from her family," Duncan replied. "Lhasa will be my home as it is hers."

"But what of your family?" Brother Peter continued.

MacLeod was beginning to lose his patience. "There is no one in Scotland I want to see more than I want to be here," he said sternly, hoping his tone would put an end to these questions.

Brother Peter opened his mouth to speak, but Brother Michael held up his hand. "Peace, my Brother," he said, then he turned to Duncan.

"Mr. MacLeod," he said, "it is truly not our intention to interfere with the happiness of this occasion, but perhaps there is a way for all to be satisfied. You say you have no wish to leave Lhasa—but that may change, or Xiao-nan herself may wish one day to see your homeland. You would not want others think less than well of her, I'm sure, or failing to recognize her as your wife. What I am suggesting is that we blend the two ceremonies—a few prayers, a blessing, nothing more. A union of East and West, as your marriage union will be."

MacLeod was grateful for Brother Michael's calm and reasoned argument. "Perhaps, Brother," he said. "I'll talk to Xiao-nan when the time comes."

"That's fine," the monk replied with a smile. "Now, let us all have another cup of tea and speak of other matters. Tell me, Mr. MacLeod, do you by chance play chess?"

MacLeod smiled. "Aye, I've been known to enjoy the game."

"Splendid—then maybe sometime you'll favor me with a match. I've a board and a set of players I carved myself, but I'm afraid they've rarely been out of their box. My brothers here to not share my fascination with the game."

"Mere foolishness," Brother Thomas said bluntly. "A waste of time."

"Not so, Thomas," said the older monk. "It is a way of opening the mind to see the possibilities. I'm sure Mr. MacLeod will agree with me."

Brother Thomas grunted noncommittally and Brother Michael sighed. "It is an old standing argument," he told MacLeod. "One of many."

"Aye, I can see that," MacLeod said as he raised the small drinking bowl to his lips.

They were very different, these three monks, yet they made an harmonious whole. MacLeod knew, with sudden and absolute certainty, that here were men he could call on if there was need—and if something were to happen to him, they would watch over and care for Xiao-nan.

Oddly, he found the thought gave him comfort.

Chapter Twenty

Nasiradeen sat astride his favorite horse far at the head of his army, where all his men could see him. They were moving at last.

Behind him rode his captains, twenty of them—men whose hearts and loyalties he knew as well as he knew his own; men he trusted above all others. Behind them, marching four abreast and stretching back for almost half a mile, was his army. *His* army, warriors that *he* had personally chosen for this campaign.

How they cheered when he rode through their ranks at dawn. They were, every one of them, proud to be his men.

The King had not bothered to come out this morning and see the army on its way. Nasiradeen was not surprised. Coming out to view the army would have meant leaving the comfort of his bed before the sun had fully risen—not something the King was personally inclined to do or something the regents encouraged. The regents encouraged little that did not keep the King under their control.

It does not matter, not anymore, Nasiradeen thought. He had obtained what he wanted from the King; he had permission to leave the court and to lead this invasion, with the crown's backing. In the end, all of the regents, even old Kumar, had urged the King's support. They were happy to see Nasiradeen go. It removed his influence over the King's imagination. They had even provisioned the baggage carts that rolled at the end of the line from out of the royal stores.

They knew nothing of the extra cart that had been added, a cart loaded with Nasiradeen's belongings including two coffers of gold and another of jewels that he had collected over the centuries. The regents in their stale, underused imaginations could not conceive that Nasiradeen and the army would not return to Nepal—except as invaders and conquerors.

The horse beneath him pranced and capered, sensing its rider's excitement. Nasiradeen laid a hand on its neck to quiet it. Like everything else with him today, this horse had been personally chosen and trained. Nasiradeen had raised it from a foal, taught it to respond to his moods and his silent commands. Like the sword by his side, this horse was an extension of himself.

Like each of the men behind him, Nasiradeen knew that this horse would willingly give its life for him, to ensure he obtained his desire. They trusted him for their reward. He would not fail them; he would give them Tibet.

He drew his sword and lifted it high over head. Behind him, hundreds of hands did likewise. Sun glinted off the curved blades of polished steel. Nasiradeen could feel the heat of it behind him, knew the terror such a sight struck in the heart of the enemy.

They would march into Lhasa—and thus, in a blaze of light, would they attack.

"Your mind is not on the Teachings, Duncan MacLeod," the Dalai Lama said.

MacLeod looked up, startled, then he grinned a bit sheepishly. "No, Your Holiness," he said. "I suppose it wasn't. I apologize."

"And where are your thoughts today? They are in Lhasa, I think, where your feet took you this morning. Yes?"

MacLeod's smile broadened. "Yes, Your Holiness."

"And you will see Xiao-nan today?"

Duncan nodded. "We're to meet later."

The Dalai Lama cocked his head to one side. His eyes twinkled knowingly. "And you will speak to her parents today?"

MacLeod sat up straighter. "How did you—?"

The Dalai Lama laughed. "Oh, Duncan MacLeod, throughout my many lives I have looked on the faces of love more times than there are stars in the sky. Always it is the same—lovers believe they live in a world of their own. They think no one else can see what they feel and that no one else has ever loved as they do. But that is good, Duncan MacLeod. Men and women *should* love each other. They should marry, have children, and love their children. Love is the best thinking, the best action. Love, compassion, truth, peace—first internal, then external. These are the stepping-stones of Enlightenment. These are the meaning of all Buddha teaches."

Once more the Dalai Lama cocked his head to one side and looked at MacLeod. He was much more at peace than when he arrived in Lhasa, but sometimes the Dalai Lama could see the darkness lurking, waiting still to close in. It was not the darkness of evil, but of sorrow.

Perhaps, the Dalai Lama admitted silently, *for a man such as Duncan MacLeod, such darkness is always waiting. The only thing that can battle or overcome darkness is light. Enlightenment.*

"We were speaking of death, Duncan MacLeod, and of rebirth," the Dalai Lama said. "I think maybe today is not the day for such words. You would rather be in Lhasa with Xiao-nan today. Yes?"

"Xiao-nan would be most upset if I were to pass up any opportunity to learn from Your Holiness."

"And you, Duncan MacLeod? Speak the truth of what your heart is feeling."

"It is true," Duncan said slowly, "that every moment I am apart from Xiao-nan I wish to be with her, but I also believe the hours I spend with Your Holiness are of great importance—and I am most humbly grateful for them."

The Dalai Lama inclined his head graciously. "Then we shall continue, but for a little while only. We feed here the mind, the soul, but the heart must be nourished also. Yes?"

Duncan smiled at him, though his eyes remained grave. "You are very wise, Your Holiness."

"Yes," the Dalai Lama replied, nodding. His voice held no pride, only honest acknowledgment. "Many lifetimes wise. You, also, have seen many lives, though you do not believe it I think. But it does not mater. The truth will come in its own time.

"So now, Duncan MacLeod," the Dalai Lama continued before good manners could make MacLeod deny his disbelief, "we return to the Teachings. Tell me, why do you think death is feared?"

"Is *death* feared, Your Holiness, or what comes after?"

"Ah, Duncan MacLeod, you ask the good question. The answer is within each individual. Is death for them an end or a liberation? Do they face it in preparation or in ignorance? Death comes to all living things and that we cannot change, but what comes after . . . ah, there we can have influence. Not by our thoughts of past lives or future lives, but by our mindfulness of *this* life. By the karma we create."

"Karma still seems difficult to understand sometimes," Duncan said. "For instance, you have said that to take the life of any living thing, even an animal, is a negative action producing negative karma. Yet the nomads with whom I stayed raise herds of yak to feed and clothe themselves. When they kill a yak for food, is that also a negative action?"

"The killing, yes," the Dalai Lama nodded. "But remember, Duncan MacLeod, the Eightfold Path speaks not only of *actions* but of thoughts and of *intentions*. Is it compassion, right action, or thought to let one's family starve or freeze? No. To kill for greed, for anger, for selfishness—these always are negative only. But the other, here balance may be found within karma with right intention."

Duncan sighed. Though he knew the Dalai Lama was waiting for a reply, an indication of understanding, Duncan found no words yet to speak. Memories of battles, mortal and Immortal, swirled in his mind. They tumbled over each other, melded together and separated yet again. So many battles.

Killing is always wrong, always negative, the words loomed large in Duncan's mind. *What are right intentions? Does survival count?*

Duncan raised his eyes to the Dalai Lama's and saw that the young man's expression had changed to a look of infinite sadness.

I'm sorry, Duncan told him wordlessly. *Even here, I cannot lay aside my sword. Few of my kind ever can. The most I can do is be a warrior of honor. Hideo Koto tried to teach me his meaning of honor, but I only understood part of what he said. You have taught me the rest.*

"Have I not told you many times, Duncan MacLeod," the Dalai Lama said, breaking the silence between them, "that the Path to Enlightenment is not easily traveled? It takes many, many lifetimes."

"So you have, Your Holiness," Duncan answered. "But what is a lifetime? How many chances are we granted?"

The Dalai Lama smiled gently. "A lifetime is a lifetime," he said, "from the moment of its inception to the instant of its end, whether that takes a season or a century. As for the number of chances we are given to advance along the Path, ah, Duncan MacLeod, that is as infinite as the Compassionate Heart. Were it not so, none of us would have hope. And now, Duncan MacLeod, we have talked enough today."

Duncan started to protest, but the Dalai Lama held up his hands. "No, Duncan MacLeod," he said. "I must meditate, and you must go to Lhasa. Xiao-nan will be waiting. I said we would not speak long this morning. Are the words you have heard not enough for you to think on?"

Duncan's laugh had a slightly sardonic note to it. "Every time you speak, Your Holiness, I find myself with enough and more to occupy my thoughts—now and for years to come."

"It is good, Duncan MacLeod, that you recognize this. Patience, with one's self and with others, is the first step along the Path. Patience is part of compassion.

"It is so much more difficult to be patient with one's self."

"That is true," the Dalai Lama agreed. "But like all else, patience *must* begin from within. If you do not possess it, you cannot give it. Yes?"

"What if there comes a time when patience with one's self and with another are in conflict?"

"There can never be such a time," the Dalai Lama said, "for the answer is *always* compassion. By showing compassion to another, one's self also benefits. The mind, the soul, these grow and expand, advancing with each act of compassion. Karma then benefits, overcoming negative with positive."

Experience from Duncan's past again flashed briefly through his mind. Sometimes the choices had seemed so clear, while others . . .

"It is not always easy to know where compassion lies," he said, not certain whether he was talking to himself or his teacher.

The Dalai Lama nodded. "True compassion is difficult. It may appear harsh or even angry. Yet, true compassion lies not in what is easy, but in what is *best*."

The Dalai stopped and cocked his head in his familiar pose. In his saffron and maroon robes, he resembled a brightly colored bird—small, with delicate features and bones. Yet Duncan knew that like the robin in the depths of winter, the Dalai Lama possessed an ability to endure and survive. Every moment Duncan spent with him, he felt that the same part of himself was somehow strengthened.

"Now, Duncan MacLeod," the Dalai Lama said with a smile, "again I must say that we have talked enough for one morning. You must not keep Xiao-nan waiting any longer. I think that you will soon have news to tell me. Yes?"

Duncan returned the young man's smile. "I hope so, Your Holiness," he said. "I truly hope so."

Chapter Twenty-one

As was so often the case after a morning with the Dalai Lama, Duncan was thoughtful as he walked through the streets of Lhasa. The sights and sounds, once so new to him, had become familiar friends, easing into his mind unnoticed and setting him at rest.

As always, the Dalai Lama had given him a lesson that contained layer upon layer of meaning. He struggled to fit it into the context of his life, past and future. It was easy to speak of peace here in Tibet, easy to imagine the luxury of living, at least for a time, as mortals do with the homes and families—no swords, no Game.

But Duncan MacLeod was no fool. He knew he could not replace reality with a dream. Immortals who tried soon lost their heads.

Even if they stayed in Tibet for all of Xiao-nan's lifetime, how long could that be? A few decades, if they were lucky, and Duncan knew he would not stay without her. After she died, and he moved on, the Game would close in again—if it had not found him already.

But perhaps, he thought as he neared her house, *by then the path between who I am and who I want to be will be clearer.*

"It takes many lifetimes," he could hear the Dalai Lama's voice speaking the familiar words. *Mine or hers?* Duncan thought in reply.

Then she opened the door to welcome him, and he put all other thoughts to rest.

"I did not expect you so early in the day, my Duncan," she said, taking his hand and pulling him inside. "The Dalai Lama, he is well?"

"Aye," Duncan answered. "Very well. My head is still spinning with all the things he said."

"That is good, my Duncan."

MacLeod laughed. "Why is it everyone here seems to find my confusion such a good thing. Everyone but me, that is."

"If you are confused, then you are *listening*, and you are hearing with more than your ears," Xiao-nan replied. "Understanding will come. You must be patient, my Duncan."

Duncan smiled as he watched her—her eyes, so calm and so serious, her low voice holding that breathless quality he found so enchanting.

"Why do you smile at me in such a way," she asked him. "Do my words make you laugh?"

Still smiling, Duncan shook his head. "No, sweetheart," he said. "It is just that I am delighted by each thing that you say and do. And just then your words echoed what His Holiness told me this morning."

"Then they are words to which you should listen."

"I will always listen," he assured her. "To His Holiness, but most of all to you. Now, are you ready to go shopping? I'm sure the merchants have opened their stalls."

"Shh," Xiao-nan said quickly, the look in her dark eyes suddenly sparking with mischief. "I've not told where we are going. I want your gifts to be a surprise for my parents."

Duncan nodded and opened the door for her. *Oh, I doubt they'll be surprised,* he thought as they stepped out into the day. *I doubt it very much.*

Duncan had only visited the market once, during his first exploration of the city, and he was surprised by how large it was and how busy.

It was a permanent market, where the people of the city could come year-round to buy or barter for goods. Two-story buildings that housed the family home upstairs and the shop below, crowded near each other, creating a jumble of alleyways down which children and dogs played. Once a year, Xiao-nan told him as they walked down a street redolent with cooking food, spices, and incense, people from the outlying villages came to Lhasa for a big bazaar, to barter their goods in exchange for others.

"It is not for several weeks yet," she told him. "It is from the middle of the ninth month until the beginning of the tenth.

Many, many people come to Lhasa then, and it is a happy time. Each night there are big bonfires where people gather to sing and tell tales. Each day the trading goes on both here and outside the city gates, where the visitors have their tents. Maybe your friends from among the high nomads will come. You will see them again, and I will be able to thank them for the care they showed to my Duncan."

She smiled at him, her eye shining with happiness, and Duncan wanted to take her in his arms, but he could not do so here in the marketplace. They might hold hands, even share a quick kiss or embrace on the streets near her home where the only eyes to see them were those of family and close neighbors. But until their engagement was officially known, public displays of physical affection were improper.

Duncan understood and accepted his, though he found it difficult to be so near Xiao-nan and not touch her. Xiao-nan found ways around the stricture, occasionally laying a hand on his arm or leaning against him softly while pointing out the wares for sale in the shops they passed.

The variety of goods was astonishing. Coppersmiths and blacksmiths offered everything from tools to cooking utensils. Silversmiths offered drinking bowls and serving trays, fine jewelry and incense burners. There were stalls of bright hand-tied rugs, finely woven blankets, merchants selling bolts of cloth and others selling garments, many covered with delicate embroidery. There were spice merchants with bins of clove and cinnamon, ginger, cardamom, and pepper and sellers of candles and incense who kept samples of their wares burning, sending soft clouds of fragrant smoke over the area.

And there was food—everywhere, cooked and uncooked, staples and delicacies. There were vats of hot soup filled with noodles and vegetables, trays of steaming pies, displays of colorful fruits and vegetables as well as merchants selling staples such as *tampsa*, the ground barley flour that was in nearly everything, butter, oil, honey, and rice. There were even a few vendors selling long strips of dried meats. The sight surprised Duncan; he had assumed from his talks with the Dalai Lama and the meals he had eaten here in Lhasa, that only the nomads ate meat and only out of necessity.

"Oh no," Xiao-nan told him, herself surprised by his reaction. "Although few in the city eat it regularly, there are many dishes made for special occasions that include meat. Some will be served at our wedding. My favorite is *momo*, the spiced meat dumpling. My mother's are the best in the city. You will like them, and I will cook them for you after I am your wife."

Duncan found himself touched by her words, by her pride in her mother's talents, but most of all, by the note of eagerness in her voice when she spoke of such a small thing as cooking their meals. It reminded Duncan of how very young she was—not in the standards of her culture, but in their vast disparity of years.

They walked through the marketplace once while Xiao-nan enjoyed showing him its sights. Then they walked back through again, this time more slowly, shopping in earnest. They found the *natag* bowl and pestle at a woodcrafter's stand. It was a beautiful piece of work, carved out of cherry burl and inlaid with coils of bright copper. MacLeod would have happily paid full price, but Xiao-nan stopped him. She haggled the purchase with practiced ease.

For her mother, they found a set of porcelain drinking bowls that were a soft creamy yellow color, the color of joy Xiao-nan told him, with little bluebirds, the symbol of good fortune, done in enamelwork around them. Duncan picked one up and held it to the sunlight. It seemed to him as delicate as eggshells.

Duncan himself picked out a silver comb for Mingxia's hair, though Xiao-nan insisted again that such a gift was unnecessary. When she was not looking, he also purchased a pair of silver and ruby earrings he thought would suit her, not bothering to bargain the price in his haste to keep the purchase secret.

The packages they carried back to Xiao-nan's home had been wrapped in sheets of thin paper and tied with red ribbon. They were cheerful-looking, and Xiao-nan was pleased by them, but Duncan could not help thinking of the paper arts he had seen in Japan and wishing he had taken time to learn something of them he could use now. Instead, as they walked back down the city streets, Duncan picked a few blossoms from overhanging trees and arranged those as best he could beneath the ribbons.

After the busyness of the marketplace, Xiao-nan's home seemed unusually silent. The family was outside in the garden, eating the afternoon meal in the soft, fragrant shade. Xiao-nan arranged the packages to her satisfaction on the small table in the center of the main room. Then, before she went to call her family, she stepped into the circle of Duncan's arms.

"Have you thought about what you will say to my father?" she asked after a kiss that was made all the more sweet by the hours they had been together, unable to touch. "My mother and sister will be easy to convince we should marry, but my father will think it his duty to be more severe."

"Don't worry," he told her, kissing the little frown between her brows. "I'm sure your father and I will come to an understanding soon enough."

Smiling at his confidence, Xiao-nan went happily off to gather her family. Standing alone in the room, Duncan found he was suddenly more nervous than he expected. *You're four times the age of her father,* he told himself—and to his amusement he realized that he could face another Immortal with a sword with more equanimity than he felt now. But then, he had faced far more enemies than parents of prospective brides.

That said more about his life than he cared to consider at this moment and as Xiao-nan reentered the room, he thrust the thought away. Instead, he put on his best smile and waited to see the mood of her parents.

Xiao-nan's father kept his face composed, trying to look stern, but there was no mistaking the twinkle in his eye; her mother and sister were smiling openly. Duncan felt himself relax.

Xiao-nan directed each of them to where she wished them to sit while Duncan remained standing, waiting. When Xiao-nan came again to stand beside him, the two of them bowed deeply and silently to the family.

"Yao-hui Choi," Duncan began, addressing her father formally, man to man as custom demanded. "I have come to ask for your daughter Xiao-nan's hand in marriage. I know that she is a great treasure to this household. I therefore present these humble gifts to you as a token that by this marriage our fortunes shall be merged."

Yao-hui made no move yet to acknowledge the package before him. "Xiao-nan is more than a treasure to our house," he replied. "She is also a blessing to our hearts. You are a man of the West. It would be too great a hardship to lose our daughter to such a distant place."

"This land is Xiao-nan's home," Duncan said, "and it will be my home, too."

"It is our belief that the law of compassion forbids us to allow even the stranger to suffer with want of food or shelter," Yao-hui continued, "but it is best for a man to have the way of providing for his family before he is wed. You are a stranger to our land, Duncan MacLeod. I must ask you what work you will do to give my daughter a home?"

Duncan had thought about this for a long time. Most of the experiences of the last two hundred years would be of no value here in Tibet. But today in the marketplace Duncan had reached a decision that made him grateful for his early life and his years as a chieftain's son in Glenfinnan.

"It is true I have traveled much," he said to Yao-hui, "and I have turned my hand to many professions. In the place where I was born, my people own land on which they raise cattle and crops. I learned the ways of this at my father's knee. It is my thought to build a farm near this city and grow food for the marketplace. If you do not think this is a correct choice, then I would gladly be guided by your wisdom. It is my wish to provide well for Xiao-nan and for this family's care."

Yao-hui gave a satisfied nod. Then he turned to Xiao-nan. "And you, daughter?" he asked. "What is your heart in this? It is my right to chose your husband, but I have no wish to see you wed without joy."

Duncan watched Xiao-nan bow again to her father. "My heart," she said softly, "is to be the wife of Duncan MacLeod."

Her words sent a quiet surge of gladness through MacLeod. Their eyes met briefly, and he smiled at her, then he turned back to Yao-hui to await the next question.

To Duncan's relief, Yao-hui picked up the package before him and turned it over in his hands, examining it carefully. He took his time before he put it back on the table and undid the wrapping. The paper fell away and a slow smile spread across his features.

"This is a fine grinding bowl, Duncan MacLeod," he said, "and a wisely chosen gift. I will first use it on the day of your wedding."

Xiao-nan's mother gave a little cry of joy. Soon she and Mingxia had opened their gifts and were exclaiming over their beauty. Duncan and Xiao-nan sat on one of the cushions, basking in the excitement that had replaced the silent tension in the room.

Duncan took Xiao-nan's hand. As her delicate fingers closed around his own, he was again filled with the desire, the need, always to keep her safe and happy. In that moment he thanked whatever force—be it God, or fate, or karma—that had brought him to Tibet.

Chapter Twenty-two

It was a long time before Duncan and Xiao-nan had the chance to be alone. After opening their gifts, Mingxia immediately replaited her hair so that her new comb could be displayed and Xiao-nan's mother made buttered tea, a Tibetan treat, which they drank from her new bowls.

Xiao-nan's father put his gift aside, reserving its use as he had said. But he brought out his old grinding bowl, and while they talked he methodically and expertly ground the spices and tobacco to refill his small box of *natag*. Duncan was pleased; Yao-hui would never grind his snuff in front of anyone who was not accepted as family.

While he ground, they talked of other options besides farming Duncan might choose to support a wife. Soldier and seaman, bodyguard and scout; these and similar occupations Duncan did not mention, but two hundred years gives a man time to develop many skills. Among the ones Duncan knew were scribe and bookkeeper, horse trainer, weaver, laundryman, farrier, and cook.

"You are a young man to have gained knowledge of so many things, Duncan MacLeod," Yao-hui said without looking up from his grinding.

"I have spent many of my years traveling," Duncan told him, understanding that there were still many questions Xiao-nan's father had not asked. Nor would he openly, now that his blessing had been given—but the questions remained, and Duncan would do his best to answer them.

"When one travels," he continued, "one must learn many skills in order to have food and lodging. The people of most lands are not as generous as those of Tibet, who open their homes to the stranger."

"A man who has spent so much time traveling may wish to

do so again," Yao-hui said calmly, still not raising his eyes. Duncan heard again the unspoken question and the concern in Yao-hui's words.

He shook his head. "It is because I have traveled that I know I will be happy to stay in Tibet. It is a precious jewel among nations, and those who live within its borders are doubly blessed, by its beauty and its peace."

And so the afternoon passed. The women chattered quietly but happily among themselves, going in and out of the room like a gentle tide as they refilled the teapot or put plates of food within easy reach. Otherwise, they left the men to their conversation.

It was a strange conversation, full of lulls of silence which grew longer as the hidden questions were satisfied. But the silence was companionable, and each time Duncan's eyes sought out Xiao-nan, he found her watching him with a soft smile that spoke not only of her joy, but of her pride in his answers.

Duncan stayed through the evening meal. It was only after that was concluded that he and Xiao-nan were at last freed to be alone. They sat in the garden, on the same stone bench by the fountain where they had sat on his first visit, and listened to the soothing sounds of the evening closing in.

Duncan still had the earrings he had bought for Xiao-nan in the pocket of his trousers. He withdrew them now and held the small package out to her. Her eyes were wide as she looked from it to his face, and he laughed gently.

"Well, take it. It won't bite you," he said.

She did not lift the package from his hand, but rather undid the ribbon where it lay and let the thin paper fall back on its own. The deep red of the rubies glowed against their silver setting; the white paper making them look as if they were resting on a cloud.

Xiao-nan still did not lift them from Duncan's hand. She ran the tip of one finger across the earrings almost reverently, as if she could hardly believe they existed.

"In my country," Duncan said, "a ruby is the symbol of hearts that are true. I wanted you to have these to know that my heart is truly yours and that there will always be truth between us."

"And I shall wear them," Xiao-nan said, finally taking the earrings and putting them on, "with the same meaning."

Shining against the softness of Xiao-nan's skin, framed by the darkness of her hair, the deep red of the rubies seemed to bring a soft blush to Xiao-nan's cheeks and lend their color to her lips. Duncan held out his arms to her, and, when he held her close, her head resting on his heart, he felt an exquisite sense of completion.

There shall be truth between us, he thought. *Soon you will know everything. Not here and now, where other ears might overhear—but soon. I promise you.*

Partway across town, other secrets were being thought, secrets their harborer hoped would have far-reaching results. Father Edward sat in his room, where he had sat for most of the short retreat of Jesuit practice. The ten days had passed quickly, filled with thoughts of invasion and revenge. These had been the fuel of his meditation; they kept his hatred alive in the silence.

He had meditated, yes, and he had prayed, though not to any Christian God, whom he considered weak beyond contempt. He nearly spat each time he looked at the large crucifix that adorned his wall. Nor had he prayed to the Compassionate Buddha whose words were revered in Tibet.

He had prayed to the great Shiva, maker and destroyer. He had prostrated himself time and again, imploring the great god for the privilege of being Shiva's hand of destruction.

And he knew the god had heard him. He could feel Shiva's strength flowing in his veins, keeping his heart alive with the fire of his aims. The great Nasiradeen would arrive, and Edward saw himself riding at his master's side. Together they would be unstoppable. Together they would conquer Tibet.

The Gurkha spy smiled to himself, playing his fantasy on the fabric of his imagination. He saw Nasiradeen's arrival, himself opening the gates wide to admit the army, Nasiradeen smiling at him in acknowledgement of his good work. He saw himself mounting one of the army's horses and, by his master's side, riding through the streets of Lhasa, fighting, hacking, trampling all who stood in their way. The carnage would be great; the streets red with the blood that fed Shiva.

He would take Nasiradeen to the Potala and up the stairs into the great monastic palace. What treasures its fifteen hundred rooms might contain, not even he could imagine. But in his mind's eye he pictured the monks cowering in fear as he and his master strode through the vast building until they found the Dalai Lama. Yes, Edward thought, he would wait until the great Nasiradeen was with him before he accomplished his mission. He would show his master his skill and strength as he killed Tibet's religious ruler.

Then he would find MacLeod.

Here the man known as Father Edward allowed his fantasy to vary just a little. He and MacLeod would fight, but always he was the victor. Sometimes he liked to envision MacLeod on his knees, begging for mercy. Other times, it was the swordplay that held his fancy—the blade in his hand flashing like lightning straight from Shiva's hand, overwhelming this Westerner who knew nothing of the Destroyer's might. In both scenes, the end was the same. His sword would pierce MacLeod's heart, and he would fall lifeless at Edward's feet.

Thoughts of defeat, of his own mortality, never entered the impostor's mind.

There was a knock on the door. Father Jacques opened it and looked in. "I am glad to see you smiling again, Edward," he said. "It has been a good retreat for you then?"

The Gurkha spy was ready to resume the role he was put here to play. His frustration had been eased by his fantasies; his unrest calmed by the knowledge all this would soon be over. He kept the smile in his face, making sure it was cheerful and did not turn into a grimace as he looked at the priest.

"Very good," he replied.

Father Jacques came into the room. He sat beside Father Edward on the bed, hands resting on his knees. Father Edward noticed that, as usual, he had dirt ground into the fibers of his cassock and caked under his fingernails. The spy suppressed a shudder of distaste.

He's as bad as an untouchable, a lowest caste, with his constant groveling in the dirt, he thought, but he was careful to keep his face neutral. He waited for what the priest had come here to say.

Father Jacques cleared his throat. "Edward," he began

slowly, as if each word was a difficult task. "I know I have not counseled you much during this retreat, but I felt you wanted, even needed, to wrestle with this temptation alone for a time."

Father Edward said nothing. After a moment Father Jacques sighed and continued. "Well—then I'll say only this and speak no more about it. It is easy when we are so far away from our home, our Community, to lose our perspective. But we must always remember that we are the face of the Church to the people we serve, and our conduct must therefore be even more circumspect than would be asked of us at home. To work in the mission field is a most difficult life. There is no shame to find one is not called to it. If your retreat has revealed that you would better serve the Church in another manner, then I will make the arrangements."

"No," the Gurkha spy answered. "I need to remain here. I am sure my . . . calling . . . is among these people."

Father Jacques slowly nodded. "All right, then," he said. "We'll start fresh—a clean slate. But you understand this must *never* happen again. Should you fall to temptation a second time, you will be sent immediately home to the Vicar General for discipline."

Edward did not reply. He kept his head properly bowed in an attitude of quiet submission, though his thoughts laughed at the priest's words.

Father Jacques stood. "Come," he said. "We'll have a Mass to celebrate your return to service, then we'll walk through the city to show the people that all is again well."

Keeping his face in a false, and he hoped, properly humble expression, Edward stood to join the priest.

"I have fed and watered your birds each day," Father Jacques said before he led the way from the room. "You will find them well cared for. I also found some writing things behind the cages. Are they yours? It is a strange place to keep them."

Edward felt his stomach tighten. He searched quickly for some acceptable explanation.

"Yes, they're mine," he said. "I sometimes write things—poems, little prayers. When I let the birds fly free, I send my writings with then. An offering, you might call it."

Father Jacques frowned. "I must remind myself often, Edward, that you come from a pagan country. But you have, with your conversion and your vows, abandoned those beliefs and practices. *We* come to God *only* through Our Lord—not through fire or wind or the wings of a bird. If you must see physical form for your prayers, then Our Lord's presence in the Eucharist is enough. Do you understand?"

The Gurkha spy again bowed his head as if accepting the reprimand. "Yes," he said. "I understand. In fact, I think that soon we shall come to understand each other very well."

"I hope so, Edward," Father Jacques replied, his voice taking on its usual, more kindly note. And as the older priest turned once again to lead the way to the little mission house chapel, Edward's smile turned genuine.

Oh, we shall indeed, the younger man thought. *When my master Nasiradeen arrives, and when I hold a sword to your throat, you shall understand everything.*

Chapter Twenty-three

The next morning, Duncan paced restlessly in the Potala garden, waiting for his daily meeting with the Dalai Lama. He had been here for nearly an hour already, and it was not like the religious leader to be so late. Duncan was becoming more concerned with each moment that passed.

The Dalai Lama was a young man, it was true, and he appeared healthy enough, but there was also something otherworldly, almost ethereal, about him. Moreover, he was mortal, and in the last two hundred years Duncan had seen many hale, energetic men fall—victims of sudden illness, badly stored food, or the unexplained and inescapable weaknesses of the mortal body. Despite the Dalai Lama's protestations about the soul's indestructibility and continuing incarnations, Duncan did not want to see anything happen to *this* cycle of the young man's existence.

He was about to go back into the Potala and find Gaikho or some other monk to ask about the Dalai Lama, when he saw the religious leader hurrying along the pathway toward him. Although he wore a slight frown on his cherubic face, he otherwise looked as well as ever.

He saw Duncan and lifted a hand in greeting. Duncan smiled at his own foolish worry, but he knew it stemmed from the affection that had grown between himself and the young man over the last several weeks—and that he would not change.

"I am sorry, Duncan MacLeod," the Dalai Lama said as he reached the clearing in the garden where Duncan waited. "I am late this morning, I know. I meant to send you word, but my mind sometimes gets distracted, and I forget many things. There is so much to do always, and now so much more, yes?"

"I do not wish these meetings to cause Your Holiness any hardship," Duncan said. "I understand that you have many responsibilities. You need not worry about me, I can find other things to do with my day if you need to be elsewhere."

The Dalai Lama held up his hands. "No, no, Duncan MacLeod," he said. "Teaching is never a hardship. For what other purpose am I here, yes? These hours in the garden are a joy in my day. But now there are preparations to be made that eat away at the time I would spend doing other things."

The young man crossed over to the stone bench where he habitually sat. As he took his place, he breathed a deep sigh and lifted his face to the sun.

"Ah," he said, "it feels good to sit in the warmth and the quiet, yes?"

Duncan nodded as he, too, sat in the dapple sunlight on the flower-studded grass. "What preparations are you making, Your Holiness?" he asked. "Is there some way I can be of service and help ease your burden?"

The Dalai Lama looked at Duncan with a slightly quizzical expression. But it was fleeting and he smiled.

"Sometimes I forget that your time in this land has been so brief and that you do not yet know all our ways," he said. "We prepare now for the great Kalachakra Mandala ceremony. In three days it begins and does not end for twelve days after that. Many, many people will soon arrive in Lhasa. Monks and nuns from the monasteries throughout this land will come. People from other towns, from farms and villages, from high mountain camps all will come to Lhasa. Some will stay here at the Potala. Others will stay with friends and family in the city. Many more will bring tents to cover the land outside the walls. Two cities almost, we will become, with the gates between us always open. There must be food available for so many, needs anticipated for their comfort. Many details and decisions."

"Before I came to Lhasa," Duncan said, "the nomads with whom I stayed spoke of this ceremony. I promised them I would attend on their behalf, but when I arrived I thought I had missed it after all."

The Dalai Lama shook his head. "We wait until this time so that no rain or cold will disturb the meditations. Even if one is trained, it is a difficult thing to sit at prayer for twelve days if the rain is pouring on the head or too much cold is filling the body. Yes?"

Twelve days of prayer and meditation; Duncan tried to put it in perspective with the hours spent on a single move in sword or *kata*, weeks spent on the open stillness of the sea, years of lonely travel. The difference, he realized, was that each of these things, occupations that had so far defined his life, were physically *active*. Even the time he had spent at Brother Paul's monastery had been quiet and restful, but it had also been filled with the gentle activities of communal life.

Perhaps it is time, Duncan thought, *to learn the activity of being still.*

As was so often the case, the Dalai Lama seemed to know what he was thinking. "Twelve days seem a long time to you, yes?" he said. "I tell you, Duncan MacLeod, they are not. It is only once, maybe twice in a man's lifetime that this ceremony occurs—only once every forty years. What are twelve days out of forty years? Nothing? But they are also everything, for they are days which build us and bind us as a people."

MacLeod felt humbled by the religious leader's words. They reminded him that this young body housed the soul of someone who was truly holy.

Duncan thought back to his own land, half a world away. What did they have, he wondered a little sadly, that could be said to bind them together, to define them as a people and a faith? Memorials of battles, athletic games, religious holidays such as Christmas, Lent, and Easter—but did these unite the clans or reinforce their separation, their sense of competition?

They had put aside their differences rarely. Most recently, many of the highland clans, especially the MacDonalds and the Camerons, the MacPhersons, and MacGregors, had united around the Bonnie Prince. Even his own clan had been divided in this cause. But why? Duncan asked himself. For war; to separate themselves from the English with blood and battle.

Was it the worthy cause Duncan had once thought? Charlie had said that peace would follow victory, but now, with the perspective of the years, MacLeod doubted that would have happened. The clans would soon have pulled apart again, each vying for the royal favor.

Well, Culloden Field had ended the dream of Scottish sovereignty, and the clans had returned to their long history of petty skirmishes and hatreds. Nothing changed.

Perhaps, Duncan thought, *it takes a land as isolated as Tibet to be able to find a way to put such differences and discord to rest.* For the sake of the years that were to come and the world he might well live to see, Duncan MacLeod truly hoped not.

"Now, Duncan MacLeod," the Dalai Lama said, his voice pulling Duncan's thoughts from the morbid path they threatened to take, "where did we leave off our discussion yesterday? Ah, yes—with the *bardo,* I think, the state of *between* death and rebirth."

Duncan could have said that he knew that state well. How many times had he "died" in the last two hundred years?—A dozen? More?—but by the Dalai Lama's words he had not died at all.

"Death does not come with the ending of our breath, the stopping of the heart and the blood," the young man was saying. "Death does not truly come until the mind changes into the clear light. This often takes three days or more. Only then, when one's mind has changed, does one enter the *bardo,* the between, and begin toward the process of rebirth. . . ."

When Duncan went down into the city he noticed the subtle changes that had come over the place. People were still as pleasant, smiling as he passed, children still played in the streets, dogs still barked and romped among them, but there was an air of expectancy and a greater sense of purpose in the way the people were going about their daily tasks. Everywhere doors and windows stood open, welcoming in the fresh air of the day. Time and again, Duncan saw people washing the front of their houses, scrubbing away the grime of winters past, trimming overgrown bushes and cleaning out garden beds. The already bright fairy-tale city of Lhasa was becoming a wonderland.

Perhaps, he admitted, these things had been happening for days and he had not noticed. His mind had been too full of Xiao-nan to notice much else but her.

When he reached her home, he found that her family was also busy. Furniture was being carried out into the garden so that the house could be scoured from ceiling to floors while the bedding and sleeping mats were aired and the rugs and cushions beaten free of dust. Duncan, who had come to appreciate cleanliness during his months in Japan, did not hesitate to join in.

He enjoyed working beside Xiao-nan. She smiled at him often while he moved and carried at her direction. It was like a gentle preview of some of the moments their life together would contain—a life he wanted more with each passing hour.

Soon all of the furnishings were outside. While Xiao-nan helped her mother in the house and her father worked on the front, Duncan aided Mingxia with the rugs and cushions. It was the first time they had been alone together since the incident with Father Edward. Duncan was uncertain what she would say to him.

Mingxia, however, acted quite happy to be working beside him. She laughed and chattered as if there had never been anything amiss between them. *Is it her youth and the natural flexibility of mind that is part of the young?* Duncan wondered as he swung the bamboo rug-beater against the heavy fabric. *Or is it something more—a practice of forgiveness woven into the very bones of this society? There is so much for the world to learn here.*

Yet, Duncan also found himself hoping that the world, with all its ways of hatred and pain, would never come to this land, never contaminate its peace and beauty.

"If you become a farmer, Duncan MacLeod," Mingxia said, "what will you grow?"

"I thought I'd let Xiao-nan and your father guide me," he answered.

She made a face at his words, and Duncan almost laughed. "They'll only tell you to grow rice and beans and cabbage," she said, her disapproval as obvious in her tone as in her expression.

"Those are good crops, Mingxia. People must eat."

"But anyone can grow them." She stopped swinging her rug-beater and looked at him. "*You* should do something else, Duncan MacLeod," she said emphatically. "You must do something *special*."

Again Duncan held back his laughter. "What would you suggest I do then?" he asked, quite seriously.

"I don't know," she replied, "but I will think about it."

They resumed beating the rug in silence, in rhythmic, alternating strokes. While Mingxia concentrated on the problem of his future, Duncan had the chance to watch her out of the corner of his eye, and he smiled to see she wore the same little frown that appeared on Xiao-nan's face when she was deep in thought.

"Mingxia," Duncan said a moment later, "what would you say if I raised horses as well as vegetables? Would that be *special* enough? I could train them and trade them with the other farmers or even the nomads."

Mingxia considered. "Yes, Duncan MacLeod," she said at last. "I think that is what you should do."

"Do you think your sister and father will agree?"

"Xiao-nan will agree to whatever you want," she answered, "and my father will wait to say anything until you have spoken all of your reasons why horses are a good choice. He will ask you many questions—then he, too, will agree."

"If you wanted to come stay with us sometimes, I could teach you to ride, and you could help me with the horses," Duncan told her.

Mingxia stopped beating the rug. She turned to MacLeod, her eyes wide with sudden excitement.

"Truly?" she asked. "You would teach me?"

This time Duncan did laugh. "Aye," he said. "I think you'd be very good at it."

He did, too. She was much like many a wild colt he had known—headstrong, vibrant, unwilling to be broken by harsh methods but responding well to a gentle touch. He thought she and the animals would quickly understand each other.

"Yes," Mingxia said with a nod as she went back to her chore with renewed energy. "I will be good at it. You will teach me, and I will become *best* at it."

Duncan smiled; it was good to be part of a family again. Soon he would have a wife to cherish and care for, a little sister to watch grow, parents . . . only children would be missing.

And he would have peace. Here in this land where peace and compassion were more than words spoken by mystics and idealists, he would live out the fulfillment of too many a lonely dream.

He had been alone far too long.

Chapter Twenty-four

Nasiradeen ground his teeth together. His hands clenched on the pommel of his saddle as he struggled not to strike the messenger kneeling in the dirt. Anger and frustration gnawed at him, but it was not this man's fault, and Nasiradeen never punished one of his men unjustly. His men knew that, counted on it, took pride in it. Punishment was swift and often brutal when it came, but it was never unjust.

No, the snail's pace at which the army moved could be blamed on no living thing. It was the mountains. Even the passes seemed determined to stay closed. There were rocks and logs and other debris, not there when Nasiradeen had scouted this route the year before, that had to be cleared so the supply carts could pass. New trenches had been formed by snows and rains and runoff that were treacherous to horses' hooves and wagon wheels alike.

Well, the incalculable strength of the mountains had just met the indominability of Immortal will. Nasiradeen would not allow even the mighty Himalayas to keep him from his prize.

"We will stop here until the wagon is repaired," he told the still kneeling messenger from the rear guard. "Take as many men as you need to get it done *quickly*. This is no place to camp for the night, if we can help it."

"Yes, Great One," the man answered before running back through the troops.

After he was gone, Nasiradeen raised one hand in gesture and immediately his second-in-command rode to his side.

"Take twenty men," Nasiradeen ordered, "and clear the road ahead until you find a wider spot to make camp. We'll catch up with you soon."

"And what if the road narrows?"

"Then we'll sleep on our feet," Nasiradeen snapped, furious

at being questioned. "Or we'll march through the night. Take the men and go!"

The man touched his hand to his heart and bowed as well as his saddle permitted. Then he wheeled his horse back toward the troops. Nasiradeen heard him shouting orders but did not bother to turn; his will would be obeyed.

Instead he kept his eyes fixed on the great peaks. *You won't stop me,* his thoughts snarled at them. *I'll dig a path with my bare hands if I must, but nothing will stop me.*

The population of Lhasa nearly doubled in the space of two days. People from throughout Tibet arrived in a steady, seemingly endless stream. Duncan watched with something akin to amazement as strangers were welcomed into the city like family members returning from a journey.

It was a wondrous sight, this example of national kindness, and one the warrior MacLeod never thought to see. Individuals, yes; in two centuries Duncan had seen individual acts that were selfless to the point of martyrdom. But this was something else. This was an entire nation living an ethic too many others merely mouthed or followed only when it suited their political convenience.

The Dalai Lama had little time to meet with Duncan now. When he was not in meditative preparation for the ceremony he would lead, he was hearing petitions, counseling and advising the people who had come to Lhasa from afar. He still invited Duncan to join him for their morning meal, but these were short and taken in the audience chamber, as of old.

Duncan missed the young man's company, but he did not mind a break from the constant influx of information and philosophy. Perhaps, he thought, the next two weeks would give him a chance to sort through all he had been told and return to his lessons with new understanding.

The other benefit for Duncan was the extra time to spend with Xiao-nan. She, however, was also busy with additional duties, and although they spent the hours together, they had little time to be alone. They had no time at all for the one talk Duncan knew they must have—the truth about his Immortality.

The air of expectation grew throughout the city as the days passed. A large pavilion was erected at the base of the Potala stairs; half of it was open to the air, containing a raised platform on which the Dalai Lama would sit. The other half was enclosed, but with steps leading both up and away.

This was the *thekpu*, the Mandala house, and in here the monks would create the great Kalachakra Mandala out of fine grains of colored sand. It would take them nine days of the twelve-day ceremony to complete their task. In the evenings of the last two days of the ceremony, the people would line up to view the Mandala, standing in line long hours for the privilege of walking around the *thekpu* and circling the Mandala that contained the path and palace of Enlightenment. For many, it was a once-in-a-lifetime pilgrimage.

Like a follower of Islam visiting Mecca or a Christian in the Holy Land, Duncan thought as he listened to Xiao-nan's explanation. He had a new appreciation for what it meant to his nomad friends when they asked him to attend on their behalf. He had agreed indifferently, not caring then where he went or what he did. Now he was glad—not only because it had brought him to Lhasa and to Xiao-nan, but because of the joy he now understood this action was providing for those who had shown him such kindness.

The morning of the third day, the day the ceremony was to begin, Duncan rose long before dawn. He spent his usual hour doing *kata*, but he did them slowly this morning, meditatively, using the movements to draw and focus his mind inward. After, he sat for a long time upon his knees, listening to the sound of his heartbeat, feeling his breath, reattuning himself before attending the religious ritual ahead.

He looked back over the last weeks and saw the changes in his life, in himself. The weight of memory that had driven him to the point of despair was no longer a burden. It was a tapestry, rich and multihued, and he saw for the first time the possibility to change the manner of its weaving.

He believed; he hoped; he prayed.

Then, from the depths of his mind came another whisper, overriding the beatific vision he was holding. *What of the Game?* it said. *The Game still exists—no changes, no choices.*

"There are always choices," the Dalai Lama's voice seemed to speak out of the air, but now as then Duncan wondered if it was true. Could there be a choice in the way one played the

Game? The rules did not vary; in the end there could be only one.

But the Game is not here, not now, Duncan's heart answered. *Not in Tibet. I am here—and for now, at least, I don't have to play.*

Dawn was approaching. Duncan could see the first shimmer of light through the long windows of his room. He rose from his knees, cleaned and dressed himself quickly. He had promised Xiao-nan to be by her side throughout the different stages of the long ceremony ahead.

The Potala was strangely quiet as he walked down the corridors. There was no sign of the monks who lived here or the many visitors. There was no sound of walking feet or whisper of human voices. Once, Duncan thought he heard the faint tinkling of a handbell, but the sound came and went so swiftly he was left wondering if he had heard it at all.

The city, by comparison, was a hive of activity. Already people were filing through the streets toward the base of the Potala, where they would spend the next twelve days at the feet of their Dalai Lama, Ocean of Wisdom, Highest Enlightened One, Priest-King.

Going against the flow, Duncan hurried toward Xiao-nan's home. She was waiting for him at her door with an anxious expression on her face and two long white scarves in her hand.

She handed one to him. "These are for blessings," she said. "They are symbols of respect."

"Aye, I've seen them before," he replied. "On the road when I first came to Lhasa."

"Then you know that you must bow when you present them and His Holiness will return them with a blessing. They may also be left at the base of the Mandala as an invocation for others. But we must hurry if we are to be there when the Dalai Lama arrives.

Taking Xiao-nan by the hand, Duncan led the way back toward the Potala. In spite of the vast number of people, Duncan noticed there was no jostling, no pushing against one another for a better place, a clearer view. It was a peaceful procession, representative of an entire nation whose collective mind was fixed on one purpose.

By the time they reached the open square at the base of the

Potala steps, many of the people had already taken their places. Monks from the Potala, some of whom Duncan recognized, sat on their knees facing each other across the square, at ninety-degree angles from the raised platform. Their presence created the side boundaries to the open area where the ceremony would take place.

Most of the visiting participants sat facing the platform, forming the fourth side of the square. Duncan noticed that the younger monks and nuns sat to the fore. These, Xiao-nan had explained, had come to be initiated by the Dalai Lama himself into the practice of the Kalachakra tantras for universal peace and compassion.

The older members of the *samgha*, the Buddhist religious life of monks and nuns, sat behind the initiates; the people of Lhasa and the mass of visitors to the city filled the rear in row upon row of silent witnesses. Their part in the initiation was to watch, to join their voices in the prayers and mantras, and above all, to add their will of compassion.

Duncan and Xiao-nan took their place among the crowd. In the ensuing silence, MacLeod had a chance to look around him. The platform and Mandala house had been completed. The *thekpu* was now painted yellow, with lotus flowers decorating the eaves and bright, multicolored banners hanging from the corners and framing the glass that would protect the sand of the Mandala from the wind.

The platform, too, had been decorated. Long silken tapestries were draped down the front, on which more lotus flowers flowed in colors of red, yellow, white, and blue. To the right of where the Dalai Lama would sit, ritual implements of polished brass rested, shining dully in the morning light. MacLeod recognized the vases that he knew held purified water and the ornate lamps that burned a combination of oil and butter. The rest he could not see from this distance, but he knew that Xiao-nan would explain each item as it was used.

Duncan turned his attention from the platform to the people. They were all dressed in their finest. The women wore soft colored shirts and short, black jackets. Their wraparound skirts were made from bands of bright cloth. Many of the older women wore headdresses that flowed down their back, studded with beads of turquoise. The men also wore bright shirts, predominately blues and greens, and their black pants were tied at the waist with multicolored sashes. Some sat on their knees, others sat cross-legged, hands folded in different patterns. Many spun prayer wheels or counted off the mantras on circlets of prayer beads while their lips moved silently. Young and old alike, all seemed to wear the same expression of looking inward in contentment.

Off in the distance Duncan heard the sound of handbells being rung. It was a pure sound, like a mountain stream rippling across stone or a young child's laughter. High up, at the top of the great stairs, the doors to the Potala opened. The monks came out, nine of them, in their plain maroon-and-saffron robes. Five more followed, wearing ornate costumes of brilliant yellow ankle-length jackets with bright red-and-orange scapulars, embroidered in intricate designs. They also wore high multisided headdresses that from a distance looked almost like crowns. Behind them, walking alone, was the Dalai Lama.

He looks so small and very, very young, Duncan thought, as the procession started down the long stairway. The monks to the fore carried the handbells, ringing them in unison with each step. As they neared, the monks in the square took up the triple-toned chant of Tibetan religious meditation, creating a rumbling undercurrent to the high tinkling of the bells. To Duncan, it seemed as if he could feel the sounds reverberating through his body all the way down to his bones.

The procession reached the bottom of the stairs. Slowly, majestically, it walked into the square and up onto the platform. After the Dalai Lama had seated himself, an expectant hush descended. Following the long minutes of chanting, the silence felt alive, as if it, too, was an entity, a participant in the ritual yet to come.

The Dalai Lama picked up the *darja* and handbell that rested on the platform in front of him. With practiced ease, he began reciting the first of the Kalachakra tantras, his voice floating out softly over the crowd. With a single motion, the rows of initiates stood and began prostrating themselves. Over and over, they stretched themselves in the dust, yet the movements were natural and graceful, like the rise and fall of waves upon the sea.

After a few moments, the prostrations ended in the same fluid motion as they had begun. Again, a deep silence followed. Without marring that silence, a single initiate stood and stepped forward. Not even his robes seemed to move. Xiao-nan had already told Duncan this monk represented all the initiates. On their behalf, he asked to become practitioners of the ancient teachings, dedicating themselves to the way of universal compassion.

When the initiate reached the base of the platform, he bowed and held out the long white cloth symbolizing his petition. The Dalai Lama leaned forward and lifted it from his hands. With this action, the chanting began again and the bells, but this time with a different cadence. Drums Duncan had not noticed were picked up and struck in a steady, heart-rhythmic beat.

As the initiate returned to his knees in the front row, the ornately clad monks descended from the platform to the open square and began a long, intricate dance. Instruments flashed in their hands. Xiao-nan leaned close to Duncan and whispered.

"The dancers now claim and purify the site," she said softly. "They carry the *purba* daggers to cut the influence of any negative thoughts or karma that might defile the ceremony, and their prayers asked the help and blessings of the Kalachakra deities. See, on their robes and crowns are the figures of 722 positive emanations."

Duncan understood now, as he would not have several weeks ago, that the deities to which she referred were not separate gods. They were different aspects of the Buddhanature. He was so intent upon watching the dancers, he almost did not see the Dalai Lama rise and, with six of the remaining monks on the platform, enter the *thekpu*. They would now begin the elaborate sand drawing that held the symbols and steps of Enlightenment.

The Dalai Lama would snap the chalked threads, the strings of wisdom, to lay out the selections and make the first marks. Then he would return to the initiation. For the next nine days the monks would apply the colored sand of the Mandala.

Duncan's thoughts went back to his nomad friends. In his mind's eye he could see each of their faces as plainly as if he sat among them. He felt again the warmth of their care, heard their happy voices as they sent him on his way to Lhasa.

Well, my friends, he thought fondly, *I have spun the prayer wheels for you many times, and I sit here holding you in my memory and my heart, as I promised. Each day I will pray for the blessings and benefits of your tribe.*

Yet, as Duncan MacLeod sat in the warmth of the Tibetan sun next to the woman he loved, he knew he was the one who had been blessed.

Chapter Twenty-five

Nasiradeen Satish led his men onward. Sometimes he rode; sometimes, when the way became too treacherous, he dismounted and walked his horse over the crumbling trails and washed-out gullies. But always he was at the fore of the army, and his men knew that if he had made it, so would they.

They followed him into the heights of the Himalayan passes where, though it was high summer, their breath still formed crusts of ice on their beards and eyebrows. At night they huddled together for warmth around pitiful fires that sputtered and smoked more than burned. The passes had felt endless, and Nasiradeen knew that without the sight of their leader struggling and suffering beside them, the men would have turned back to Nepal.

But they followed him. They would follow him wherever he led, and they would give him his dream.

Now the passes were behind them. Last night, Nasiradeen and his men slept on the Tibetan plateau—or rather, his men slept. Nasiradeen had tried, but for the first time in over a century, he had been haunted by childhood dreams, nightmares of the rotting corpses of the two whom he had known as parents.

The dreams would not leave him. Each time he closed his eyes they returned until, finally, Nasiradeen had risen in the darkness. He would be awake to greet his first dawn in Tibet— and rather than weaken him, the dreams served only to strengthen his resolve to succeed, to conquer.

He did not mind the darkness. It was neither silent nor lonely. It was filled with the voices of his plans, the company of his desire. He could feel Tibet like a living fire in his bones. Possession would be a consummation greater than any physical union or release.

And after Tibet? a small voice inside of him whispered.

When this land kneels at your feet, what then? You have centuries ahead, endless, ageless time.

In that moment, Nasiradeen felt the hand of destiny close about him. He would take Tibet; he was sure of it. By the time the children now living had passed to dust, Tibet would become a warrior nation, *his* warrior nation. He would lead them back into Nepal, into India, perhaps into Mongolia and China. With a nation of warriors behind him, he could conquer the continent and build an empire such as the world had never seen. He, who had begun his life as an untouchable, would rule over the mortals as the Emperor and demigod his kind were meant to be.

As the first light of dawn blushed in the eastern sky, it was greeted by Nasiradeen's laughter.

His army had not been marching long when smoke rising from a village greeted them. Here they would strike their first blow. Nasiradeen had no illusions about it being a worthy battle, but his men needed something to whet their appetites for what lay ahead. They needed the sight and smell of blood, the screams of dying men, of women for the taking, and the heat of battle and victory to wipe out the memory of their long, cold march.

Nasiradeen would give those to his men now, their first full day in Tibet. They would feel the power and the rewards of being his army, and from this day on they would be unstoppable.

He raised a hand to call a halt, then beckoned his captains to his side. They, too, had seen the smoke and knew what he wanted. A moment later a rider was sent out to scout the distance, terrain, and size of the village.

While they waited, Nasiradeen could hear his men drawing and checking their weapons. Here and there was the rasp of stone upon steel as an edge was made more keen, more deadly. Nasiradeen smiled savagely; they were ready, even eager, for battle.

The rider returned quickly. His expression was almost a sneer as he told his leader what he had found.

"It's a small village," he said. "No more than a hundred people at most. Crops grow in the fields. No sentries—a few dogs. I'm not even sure they have weapons."

Nasiradeen nodded and gestured the man back to the line. If this had not been their first encounter, Nasiradeen might have been tempted to take his warriors around the village in search of larger prey. But he would not deny his men the first of their warriors' pleasures.

He drew his sword and raised it. Behind him, the others did the same.

It was not a battle, it was a massacre, and it lasted even less time than Nasiradeen expected. He held his captains and his cavalry back and let the foot soldiers swarm into the village. Men, women, children, even household pets had been cut down at their morning meal, offering little or no resistance for their own survival.

I've seen sheep put up more of fight on their way to slaughter, Nasiradeen thought as he rode his horse through the carnage. Dead bodies, human and animal, littered the ground. The smell of blood was heavy in the air. Overturned cooking fires had caught two of the houses on fire, and Nasiradeen gave no order to control the blaze.

Let them burn, he thought. *Let the whole village burn. Let the smell of burning flesh be an offering to Shiva and let the smoke carry the message of our presence to the other villages. Maybe next time we'll find a worthy battle.*

Around him, he heard the screams of women his men had captured for their pleasure. This, too, he made no effort to stop. Most of the women would die from their wounds or from the shock of grief and rape. But the ones who lived would give birth to sons who would be warriors. They would grow up under a different regime—his regime—and they would be strong enough not to let this happen to their mothers and sisters, wives and daughters.

Nasiradeen drew his horse to the outskirts of the village, inclined to wait this once until his men had wearied of their victory. Then they would press onward toward the city of Lhasa, leaving a conquered country in their wake.

The days took on a surreal quality for Duncan MacLeod. It was as if he had entered into a time without time, a place where pageantry and superstition, ancient symbols and future intent melded in elaborate union.

In his long life Duncan had been witness to countless rituals. He had attended weddings and ordinations, coronations and knightings, births, deaths, and rites of passage. Yet this ceremony was different from anything he had seen.

For nine days, amid the tantric prayers led by the Dalai Lama, the initiates were made part of a spiritual lineage going back centuries. The intricate dances of the first day, to claim and purify the site of the ceremony, had been only the beginning of the rite.

After the first day the emphasis shifted to the preparation of the initiates, who were, in the essence of their beliefs, asking for spiritual rebirth as children of the *varja* master, the Dalai Lama. Amid ever more elaborate prayers and blessings, the initiates made their *bodhisattva* bows, pledging themselves to eternal altruism. Offerings of flowers, incense, butter lamps, and food were exchanged between initiate and master, symbolizing their union in Enlightenment.

Divinations were also made on behalf of each new practitioner of Kalachakra, so that they might individually know how best to purify themselves along the Path. Even their sleeping each night was an ordered part of the ceremony. Blades of Kushi grass, the grass upon which the Buddha was sitting when he attained Enlightenment, were handed out, to be put under the initiate's pillow and mattress—one to clear the mind of obscuring thoughts and the other to aid in the generation of beneficial dreams.

While the initiates were being thus prepared, the monks in the *thekpu*, the Mandala house, continued their work on the Great Kalachakra Mandala. Theirs was another ritual, as elaborate as the one taking place outside. All 722 emanations of Kalachakra had to be visualized and their individual mantras recited, the different sections of the Mandala purified with scented saffron water and each of the monks inside the *thekpu* likewise consecrated before the actual sand construction could begin.

All of this lasted for nine days. On the morning of the tenth day, the sand Mandala was completed, and the final steps of the ceremony began. Duncan and Xiao-nan were seated on the ground in their accustomed places amid the crowd. She had carefully explained each day's action to him, wanting him to share this experience as fully as possible.

And Duncan knew he had reaped the benefit here. He felt no closer to understanding the Buddhamind, as the Dalai Lama called it, or to attaining Enlightenment. Those were both still concepts in words only. What he had found was peace. The restless strivings that had filled him for so long had finally, somewhere in the last nine days, been set to ease. All of the ghosts were quiet.

For Duncan MacLeod, that was Enlightenment enough.

Xiao-nan leaned close to him and whispered. "Do you see, my Duncan," she said, "the blindfolds they are given now. These show the spiritual blindness they must overcome."

Duncan watched as strips of red cloth were handed out to the monks and nuns in the first rows. These were tied in symbolic actions around their foreheads. Then pitchers of scented water began to make the circuit through them.

"The sips of water they now take," Xiao-nan continued her explanation, "three sips to cleanse the gates of their bodies, speech, and minds. Now they will make their pledges to turn from all wrong ways of conduct and repeat their vows of *bod-hisattva*, then they will be taken to view the Great Mandala. We must pray for their benefit, my Duncan, as they will pray for ours and for that of all beings."

All around Duncan, the people were chanting again. The soft syllables of this mantra had a soothing, almost hypnotic effect. Duncan joined his voice to the others. He had done so often over the last days so that now the sounds rolled easily off his tongue.

OM AH HUNG HO HANG KHYA MA LA WA RA YA HUNG PHAT.

The sounds, though chanted softly, seemed to hold the air in sudden stillness, a barrier against the evil of the world. The mantra would continue for hours, until the initiates had all viewed the Mandala and retaken their seats before the Dalai Lama.

As Duncan chanted, he let his mind drift over the days past and the days yet to come. Tomorrow, the initiation rite would be concluded and the Mandala house opened to the people so that all could see the great sand map of Enlightenment. The day after that, the twelfth day, the colored sand would be swept up and placed in a special receptacle, then carried to the river and poured into the moving water so that its blessing power could move across the land. On that final night, the city would have a festival of celebration.

Then, finally, the visitors would leave Lhasa, and life would return to normal. Duncan was eager for that to happen. Although he had spent each day and most of the evenings with Xiao-nan, there had been no time to be *alone* together. For Duncan, missing those times of shared solitude was like a subtle ache in his bones.

As eager as he was to be alone with Xiao-nan, to hold her again as they sat in the sun by the river or amid the sweet scents of the garden, the thought also brought a little whisper of dread. Soon, before their wedding plans were allowed to go much further, he had to tell her the full truth of who he was. He did not doubt the love, but a small part of him still feared that the difference between them would be too much for her to accept.

His thoughts were interrupted by the feel of Xiao-nan's hand sliding gently into his own. He turned to see her watching him with eyes so full of love that all else in the world ceased to matter.

Duncan had seen many wondrous things in his two hundred years. He was living proof that the inexplicable existed. But it was from Xiao-nan he was learning the true magic of life. It was the magic of needs met without speaking, of human hearts united.

It was the eternal magic of love.

Chapter Twenty-six

Father Edward knew Nasiradeen must reach Lhasa soon, and the charade he was playing would finally be over. What he did not know was whether the army would arrive before this Tibetan ceremony that occupied the city was over or after, when all was quiet again. Either way, Father Edward would be prepared.

A part of him hoped Nasiradeen would arrive before all of the many visitors had departed. He had no doubt the army would cut them down to a man; Nasiradeen was not known for his clemency to the vanquished. But the ceremony was almost concluded now. Tomorrow was the twelfth and final day; after that, the people would go home. How many of them would Nasiradeen meet on the roads? he wondered. They would have to be killed before they could bring back a warning.

So much fighting going on without him; Edward wanted his share in the victories.

For the last few days, Father Jacques had gone to watch the activities in the city square. He had tried to persuade Father Edward to accompany him, saying that the more they understood about the people of Tibet, the better they could minister to them, but Edward had refused. Oh, he used the phrases Father Jacques expected to hear about heathen practices and beliefs— but the truth was far different. He needed time alone to find something he might use as a sword.

It had been a frustrating and fruitless search. The house, including Father Jacques's belongings, yielded nothing but a few kitchen knives, appropriate for cutting vegetables but useless for anything else. Edward tucked one into his boot and went to search through Father Jacques's tools. Here, too, he was frustrated. Two hand trowels, a shovel, a small hand rake, and a pair of shears; nothing he could turn into a weapon to fit his hand and his training.

This morning he waited until Father Jacques was out of sight, then headed in the opposite direction. His goal was the marketplace. Surely, he thought, some of the stalls would be open for business—and if they weren't, well that would not stop him, not if he saw what he wanted.

And if he could not find it there, then what? he wondered as he walked down the silent streets. Start going through the homes in the city? It would be an easy task; there were no bolts or bars to the doors in Lhasa. Or, perhaps outside the gates, someone among the visitors would have something he could barter and then sharpen into the weapon he wanted. But he had only today and tomorrow to find out.

He entered the market to find most of the stalls closed. Here and there, a vendor selling incense or fresh hot food still had his shutters open to any who might pass by, but otherwise all was still. That suited Edward. Ignoring the vendors who looked up hopefully at the sound of his steps, he headed toward the far end of the market where the various metal crafters had their shops.

He passed the stalls of jewelers and artisans without a glance. He was not after something ornamental. The blacksmith's shop was another matter. Edward had heard Father Jacques speak of this man as an artist in his own right, creating farm tools and blades as well as decorative work. Here, Edward would begin his search.

What he wanted was not likely to be found in the front shop, so he did not waste his time searching amid the candlesticks and cooking pots, the kitchen knives and household tools. Making certain no one was watching his movements, he went around to the back of the building where the smith had his forge.

Like the other buildings in Lhasa, this, too, was unlocked, and Edward had no trouble slipping inside. He left the door ever so slightly ajar to admit some additional light, then set to work, trying not to make enough noise to alert the few shopkeepers down the road.

Minutes of mounting frustration passed as he found only hand plows and ropes of chain, ornate grillwork and large iron kettles, brazier grates and small cooking stoves. There were some long metal stakes that, with enough time and the right tools, Edward thought he could turn into pikes—but time was something he did not have, not that kind of time, and there was no place to do that kind of work.

Then, in the back of the shop he found the knives. There were blades and cleavers of several sizes, many not yet fastened to handles and all of them still not sharpened. That did not matter; there was a sharpening stone back at the mission house that Father Jacques used on his shears. But a handle was necessary; that Edward could not fit himself.

He began to rummage through the blades, carefully, still trying not to leave too much evidence of his passage. If the theft was not discovered for a few days, it would be too late.

Finally he found what he wanted and lifted it close to examine in the dim light. The blade was about twenty-eight inches long and thick. It was the type of blade used to cut through brush and small trees. But the handle felt good in his palm. He swung it a few times, testing the feel. It was not the curved blade he was used to, and it did not have the balance of a true sword, but it would do. Oh, it felt good to be armed again.

For the first time Edward was glad of the cassock he wore. He hid the blade beneath the long black robe and carefully exited the shop. He would not take the chance of walking back through the marketplace, but instead began to cut between buildings, taking the quickest way possible back to the mission house.

Soon, the blade would be honed, and he would be ready for the army to arrive. He would be Shiva's warrior once again.

It was the final day of the ceremony, the day the sand Mandala would be destroyed. Yesterday Duncan and Xiao-nan had stood in line far into the evening for their chance to view the Great Wheel of Time and symbol of the Path to Enlightenment, and the sight of it was more amazing than Duncan anticipated. The colors were bright, vivid, the design so intricate he knew he could study it for hours and still not take in every detail.

In his travels he had seen masterpieces from all over the world, works of art crafted in paint or stone, bronze or wood, ivory, gold, and jewels. He had seen pictures in caves and designs cut into rocks that dated back to the time when humankind had no other language, messages so old their meaning had been lost. He had also seen artwork so new the paint was still wet and the chisel marks had not yet been polished away.

But the sand Mandala was somehow both; like the whole ceremony, it was a bridge between the past and future. Its symbols were stepped in antiquity but it was a living, breathing past that drew the mind not backward to what had been, but forward into what might someday come to pass—for the individual viewer and, Duncan found himself hoping, for the peace of the world.

As he continued his slow progress around the Mandala that measured seven feet to a side, he could not help but wonder if it was a vain hope.

As she had with everything he had witnessed over the last twelve days, Xiao-nan acted as guide to what he was viewing. He learned that the bands of colored sand surrounding the great inner structure, which was the Mandala itself, all had their meanings:

The outermost circle was done in stripes of different colors. This was the circle of fire that protected all within the Mandala and represented bliss consciousness and pristine awareness. The green circle within that was the symbol of space. It contained a chain of *varjas* which were the indestructible mind. Next came the gray sand of wind and the pink-red of fire, the white of water, and the yellow of earth. Within the band of yellow, a greet pattern swirled, representing stability.

The circles were the six elements, and inside them was an ornate square surrounded by four crescents. These were the gardens which contained offerings to the deities and the gates into the heart of the Mandala. The square itself was the palace of Enlightenment, each floor a step closer to that perfected state.

The outer square was the Mandala of the Enlightened Body. Inside that were the Mandala of Enlightened Speech, of the Enlightened Mind and the Enlightened Wisdom. Finally, the innermost square was the Mandala of Enlightened Great Bliss.

Within the different levels of gardens and squares, were figures of animals and dancing deities, humans in different poses, flowers, trees and the heavenly wheels. So much to see; Duncan could only open his mind and let it imprint itself on his memory, to be called up later and pondered.

But now it was all being swept away. The colored sand was being pulled together into a pile, into a vase to be poured into the river. Duncan felt a vague sense of loss to know that the beauty of these last days would not be repeated for another forty years. The Dalai Lama had been right when he had said they would pass swiftly. But then, Duncan admitted to himself, the young man was usually right in the things he said.

Usually.

Duncan and Xiao-nan walked with the rest of the people, following the Dalai Lama to the river to watch the sand cascade into the water and be carried on to bless the land. The ritual completed, the mood turned to one of celebration.

Returning to the city as dusk fell, large bonfires had been lit in the square where the initiation had taken place. While the Dalai Lama and monks returned to the Potala, the people of the city gathered in the square for a night of social gaiety and the usually quiet city of Lhasa seemed to erupt in laughter.

People brought food from their homes and from the camp outside the city walls. Musical instruments—drums and cymbals, flutes, bells, and horns—appeared and added their noise to the night. Children set off firecrackers, ran and danced around the fire while the adults talked and sang and told stories from the past.

Duncan left Xiao-nan chatting with a group of friends while he went to stretch his legs. The last twelve days had been a wonderful experience, but now that it was over he found himself weary of sitting.

He walked through the crowd, listening to the sounds of Lhasa at play. Now and then, someone would beckon to him, inviting him to join their conversation. But he would only smile and wave and move on. Then he spotted Brother Michael, the eldest of the Capuchin monks, standing along the edges of the crowd, and went to join him.

"Good evening, Brother Michael," he said when he drew close. The monk turned and looked at him, squinting in the growing darkness. Then a bright smile spread across his face.

"Ah, good evening, Mr. MacLeod. It is indeed a fine night

for a party. I saw you sitting among the people at the ceremony these past days. Tell me, what did you think of it?"

"Like everything else in this land, I found it to be unique—beautiful, moving, and yet often difficult to comprehend."

Brother Michael laughed at his words. "And there, Mr. MacLeod," he said, "you have truly described Tibet."

Duncan also smiled. "I have to admit I'm surprised to hear you attended the ceremony," he told the monk.

Brother Michael shook his head. "Attended is too strong a word," he replied. "Watched, perhaps. It was too great an opportunity to miss. Even Father Jacques was there, though his brother priest was nowhere to be seen."

Brother Michael's words reminded Duncan that he had not seen the younger Jesuit since that day outside the Choi house with Mingxia, and, content in the pattern of his days, MacLeod had let the absence calm his previous suspicions. Perhaps they had been based on nothing more than personal distaste after all, he thought briefly.

But another part of him still whispered a warning, and MacLeod silently promised himself to be more wary. It would be so easy, here in this land of pace, to drop his guard—but if he did, who might pay the price of his negligence?

Duncan knew he would continue to heed that small inner voice he had come to trust over the centuries. He would renew his vigilance.

Brother Michael's gesture recalled MacLeod's attention. A little distance away he saw Father Jacques sitting surrounded by a group of children. What story the priest was telling MacLeod could not hear, but the children squealed with delight as he made faces and changed his voice with the characters.

"He's a strange man, is Father Jacques," the monk said softly, unaware of the misgivings his words had caused in MacLeod. "One would hardly guess that someone with a soul of such genuine love and simplicity also has a brilliant mind. He was a professor of botany back in France, you know. He taught for many years, but when he heard this mission was opening up, he begged to come here. The children adore him. They call him Bo-Bo."

Duncan smiled again. "Aye, I've heard them," he said.

"Well, don't let his gentle spirit fool you, Mr. MacLeod. Father Jacques also plays a very mean game of chess. Speaking of which, you said you might come by for a game."

"Aye, so I did. Next week?"

"I'll look forward to it. Perhaps you can explain the ceremony to me. There was much I could not see from where I was and less I understood."

The conversation was ended by a loud crash of cymbals. All around them drums began to pound in a steady rhythm. MacLeod looked toward the center of the square and saw dancers in costumes and headdresses performing around the fire. One had the head of a deer, another of a dragon. The third was wearing a huge black hat with the face of a fierce deity. All were dressed in bright multicolored robes that flowed around them as they moved.

"This dance I have seen before," Brother Michael said over the noise. "It is the Tibetan version of a morality play. Soon they will bright out an effigy representing evil that they will dance around and eventually destroy. When that is accomplished, the dancers climb to the next step of rebirth by the animals becoming human and the fierce deity changing to a face of compassion."

Duncan stayed by Brother Michael to watch the dance, and he clapped with the rest of the crowd at its completion. When it was over, he headed back to Xiao-nan to spend the rest of this celebration in her company.

Tomorrow, he told himself as he slid an arm around her waist, *tomorrow there will be time to be alone. Tomorrow I will tell her the truth of who I am.*

Chapter Twenty-seven

There was no time for Duncan and Xiao-nan to be alone the next day, or the day after that. Finally, on the third day after the Kalachakra ceremony concluded, when the last of the visitors had truly left Lhasa, Xiao-nan packed a basket of food for them, and they headed out into the hills.

It was a warm day, the warmest Duncan had known in Tibet. He wanted to go down to the river and sit on the rocks in the sun and the quiet, but Xiao-nan knew it would not be quiet today. On a day such as this, many of the women from the city took their washing to be cleaned in the river and laid out to dry on the rocks and bushes near the water's edge.

Instead they went into the hills. Neither had a destination in mind, yet they both headed toward the same place—back to where the blue orchid grew, where they had spent their first day together and begun to fall in love. Xiao-nan chattered while they walked, far more talkative than usual, but Duncan was only half listening. With each step he could feel the tiny spark of dread in his heart growing. He struggled to find the words that he would say to her, knowing that no matter how eloquent his explanation, Xiao-nan might still choose to turn away from him.

It was not an unreasonable fear. It was born of experience and sorrow. Had not his own clan cast him out, people with whom he had spent all the years of his youth, who knew him better than any others on earth? The man whom he had called Father, whom he had honored and revered and loved, turned from him, calling him a demon and devil's spawn. Even after two hundred years, Duncan still felt the pain of their last meeting on the road near Glenfinnan.

Of all the clan, only his mother had still loved and accepted him. It did not matter who had borne him or what others might say about his life—he was *her* son and ever would be.

It was only the memory of her love that gave Duncan hope now.

The blue orchids still bloomed in rich profusion beneath the slender trees, sending their sweet fragrance into the summer air. More than ever, the place had a feeling of enchantment as the slight breeze moved the leaves overhead, sending dappled pools of golden light dancing across the brilliant blue flowers.

The summer heat had dried much of the ground beneath the trees, but Duncan still spread out a thick blanket so that they could sit in comfort. Xiao-nan quickly unpacked the basket she carried, then sat back and breathed deeply, smiling at the fragrance of the flowers.

"I have been thinking, my Duncan," she said, as she moved close, nestling into the circle of his arms, "that our wedding might take place at the time of the next new moon. I know that is only three weeks away, but you have not family with whom marriage property must be settled and if we marry soon, we will have many weeks of fine weather ahead to build our home."

"Marry in haste, repent at leisure," Duncan said in English, under his breath. Xiao-nan looked up at him, puzzled.

"What did you say, my Duncan?" she asked. "I did not understand."

Duncan shook his head slightly. " 'Tis nothing," he said. "An old saying of my people that popped into my head."

"But I would like to learn the words of your people."

Duncan looked down at her head resting on his shoulder and gave her a small smile that did not quite cover the worry in his eyes. He knew he was just postponing the inevitable. He took a deep breath.

"It is a saying that means to be certain about the person you marry. Are you certain you want to marry me, Xiao-nan? No doubts or reservations?"

Xiao-nan pulled away from him. Duncan watched her dark eyes cloud with concern, losing the spark of joy that had been there all morning.

"I am certain, my Duncan," she said. "Are you no longer?"

"Oh, sweetheart," he said as he reached out and ran a finger down the softness of her cheek. "I've never been more certain of anything. But if we are to marry, then there are things about me that you must know. No secrets—the whole truth."

Xiao-nan took his hand and held it in both of her own. Duncan looked down at her fingers, so slender and delicate, clasped around the squareness of his palm. In a moment she would likewise hold their future; would she be strong enough, or would the truth shatter their lives? Even in the love Duncan saw staring out of her dark eyes, he found no answer.

He searched for a way to begin this conversation. "Do you remember when your father asked how I would provide for a wife and after I told him, he said I knew many trades for a man so young?" he said at last. "Well, he was wrong. Oh, not about my knowing many trades—I've had more occupations that I chose to tell him—but about my being young. I have lived a long time, Xiao-nan, far longer than you can imagine."

Duncan waited, giving Xiao-nan a chance to speak, but she sat, staring at him with her serene expression and waiting for the words yet to come. Again Duncan drew a breath. He held it and let it out slowly.

"I am truly Duncan MacLeod of the Clan MacLeod, as I have told you," he said. "I was born two hundred years ago in the Highlands of Scotland. I do not age; I cannot die as other men do. I am Immortal. . . ."

Xiao-nan remained very still while she listened, letting her silence encourage Duncan to speak. She had questions, certainly, but she knew that if she spoke, Duncan would stop. He would answer only what she asked and, perhaps, not say all the things he needed to say.

With the full empathy born in womankind, strengthened by the depths of her love, she knew that Duncan needed to purge the secrets of his soul. She knew, too, that by letting him talk without imposing direction on the things he said, she would learn far more about this complex man before her.

He filled the silence with his memories, telling her of his life, of his years of wandering and the loneliness they contained: no true home or family, no wife to share his truth, no children to lighten his burden, friends lost to old age and death. He had

seen wonders, too, the glories of land and sea but, Xiao-nan
wondered, were they recompense enough for all the sorrow?

He told her then of the Game and what it took for him to stay
alive. She did not doubt his words; his eyes held the years and
the deaths he had seen, had caused. Xiao-nan felt as if her heart
would break for him. A single tear slowly ran down her cheek.
At the sight Duncan stopped. With his free hand he reached up
and gently wiped it away.

"Oh, sweetheart," he said, "I'm sorry. I did not want to hurt
you, but you had to know the truth. I love you, Xiao-nan, and I
won't have my life causing you sadness or remorse. Now that
you know the kind of man I am, if you want me to go, I'll understand. I'll think of something to tell your family, so they
know it's my fault and no shame to you."

Xiao-nan put a hand to his lips. "Shh, my Duncan," she said,
"You speak with foolishness now. Do you think my feelings are
so weak, that I am so changeable, that I will love you less for
having opened your heart to me? No, my Duncan. I think I shall
love you not only in this life, but in all the lives to come."

Xiao-nan saw that despite her words, there was a haunted expression lurking in the depths of Duncan's eyes. Part of him
still doubted, still expected her to reject him, to turn away in
horror at who he was and what he had done in his life. *What a
sad thing,* she thought, *to have so little knowledge of love.* For
all his two hundred years, at that moment Xiao-nan felt infi-
nitely older and wiser than he.

She leaned her face into his and brushed his lips softly with
her own, knowing in her woman's heart that the assurances he
needed were not given with words. He returned her kiss, but
she could still feel his hesitancy. She moved closer to him,
wordlessly inviting his touch.

She kissed him again, her hands pressed lightly against his
chest. She was not experienced in the ways of physical passion,
but neither was she ignorant, and she knew that she must guide
him into this, at least for now. His gift to her had been the secrets of his heart; her gift to him was the fullness of her body.
From this day onward, they would truly be as one.

As his kiss lingered, she slowly slid her hands under his
shirt, feeling the hard muscles of his back, the smooth supple-
ness of his skin. With a single, graceful movement she lay

down, drawing him with her. He pulled his face away and looked deeply into her eyes.

"Xiao-nan, there is no need—"

"Shh, my Duncan," she said, once more raising her fingers to his lips. "It is time."

He kissed her then, slowly and tenderly. Xiao-nan gave herself up to the feeling of his lips warm and soft upon her own, of his hands, so gentle as they brushed the hair back from her face. His lips moved to her eyelids, her ears, the juncture of her neck and shoulder, lingering in a rain of soft touches that sent shivers of delight through her. Once more she slid her hands under his shirt to feel his skin beneath her palms.

With a swift motion he pulled the shirt over his head and cast it away. Gently, Xiao-nan ran her fingers through the mat of dark, silken curls in the center of his chest, up over the muscles of his shoulders and back again. Her movements were slow, savoring each second, exploring the sensations that touching him gave her.

Duncan moved slowly too, as he began to unfasten her clothing. He watched her carefully, and she knew that with the slightest indication he would stop. But she did not want him to stop. With each passing second, each touch of his fingers and lips, she desired more of him.

He bent his head to her breast, his tongue sliding across the sensitive flesh. Xiao-nan could not halt the gasp of pleasure as his lips closed upon her nipple. His hand slowly explored the softness of her flesh, stroking across her arm, her stomach, her thigh. Her back arched to meet him as lips followed hand, leaving a shivering trail everywhere they touched.

Xiao-nan felt alive in ways she had never felt before. She found herself ill-content just to lie there. She wanted to feel, to touch, to taste him in the same way he was touching her. With a gentle push, she rolled him onto his back. He pulled her with him, strong arms holding their bodies together, flesh against flesh.

Lying on top of him, Xiao-nan slowly slid down his body until she rested her head upon his chest. She could hear the steady beating of his heart. She moved her head from side to side, brushing his skin with her lips, letting the soft hair caress her cheeks as she breathed in the warm male scent of him. With her lips, she followed the hair down to the flat of his stomach and heard his sharp intake of breath.

Bold as she had already been, she was not quite brave enough to undo the rest of his clothing as he had removed hers. Instead, with lips and tongue she followed the outline of his rib cage back to his chest, his neck, his lips. His hands entwined themselves in her hair as their kisses grew deeper and Duncan again took control of their lovemaking.

He rolled her beneath him, letting her feel his strength, the very *maleness* of him in the action. Xiao-nan opened her lips to his kiss and felt his tongue caressing the inside of her mouth. She felt herself filled with a growing hunger for which she as yet had no name.

Still Duncan did not hurry. Their kiss went on, became another and another. Xiao-nan hardly noticed when he removed the last of his clothing, but soon there was no impediment between them. He moved his hand to the soft inner part of her thigh, stroking, fingers gently grazing her skin. She opened herself to him as his hand traveled to the dark triangle of hair and found the warmth awaiting him.

He moved himself more fully on top of her. She opened herself wider to him, every part of her body aching to have him inside her, male to her female. She knew there would be pain the first time, but when it came it passed quickly, the memory of it erased by the pleasure that followed.

Duncan's movements were slow and sure, teaching her body how to meet and move with his. Her breath came in gasps as the sensations built. Her hands roved down his back, to his hips, the firmness of his buttocks, the power of his thighs. He seemed to know her body's needs before she did as he slowly brought the rhythm of their joining to match the pounding of their hearts in movements as old as life and as elemental as the mountains around them.

Xiao-nan had not know such pleasure existed. She wrapped her legs around his thighs, bringing him deeper into her as the sensations built in waves through her body. Her back once more arched, her hands gripped his arms as light erupted inside of her. She rode the crest of it for a long timeless moment, feeling as if the light wrapped around the two of them, binding their souls together and reaching on toward infinity.

As the sensation began to fade, she felt Duncan give the deep shudder of his release. Then he, too, was still and they lay there as their breath quieted, wrapped in the warmth of their love and each other's arms.

He rolled off of her and pulled her to him. She nestled, cradling her head in the hollow of his shoulder; she felt as if she could stay here forever. Duncan kissed the top of her head and Xiao-nan turned to look at him. All of the doubts were gone from his eyes. She saw only peace, and love.

"In my country," Duncan said softly, "when a man and woman marry they are said to become one flesh. I know we have not yet said the words of marriage together, but no words can add to what I feel in my heart."

"Yes, my Duncan," Xiao-nan replied, "we are one. Now and forever—through all the lives to come."

Chapter Twenty-eight

They stayed in the hills for most of the day, talking and touching, loving each other in that enchanted place where the blue orchid grew. Duncan could think of no more beautiful spot for their lovemaking to have begun than here, with the sweet scent of the flowers surrounding them and the warmth of the sun playing its golden fingers across their bodies.

They made love again in the afternoon with quieter passion, each enjoying the discovery of the other. Then, as the sun passed behind the tallest of peaks to the west, ending the heat of the day, they knew it was time to return to the city.

Duncan had agreed to Xiao-nan's date for the wedding; it could not come soon enough for him. Tonight they would speak to her parents, and tomorrow the arrangements would begin in earnest.

When they reached the city, Duncan thought he felt a subtle change to the atmosphere. There was a tenseness that reached him even through the euphoria of the afternoon. It was like an itch between his shoulder blades that made him want to reach for his sword. But his sword was in his room at the Potala and its absence at his side, for the first time in many weeks, filled him with disquiet.

Xiao-nan's father came out to meet them as they neared the house. "Good, my daughter, you are home," he said, "and you, Duncan MacLeod. We feared you would not be in time."

"In time for what, Yao-hui," Duncan asked sharply, the uneasy feeling within him focused into a flood of dread. "What has happened?"

"One of the monks who attended the Kalachakra ceremony has returned with his robes bloody and torn. Now there is talk of closing the city gates."

"What happened to the monk? Do you know?"

Yao-hui shook his head. "I know nothing for certain. He is at the Potala now, speaking with His Holiness the Dalai Lama. But there are whispers of an army on its way toward Lhasa."

Duncan knew he must return to the Potala at once. He pulled Xiao-nan into his arms for one quick embrace.

"You stay here, in the house where it is safe," he told her. "I'll return as soon as I can."

Xiao-nan nodded. Duncan did not like to see the fear that suddenly filled her eyes. He ran a fingertip down her cheek.

"Don't worry, sweetheart," he said softly. Then he turned and began to run toward the Dalai Lama's palace.

He met two monks from the Potala on their way to close and bar the city gates. From them he learned the rest of the news. There was indeed an army marching toward Lhasa; its arrival could come at any time. The injured monk and his companions had been set upon as they walked toward their home monastery. Though they were unarmed, they were attacked mercilessly. Only this one monk escaped. He had hurried back to warn the city as fast as his wounds would allow. A messenger had been dispatched for help from the Chinese Emperor, in accordance with an agreement that had been signed many years ago. It was the Dalai Lama's hope that by barring the gates, Lhasa could withstand the army until such help arrived.

Duncan's frown deepened as he heard this last part. He doubted the inhabitants of Lhasa had any idea what it took to withstand a siege or how to fortify their city against the coming attack. But, Duncan thought as he headed once more toward the Potala, he did—and he knew where he would go for help. If he was any judge of men, Brother Michael had been a soldier before taking the cloth. There MacLeod hoped to find the aid he needed.

He raced up the Potala steps, taking them two at a time. Once inside the great building, he hardly slowed his pace down the long corridors to his room. His only thought was to retrieve his *katana* and return to the city.

He found the monk, Gaikho, waiting at his door. "His Holiness has sent me to find you," the young monk said. "He requires your immediate attendance."

Duncan shook his head. "Not now," he said, "but I'll return soon."

He stopped, wondering how to make Gaikho realize the urgency. But no, there was nothing in the monk's experience to make him understand—nor, probably, in the Dalai Lama's, for all his incarnations. Duncan knew he must act now and explain it to them later, when there was time.

"Tell His Holiness I'll return as soon as I can," he told Gaikho. "Shortly after sunset I hope. Right now there are too many things I must do."

The monk opened his mouth to protest, but Duncan pushed past him and into his room. Gaikho was still there when he emerged a moment later carrying his *katana*. The monk backed away at the sight of the sword. Duncan saw the shocked and fearful look on his face, but took no time to stop and reassure him.

MacLeod ran back down the corridors and out the great doors, his mind already turning over various options he had seen work in battle. He would go first to Xiao-nan's house to make certain the family was safe, then he would find Brother Michael. Duncan was certain that between them, he and the monk would find a workable plan.

When he reached Xiao-nan's house, he found her mother and father waiting for him. "Xiao-nan has gone to find her sister," they told him. "Mingxia went to help old Huilan earlier today, but when we sent for her to come home, she was no longer there. Xiao-nan said we must wait here and tell you where she has gone. She said she would start looking for Mingxia at the city well."

Damn the girl—why couldn't she have been where she was supposed to be just once? Duncan thought as he rushed off. He had to find Xiao-nan—and now Mingxia—or he would not be able to keep his mind on anything else.

The area around the well was deserted when Duncan arrived, unnaturally quiet without the bustle of women chatting and children playing. It was like the silence that came upon you at sea just before a storm.

And the storm was not long coming. Duncan felt the sound before he heard it, rising up through the ground and into his bones—the tramping feet of a marching army, the heavy thud of horses and men coming to attack.

More terrible still was the woman's scream that pierced the

city's silence. Duncan's heart seemed to freeze at the sound, but not his feet. He was running even before the thought could form.

He ran toward the city gates that had been closed and barred against invasion. But no—one side stood open to the road. And in its frame played a scene from the mouth of Hell.

The bodies of two monks, the servants of the Dalai Lama Duncan had passed such a short time ago, lay limp and lifeless on the ground. The maroon and saffron of their robes was stained with the wet crimson of fresh blood. Duncan's eyes slid across them almost without seeing, their deaths paled by the other horror, the moving horror, that he saw.

Xiao-nan, creature of love and tenderness, sweet, gentle Xiao-nan, struggled with a man. His upraised hand gripped an odd-shaped sword; even from the distance Duncan could see the blood upon the blade. With all the strength of her slender body, Xiao-nan was holding against him. She fought him for her city, her home, for the people she loved.

She fought against—

Father Edward.

Icy fingers gripped the base of MacLeod's spine. They reached into his soul as all his half-formed suspicions coalesced.

Duncan knew the man for what he was.

He screamed Xiao-nan's name, to warn her away—*Oh God, she should not be here. She should be home where she was safe, where he could keep her safe*—just as the spy's free hand whipped out hard across her face. Xiao-nan stumbled back, but she did not let go. She struggled to keep her feet as she pulled her enemy with her.

Away from the gate . . .

Outside, off of Holy Ground. . . .

Again, Edward raised his hand and struck at Xiao-nan. Even from a distance, Duncan could see the blood on her face, pouring from the cuts to her lips—lips Duncan knew to be so gentle, so soft. Anger, hot and primitive, erupted in him. He pushed his body to its limit and beyond, but they were still so far away—too far away.

The man who was no priest looked straight at Duncan. An

odd smile twisted his face. Suddenly Duncan knew what was to come.

The cry began down in the pit of his stomach. Two hundred years of civilization fell away to the sound. The war cry of his clan, a sound as untamed as the hills that gave it birth, poured from Duncan's throat. He screamed; he roared as Father Edward raised his makeshift sword an inch higher, turned it, brought it down.

The pitch of Duncan's cry heightened; the false priest's hand hesitated, but only for a second. Not long enough. He stabbed, piercing Xiao-nan's body. Duncan felt it in his own as he lunged, throwing himself onto his enemy. But too late.

Too late.

Xiao-nan crumpled to the ground as Duncan hit, taking Father Edward with him. The Nepalese man scrambled frantically to gain his feet, but for all his fantasies he was never a match for Duncan's size and power.

Duncan could not draw his sword. He did not need, did not even want a weapon for this first blow. He needed to strike, to rend, to wound with his bare hands. Eyes nearly blinded by the red haze of rage and pain, Duncan's arm shot forward. He felt his fist connect. Facial bones smashed beneath his fingers; blood spurted across his flesh and his opponent went limp. Duncan tossed him away like a rag doll and crawled quickly to Xiao-nan's side.

She lay with one hand covering the wound of her stomach. Blood stained her long, delicate fingers. Once more, Duncan felt the pain of it in his own body, though it was his soul that bore the cut. He gently brushed the hair away from her face; her skin was growing ashen, the blush of life draining so quickly away.

Her eyelids fluttered open with his touch. Her eyes were still so serene, so full of love.

"My Duncan," she whispered through her swollen lips, now so pale—lips that only hours before had been so warm and sweet with passion.

"Xiao-nan, don't move," he said urgently. "I'll get you home. I'll get—"

She raised her other hand to his lips. He ached to feel the cold already seeping through her skin.

"Shh," she said. "I am glad of today, my Duncan. We are one now. And forever."

Her voice was growing weaker. But Duncan heard her clearly. With his heart.

"And for all the lives to come," he answered her.

A little smile moved her lips as her hand caressed his cheek. Gently, a bare flutter of a touch. Then her eyelids closed again and the hand dropped. She lay still.

A single sob filled him, rose, caught in his throat. It cut off his air; he could not breath around the pain. He felt as if his soul had shattered.

"*Duncan,*" came a scream behind him. Instinct moved him now as he whipped around. He looked up and saw Mingxia crouching, half-kneeling, in the opening of the gate. Her arms were clasped around her middle; her face was bruised, yet white with the shock of what she saw.

Duncan had not time to go to her. Father Edward was up, rushing at him with sword raised. Blood streamed from the man's broken nose, and his face twisted into a mask of hate.

Duncan should have been vulnerable kneeling beside Xiao-nan's body, no time to come to his feet. But for this he had trained, to kill by any means, and by his training he survived. Gathering his power into his legs, he waited for the moment to strike.

Two more steps; Father Edward was almost upon him. Duncan took his weight on his arms, muscles rippling as he put all his force into the kick. His legs snapped out, turning Edward's own momentum against him.

The Nepalese man flew backward. He hit the ground and rolled. Duncan stood and followed him, sword in hand.

Edward leapt to his feet, holding his homemade weapon out before him. They circled each other, measuring movement and strength. Duncan saw what weapon his opponent carried and knew it was no match for the perfection of his Japanese steel. Another man he might have let escape certain death, but not this one.

Xiao-nan, his heart cried in anguish. Duncan pushed his grief away. Not yet. He could not feel yet. He covered his pain with anger.

"Why?" he asked through gritted teeth. "Why did you kill her? She couldn't have hurt you."

"She tried to stop me. It doesn't matter—my master will soon be here, and you will all be dead."

"And so will you," Duncan growled.

Duncan attacked, his steps quick and sure. The false priest parried, but his weapon had no balance and threw his weight to the wrong side. He could not bring it back before Duncan's *katana* slashed deep into his arm. He screamed as the blood gushed, but he did not stop.

The spy lunged—Duncan spun away and brought his blade in a straight cut behind him. He felt it connect, slicing across his opponent's middle, biting deeply into flesh and viscera.

Father Edward dropped his sword. He fell to his knees, his hands clutching at the long wound of his stomach. Blood flowed out through his fingers, turning the black of his cassock crimson. He looked up at MacLeod with a surprised expression.

"You were not supposed to win," he said in wonder as the light began to fade from his eyes.

"Xiao-nan was not supposed to die," MacLeod answered, unmoved as the body fell forward, lifeless.

Xiao-nan.

Duncan was vaguely aware that the sound of the army's approach had ceased. He turned to find a single rider nearing. With him came the one feeling Duncan did not want to feel: the searing presence of another Immortal.

The rider stopped a few feet from where Duncan waited. "You have killed my tool," he said, "and he was useful to me."

"He deserved death," Duncan answered, quickly assessing the Immortal's size, his dress, his speech, the way he sat his horse. Here would be no easy victory like the one just past.

"He no doubt did," the Immortal replied somewhat dryly. "But I do not like my tools ill used by anyone but myself. I am Nasiradeen Satish, leader of the Gurkhas, and we have business together, you and I."

"I am Duncan MacLeod of the Clan MacLeod, and you've only to dismount for our—business—to begin." Duncan raised his sword to the ready.

"Come now, Duncan MacLeod of the Clan MacLeod, you know our battles are not for mortal eyes." Nasiradeen looked around then pointed to the west. "My army will camp where they are and they will obey my orders not to disturb us. Let us meet over that rise at dawn. Spend this night praying that whatever gods you serve will welcome you, for tomorrow Shiva will drink the blood of your sacrifice."

"Or yours," Duncan said, still not lowering his sword. Nasiradeen laughed as he turned his horse and rode back to his waiting men.

Duncan watched him go, not lowering his sword until the Gurkha commander had reached his men and Duncan saw them move out of attack formation. Then it was as if a fist closed around his heart. The pain of it made it almost impossible to breathe. To live.

Xiao-nan . . .
was . . .
Dead . . .
Dead . . .
Dead . . .

Chapter Twenty-nine

Mingxia was kneeling by her sister's body when Duncan turned again toward the city. Nearby, back through the gate, the bodies of the monks lay limp and twisted in death, but Duncan could spare them only pity. The world swam, swirled around him as his eyes focused on the one sight his heart wanted to deny.

Oh God, Xiao-nan . . .

Duncan's step faltered once. At the sound, Mingxia turned her tear-streaked face toward him. Duncan saw more clearly the deep bruise upon her cheek, the cut lips, and that one eye was starting to discolor. He knelt beside her.

"Tell me what happened," he said. He put an arm around her shoulders, and she sat trembling while she talked.

"I went to old Huilan's," she said, her voice thick with tears. "She needs help with her garden, and I had not been there in two weeks. But when the order came to close the gates I knew I should return home. I left almost at once. I was not far from Huilan's house when *he* came hurrying down the street—Father Edward. He laughed when he saw me. He grabbed me and kissed me. It was horrible. I tried to pull away from him, but he hit me. I screamed, and he hit me again. Then he kissed me again and began to pull me with him. I tried to get away, but he was too strong."

Her breath was coming in big gulps and trembling shook her body. Duncan tightened his arm around her.

"Shh," he said. "You're safe now. What happened next?"

"We reached the gates. The monk who was guarding came hurrying toward us. He told us to go home. Father Edward laughed. He drew his sword . . . I screamed . . . I tried to pull away, I wanted to go home. He threw me against the wall . . . I hit my head . . . I couldn't . . ."

Mingxia's voice shook with tears and shock, making it difficult to understand her words. She took a deep breath and ran a hand across her face, wincing at the pain of her own touch as she tried to collect herself enough to go on.

"The other monk was on the wall, watching for anyone who might still need to come inside," she continued. "He hurried down the ladder. Father Edward started to open the gates. The monk tried to stop him, but the sword . . . it went right through him . . . I saw it. He screamed . . . I screamed, too. I tried to get up, but my legs would not work.

"Then Xiao-nan came. She ran to him and grabbed his arm, his sword. She tried make him stop. He hit her . . . he . . . killed her. . . ."

A sob tore up from Mingxia's throat, and she turned her face into Duncan's chest. He let her cry until the worst of her tears were past. He wanted to cry, too. He wanted to rage against the heavens for the death of his love, but he could not. Not yet.

Xiao-nan . . .

Father Jacques came running toward them, hair and cassock in disarray. He stopped, his face white with shock at the vision of grief before the gates of the holy city. Duncan saw him cross himself before he took the last lasting steps toward them.

"Blessed Jesu. I heard—" he said. "What has happened here? Where is Father Edward?"

"He was no priest to be called Father," Duncan snapped. "He's dead. Over there," Duncan gave a curt gesture with his head, not caring to even look in the dead man's direction.

Father Jacques started to turn. "I must go to him. Shrive him—"

"Leave him," Duncan ordered.

"But he must be shriven, no matter what has happened. Prayers must be said for his soul."

"Leave him, I said," Duncan let his grief turn to anger. He welcomed it; it was a safer emotion for now. "He was a spy for that army out there. Let his own kind deal with his body."

"A spy?" Again Father Jacques crossed himself. "Oh, Dearest God, forgive me. This is all my fault.I should have seen, should have listened to my suspicions. But I wanted to believe . . . Oh, I should have stayed in France studying plants, not people."

"Stop it," Duncan snapped. "What *should* have been done doesn't matter. There are *living* souls that need your help now."

"Yes . . . yes, of course," Father Jacques said quickly. "What can I do?"

"Help me with Mingxia. We have to send word to the Potala about the monks—and we have to take Xiao-nan's body home."

Duncan's voice cracked on the words. *Oh God—Xiao-nan . . .* The black abyss of grief opened, threatened to pull him down. *No, not yet. He could not give in yet. . . .*

Duncan stood, bringing Mingxia up with him. Her sobs were quiet now, though silent tears still ran down her cheeks. Duncan knew there would be tears in her household for a long time to come.

He gave her over into the priest's waiting arms, letting her be comforted as he, himself, could never be. As they turned away toward the city to wait by the gate and close it when Duncan has passed through, Duncan knelt again beside Xiao-nan.

He looked at her face. Even in death she was so beautiful. His fingers trembled as one last time he touched the softness of her cheek.

"For all the lives to come," he whispered to her. He truly wanted to believe, at that moment he had to believe, they would someday be together again. Drawing a deep ragged breath, he put his arms beneath her and lifted.

How light the body felt, as if her soul had been all that weighed her to this earth, and with its departure she had become a creature of air. Duncan shifted her position in his arms. Her head fell against his shoulder where a few hours ago it had lain in love. He could not stop the tears that filled his eyes. For one too-brief moment, he let them flow, burning like hot lava down his cheeks. Then he shut them off, shut every feeling part of himself away, and turned to follow Mingxia and Father Jacques.

Duncan did not stay long with Xiao-nan's parents. Their grief threatened the numbness in which he wrapped himself. He left them in Father Jacques's care, knowing that for all his protestations, he would be better suited to comfort them.

Duncan had no comfort to give anyone—not even himself.

Xiao-nan . . .

Her presence was there in every beat of the heart he could not allow himself to feel. It was part of every breath he must force himself to take.

Xiao-nan . . .

The silent streets of the city accused him. He had not protected her, not kept her safe. She was dead.

Oh, God . . . Xiao-nan was dead. . . .

Duncan stopped and drew a deep shuddering breath. Another. He forced his thoughts away from the pain in his soul and focused on strategy, on what could be done to keep this city safe if he was defeated tomorrow.

Lhasa would only have to hold out a few days, only until the troops from the Chinese Emperor arrived. With help, he should be able to accomplish that much. For Xiao-nan's sake, he would save these people she had loved as he had not been able to save her.

Xiao-nan . . .

A slow, loud pounding echoed through the mission house as Brother Michael hurried toward the front door, the soles of his sandals slapping on the hardwood floors, the long brown robe of his habit hampering his haste. Deep inside, some half-forgotten part of him tensed; this intrusive pounding was so unlike the well-mannered tap usually heard in Lhasa.

Brother Michael reached the door and pulled it wide, interrupting the next blow of the closed fist. With a quick glance he saw MacLeod standing there, a glance that filled with horror as the monk's eyes took in the sight of the blood staining the blade in Duncan's hand, the clothes spattered and smeared with drying gore.

But that was not what make the monk tremble. It was the face—Oh, Dearest God, the face.

Duncan's face was cold—hard as iron. His eyes were burning coals of rage and pain straight from the deepest pit of Hell. Brother Michael knew that face; those eyes were burned into his memory. He had taken his vows, praying to God never to see them again.

Many years ago Brother Michael had worn that face.

He stepped from the mission house and closed the door behind him. His Brothers, gentle and young, must be spared this.

"Oh, my friend," he said, "you have been in a fight." It was a statement, an understanding offered and he saw MacLeod's relief.

"Aye," the Highlander answered, briefly closing those death-embittered eyes. "And I must face another at dawn. If I fall, can you defend the walls of Lhasa against an army?"

For a single moment Brother Michael stood still, feeling the impact of Duncan's words. It was like a hammer blow to his insides; how could he become, even for a day, the person he had turned from, he had fled. Yet if he did not, how many more deaths would his soul carry?

Wordlessly, he nodded once, accepting the role into which he was once more—*Oh, please, Sweet Jesus, let it be for the last time*—being thrust.

Stepping away from the mission house, he let his eyes rove over the parts of the city walls that he could see.

"It's meant more to keep out sheep and goats than an army," he said, raising an eyebrow in the black irony of the statement.

"Can you hold the wall?" Duncan asked again.

Brother Michael shook his head. "Myself, my Brothers, maybe Father Jacques—four men to hold three, no, five miles of wall?"

He saw MacLeod open his mouth to speak and held up a hand to stop him. Then Brother Michael rubbed his chin, the sergeant once more, and considered with a soldier's eye all that he had seen since coming to Lhasa.

"The merchants sometimes cross the borders and travel through lands thick with bandits. They do not trust to spinning prayer wheels for the safety of their goods and profits. I have seen them hide their weapons when they reach this city. They honor the Dalai Lama and the teachings of Buddha, but—"

He turned back to MacLeod. Glancing around at the few people hurrying through the streets, he continued, "I think there are others who will understand that the cost of keeping a peaceful mind will be the rape of their wives and daughters, the murder of everyone they love—their lives torn into shambles and horror. They will join us."

Brother Michael heard Duncan's sigh, saw the weariness take hold of the man. His eyes asked the question once again.

"Tomorrow morning," the monk answered him, "I will be on

the wall with every soul I can muster. The rest will be in God's hands."

Duncan nodded and turned, his footfalls leaden as he started toward the Potala.

Brother Michael reentered the mission house, preparing to call his Brothers together. His eyes fell on the crucifix hanging from the wall. Two quick steps, then he dropped to his knees. The last few minutes had reopened scars the monk bore upon his soul, and he felt them now as the wounds in the Sacred Body.

"Sweet Jesu," he whispered, "help me. I know my vows have called me to another path, but I cannot let these gentle people die. Give me strength to do what must be done."

Brother Michael bowed his head. When this was over he would have to do penance, forty hours of fasting and prayer before his Lord in the Eucharist. He would pray to cleanse his heart—and he would trust that a carpenter who had made tables and chairs from imperfect wood would not fail to forgive his imperfect servant.

Crossing himself, the monk-now-sergeant, rose. "Brother Peter, Brother Thomas, to me," he called in a booming voice he had not used in years. "We have many things to do and only a night to do them."

Duncan fought the weariness of black and heavy grief as he walked with dragging feet up the Potala steps. He should go back to Xiao-nan's house and be with her family, but he could not make himself look again so soon at her dead body.

He wanted to remember her warmth, not her death.

His grief was a private thing, and he would work it out as he always did. He would go to the silence of his room and to his *kata*. Sweat and tears would mingle as he pushed himself through the pain.

And on the other side of it, what would he find? Acceptance? Peace? No. Only his own Immortality.

He reached the great doors of the Potala and stood with his forehead pressed against them. For a moment, he did not even have the will to open them.

Xiao-nan, his heart screamed, and this time he let it have voice. The sob that rose from his throat was like the cry of a wounded beast. His knees slowly buckled beneath him. He slid to the ground and let the worst of the tears come.

Finally, long minutes later, he could breathe again. He dragged himself to his feet and once more put his hand to the great doors.

They opened silently and he stepped inside. The Dalai Lama stood waiting for him. The young man's face was an impassive mask as he looked Duncan over. His expression held neither welcome nor condemnation, but MacLeod could feel the sudden unassailable resolve about him, several lifetimes strong. In that instant, more than any other, Duncan felt an absolute certainty that all the Dalai Lama's claims of reincarnation were true and that youth was only a facade.

"Come with me, Duncan MacLeod," the Tibetan leader said in a tone as hard as forged steel. "We must talk."

Duncan bowed. The Dalai Lama turned away and began walking; with heavy steps Duncan followed. He knew what now must come.

Chapter Thirty

They went into the audience chamber where so many pleasant hours had passed in conversation. Today, however, when the Dalai Lama took seat upon his cushion, he sat it like an imperial throne. The atmosphere in the small room felt charged with the energy of his emotions.

Is it anger I'm feeling from him? Duncan wondered. *For what—trying to save his city from invasion and his people from death?*

One look in the Dalai Lama's eyes and he had his answer. There was nothing merry in them today. They did not twinkle; they stormed as they looked Duncan over, stopping at the sight of the blood on his clothes and the sword hanging at his side. Duncan waited for the storm to break.

"Have you understood nothing I have said to you, Duncan MacLeod?" the young man said. "Have my words fallen on a heart of stone, that you would bring violent death into my city?"

"I did not bring it here, Your Holiness, nor was the first death at my hands," Duncan replied.

"Do you deny that you have killed this day?"

"No, Your Holiness, I do not—but I had no choice."

The Dalai Lama's eyes flashed like lightning in a thundercloud face. "There are *always* choices, Duncan MacLeod," he said, repeating the lesson he had used before.

Duncan closed his eyes for a moment as again weariness engulfed him. For all his incarnations and the ancient wisdom that came so easily to his lips, the Dalai Lama lived in an ivory tower of dream and ideals. It was a beautiful place when those around you shared your views. When they did not, it was only a place that invited death.

Duncan opened his eyes and straightened his back, standing unrepentant and unflinching before the Tibetan leader's stare.

"Yes, there are choices," he said, lifting his chin a bit higher, "and I made mine. He *killed* Xiao-nan. I killed him."

"One death begets another."

Duncan nodded. "Yes," he said, "it often happens that way, too often. But the man I killed today was a spy for that army out there. He opened the gates to them—gates you had ordered closed. Two of your own monks are dead at his hand. Should I have stood back and done nothing while that army swept into the city? There would have been hundreds of deaths."

With this last word, the grief closed in again. It took almost all his strength to push it away. Control; he still must remain in control.

"And was this your only intention, Duncan MacLeod?" the Dalai Lama asked. "Look into your heart and tell me you felt no anger."

"Of course I was angry," Duncan snapped, nearly shouted. "I was almost blind with anger. Must I say it again? *He killed Xiao-nan.*"

"And you took pleasure in *his* death."

"Yes," Duncan answered through gritted teeth. He would not deny what he had felt, still felt. He began to pace restlessly, feeling like a trapped animal.

The Dalai Lama watched him silently, waiting for the worst of his inner storm to pass. "And what of tomorrow, Duncan MacLeod," he said at last. "I know you go to meet the leader of the army in combat. Will you kill again?"

"If I must."

"And will this death also give you pleasure, Duncan MacLeod?"

Duncan stopped pacing. He closed his eyes again, against the despair he felt welling in his soul.

"No," he said softly. "There is no pleasure—only necessity."

"Why, Duncan MacLeod? The death today might be called justice by some, but not tomorrow. I forbid you to do this."

"I must," Duncan said. He was tired, suddenly so tired his legs almost refused to hold him up. He wanted no more questions, no more half-said explanations. He was what he was. It was time the Dalai Lama knew the full truth.

"You said there are always choices, but that's not true, not for my kind," he said, turning to look at the youthful face of the Tibetan Priest-King.

"Your kind?" the Dalai Lama cocked his head to one side in his old familiar gesture. "You are a man as other men."

Duncan found he wanted to laugh a the black, sardonic humor of the Dalai Lama's words. But it was the laughter of tears and exhaustion so close a hand.

"No," he said. "Not as other men." Once more he pulled himself up straight and looked into the Dalai Lama's eyes.

"I am Duncan MacLeod of the Clan MacLeod. I was born in 1592 in the Highlands of Scotland. I am Immortal. . . ."

The Dalai Lama listened while Duncan told him of his "death" in 1622 during a battle with a neighboring clan and of his many "deaths" since then. Duncan was not sure whether it was horror or sorrow he saw on that gentle face when he told of the many true deaths that had come at the end of his sword. He held nothing back, speaking of the wars he had been in, the causes he had supported, the deaths that had brought him the satisfaction of justice and the others that had shown him only grief. The tale of his life unfolded like the lotus flower of Buddhist lore, revealing at its heart a man of honor who longed for peace but who was also a warrior; a man who accepted, sometimes with deep remorse, that he must kill to stay alive. It was both his weakness and his greatest strength.

They talked long into the night. It was better to accept death, the Dalai Lama said, than to carry the stain of killing into the next life. Duncan listened, sometimes in silence, sometimes vocal in his disagreement. He wanted to believe as the Dalai Lama did, but he could not.

Finally, they both knew there was nothing more to say. The Dalai Lama remained seated while Duncan went wearily to the door of the audience chamber. He must now get what sleep he could before the dawn. As he put his hand to the latch, the Dalai Lama spoke one last time.

"I tell you again, Duncan MacLeod," he said, "do not do this thing. Do not go to kill."

Duncan stopped and turned around. He stared at the young man who for the last weeks had been teacher, mentor, and friend, wishing there were some way to make him understand. But the differences were too great. Duncan had never felt so very alone.

"I'm sorry, Your Holiness," were in the end the only words he had left.

Duncan walked through the door, closing it softly but firmly behind him.

A half mile outside the city gates the Gurkha army made camp, spreading like a blight across the gently sloping land. Smoke from their campfires filled the air like a thousand specters, and the wind carried their voices through the silence of the night.

Nasiradeen walked among his men. Everywhere he went, the eyes that watched him shone with pride and devotion. He was their leader and their champion. Nowhere did he see the slightest doubt that he would win on the morrow.

Nasiradeen drank in his men's surety. It fed his own confidence. Why should he *not* expect to win tomorrow? The Immortal he had seen today was good, and the sword he carried was an impressive weapon, but over the centuries Nasiradeen had killed hundreds of men, mortal and Immortal. He knew his own power was formidable.

He left his men to their food, drink, and song. They were in good spirits tonight. Their campaign was nearly over; Tibet was nearly theirs. Once Lhasa fell, their claim to this country would be complete.

Nasiradeen went to stand at the top of the rise where he could see the holy city and the great palace of the Potala. In the moonlight, its whitewashed walls shimmered like silver. The light shining from the many windows made it look studded with slabs of gold. The sight of it made the hunger grow in him again.

Yes, he thought, *it is a fitting palace for a conqueror—and a King. An Immortal King.*

Then Nasiradeen frowned as he noticed the dark spot outside the gates where the body of his spy still lay unattended. The man had been a nuisance through much of his training, given to flights of fantasy his skill with a sword had never been great enough to fulfill. But he'd had other talents and had been a useful tool. He deserved to have his soul sent home to the gods.

Nasiradeen turned and called back to the camp. Immediately, half a dozen men left the nearest campfire to answer his summons.

"Build a funeral pyre," he told them when they reached his side. "Then go down to the gates and retrieve the body. Prepare it, but do not light the fire yet. Tomorrow I shall lay the body of an enemy at his feet as an offering to Shiva."

"Yes, Great One," the men said, touching their hands to their hearts. Then went quickly to do his bidding.

Nasiradeen turned back to his contemplation of Lhasa. His thoughts went to the battle the would face at dawn.

A man from the West was a new experience for Nasiradeen. *Who are you, Duncan MacLeod of the Clan MacLeod?* he wondered. *What will I gain from you when I drink your Quickening?*

And there was the Quickening itself. It had been too long since he had felt that raw power surging through him like the thunderbolts from Shiva's hand. *How long?* Nasiradeen tried to remember. *Ten years, twelve?* No matter; he had kept his skills sharp, honing them on mortal blood.

In Kathmandu, he had often spoken to the boy-King of the glories of a warrior's life, trying to convince the boy to become a man. But such glories were nothing compared to a Quickening. Riding into battle, sword tasting the blood of the foe, seeing your enemies fall at your feet, even taking a dead man's woman when the battle was won—these mortal pleasures paled when compare to what one Immortal felt when the Quickening of another entered him in the searing, savage ferocity that shook the heavens. Here was proof, Nasiradeen believed, of an Immortal's power, of their strength and superiority over the poor mortal creatures that surrounded them.

And you, Duncan MacLeod of the Clan MacLeod? he thought, staring down at the city of Lhasa. *What are these mortals to you? Have you lived long enough to see them for what they are—instruments of passing pleasure, tools to be used and discarded at leisure—or do you foolishly still count yourself among them?*

Nasiradeen hoped MacLeod's time in Tibet had not made

him soft. The Gurkha was tired of conquest without fitting battle. He had hardly unsheathed his sword since they crossed the mountains; the villages his army had destroyed had not been worth the effort.

But tomorrow, he grinned into the night, tomorrow he hoped for better things. First a Quickening—and then *Lhasa*.

Nasiradeen turned back to the camp behind him. With strong, purposeful strides, he reentered the circle of firelight and called for wine. Men scurried to serve him, returning not only with drink but with a platter of hot meat carved from one of the yaks they had taken from a village.

He squatted by a fire and his men clustered around him, eager for anything he might say. Looking at their faces, Nasiradeen knew that not even the gods held as high a place in their hearts as he.

And he accepted their devotion as the fitting tribute a mortal must pay. He grinned at them in the dancing firelight.

"Tomorrow," he said, "we dine in Lhasa."

To a man, they cheered him, their cries slicing the silence of the Tibetan night.

Chapter Thirty-one

It was a long hard night for Duncan MacLeod. The sleep he needed came only in fits, and then without rest. Xiao-nan was there every time he closed his eyes; there in memories of her smile, her laughter, her touch, of the warmth of her body beneath him, around him . . .

Of her body cold and still in death . . .

Of blood. So much blood . . .

Dreams of longing twisted into anguish and loss, into sweat-drenched wakefulness that brought no relief.

The nightmare was real. . . .

Xiao-nan was dead. . . .

Xiao-nan . . .

Finally, two hours before dawn, Duncan rose from his bed. To remain there was not only futile, it was exhausting his spirit even more than his body. If he was going to survive, he needed to clear his mind of everything but the day ahead.

He sat on his knees in the darkness of his room, legs wide, weight balanced, hands resting lightly on his thighs, and began deep focused breathing. At first he could not concentrate past the gaping hole that had once—was it only yesterday?—been filled with hope and love. But he knew he must; of all the battles he had fought, with sword and body, this one fought without movement, fought in the darkness and silence, was his most important—and the most difficult. The prize was the future and possession of his soul.

He breathed in and held it, picturing the air as a stream of light flowing down to his *tant'ien*. This was his center, the place of his *ch'i*. He exhaled, breathing out the turmoil that still coiled within him, wanting to drag him down into the deep abyss of despair.

Slowly, breath by breath, he backed away from that chasm.

True healing, he knew, was a long time away; the scar of his loss, perhaps, would never heal. But as he breathed he found the strength to face the future.

He rose from his knees and began to stretch, muscle by muscle, moving out of stiffness, releasing the tension. He went from stretching into *kata*, and there in the movements he met himself again; he found balance.

His body warmed, and Duncan knew it would be folly to push himself further. He lit one lamp and dressed, then retrieved his *katana* from the corner by the door where he had placed it to wait in readiness. As his hand closed around the hilt, feeling the familiar grooves of the intricate carvings fit themselves into the calluses of his palm, he was flooded with the surety of his life come full circle. There *were* things worth fighting for, worth killing or dying for; all a man could do was choose his causes carefully and walk the path his heart told him was right.

Dawn was now less than an hour away. Duncan still wanted to walk through the city and check that the defenses were in place. He needed to talk briefly with Brother Michael—then Nasiradeen would be waiting.

Duncan paused at the door, turned, and looked around the softly lit room. On the morning of Hideo Koto's death, the samurai warrior had composed a Haiku, a poem of gratitude for the life he had lived. After reading it to the rising sun, he had peacefully faced his death. Duncan did not know if death awaited him this day, but his own poem was carried in the beating of his heart.

We are one, Xiao-nan, it said, *now and for all the lives to come.*

Duncan walked the halls of the Potala with swift, long steps. Through many campaigns such a pace had eaten up the miles. This morning it took him quickly through the halls of the great monastery and down its steps. He did not see a single monk.

His mind was elsewhere, but his feet took him toward the main gate. He made only one detour along the way. He stopped for a moment outside Xiao-nan's home and put his hand silently on the door.

"Good-bye," he whispered to the still and lifeless body of the woman he loved, to the family he had hoped to call his own.

Then he turned away and strode toward whatever destiny lay ahead.

When he neared the city gate, torches set into the wall flickered in the darkness before dawn and in their light what Duncan saw both relieved and saddened him. Brother Peter, young and innocent, squatted among a group of Tibetan women. He was helping them tear apart firecrackers left over from the celebration and pour the gunpowder as well as nails and bits of metal into small libation jars and twist cloth into wicks. A pile of filled jars was already stacked in the center of the circle.

Duncan looked up and saw fires burning at intervals along the top of the wall, with small cauldrons set in the heart of the coals. MacLeod did not have to look to know they would contain oil that could be poured in hot, sputtering agony on anyone below. Brother Thomas stood amid a group of young men, giving instructions to those who held bows and cloth-wound arrows that could be quickly ignited by the fires beneath the cauldrons.

All along the top of the wall, men clustered as if trying to give each other courage. There were so few—maybe thirty in all—yet more than Duncan had hoped to see. Some of them held long knives, others had sharpened poles in their hands. All of them wore grim and frightened expressions. Brother Michael walked back and forth among them, offering a word here, a clasp on the shoulder there—a commander to his men.

Duncan's glance slid over the scene quickly. He knew that all that could be done was here. He started to turn away when two figures caught his eye. Mingxia and Yao-hui stood together, father's arm around his remaining daughter's shoulders. They clutched short poles like clubs, poles that might have once been table legs, things of beauty in a peaceful home. Their faces wore the same look of determination overlying grief.

Duncan started toward them when Brother Michael noticed him and descended the ladder.

"Xiao-nan's family should not be here," Duncan said as the monk neared. "They have already paid too dearly for this city's defense."

"I could not deny them the right to fight for that which Xiao-nan gave her life. Her mother sits vigil over her body. These two stand here to honor her as well. I could not turn them away."

Duncan knew Brother Michael was right. "When the fighting starts—" he said.

Brother Michael nodded, understanding. "I will try to keep them separated from it," he promised.

"Thank you."

Brother Michael paused for a long moment. "My friend," he said at last, searching Duncan's face for the sign of hope MacLeod knew was not there. "I have seen an army so dispirited by the death of its general that it tucked its tail between its legs and ran like a dog. I have seen others fight like demons to avenge a fallen leader. Is this battle you go to wise?"

"Wise or not, I must go to it."

"I feared you would say no less. Then, my friend, may God go with you."

Duncan accepted the monk's blessing with a single nod. For one more moment, the two men's eyes locked, each understanding what the other did not say. Duncan turned away. He strode toward the city gate, leaving the monk behind.

At the gate, Father Jacques waited. The priest stood alone. His head was bowed and shoulders slumped even more than usual, as if he carried a great burden. Duncan knew he blamed himself for the treachery of his false companion.

Duncan went to him and laid a hand upon his shoulder. It was all the comfort he had to give.

"Father Jacques," he said. "I have something to ask of you— a favor."

"Anything, Monsieur MacLeod."

"Xiao-nan's family—when this is all over, take care of them for me."

The priest nodded silently. MacLeod's fingers tightened briefly on his shoulder. Then Duncan dropped his hand. He turned slowly and let his eyes sweep over the city, saying goodbye to what this place had been to him, to who he had been while he lived here and to all he had hoped to be.

As he turned back toward the gate, Father Jacques called out to him. "Is there nothing more we can do for you, Mr. MacLeod?"

"Bar the gate," Duncan replied. "Pray, if you will," he added softly.

Duncan walked through the city gate. He stood until he heard the bar drop into place behind him, then he strode toward the rise to the west where Nasiradeen—and the Game—were waiting.

Over the rise and down into the hollow between the hills; the Gurkha Immortal was waiting. He was an impressive sight, standing statue-still, his hand resting lightly on the hilt of his long curved sword as the first light of dawn washed the air in gray and gold.

He was taller than Duncan had thought when he had seen him on his horse yesterday, and his long arms would give him the advantage of reach—but, Duncan hoped, not of speed or of agility. Duncan silently raised his *katana* in salute; Nasiradeen smiled and did the same. They both dropped into ready position.

"We don't have to do this," Duncan said as they began to circle each other slowly, each instinctively taking the measure of the ground and his opponent. "Leave this land in peace, and neither of us has to die."

Nasiradeen laughed. "For three centuries I have worked toward this," he said. "I'll not walk away from it now. Are you afraid of death, Duncan MacLeod of the Clan MacLeod? For that is your destiny this day—just as mine is to conquer, to rule throughout time."

Arrogance was one weakness, and if there was one, there might well be others; all Duncan had to do was find them.

"There is no *destiny*," Duncan answered. "Nothing is *written*."

Suddenly, Nasiradeen lunged. As he moved, he dropped his left shoulder, telegraphing his action. Duncan parried; he spun to the right. Nasiradeen brought his sword around in a sideways sweep, but Duncan was ready. His *katana* arched up and back, stopping the curved blade's slice. As the swords collided, Duncan kicked, catching the Gurkha in the stomach and sending him staggering backward.

But he kept his feet. He grinned again at MacLeod. "Good," he said. "Very good. A worthy battle at last."

Duncan did not answer. He kept his stance low as he watched Nasiradeen's body for any subtle signs of attack.

The left shoulder dropped again and turned slightly, allowing Duncan to prepare for the upward slice that came at him. He parried and spun. This time his sword cut deeply into the Gurkha's bicep.

He heard Nasiradeen's gasp of pain. The grin was gone now from his face. His sword swung; Duncan caught it, parried, swung his own. Metal to metal, they flashed in the growing sunlight.

The heat and power of battle swept over Duncan; necessity and training kept his arm from feeling the weariness of too little sleep and too much emotion.

The Gurkha's curved blade arched toward Duncan in a disemboweling sweep, blood-grooves on the blade whistling their deadly melody in the morning air. The uneven ground beneath Duncan's feet made balance uncertain as he dropped his stance and let the blade swing through the empty place where his body had just been.

Your hand might hold a sword, May-Ling had once said to him, *but what of the rest of your body? Learn to use all your weapons.*

Duncan rolled, crouched, whipped one leg around in the move called *iron-leg*. It knocked Nasiradeen's feet from under him. The big man went down, but he, too, rolled and was up almost as quickly as Duncan.

Again they circled each other. *Yes, this Gurkha is good,* Duncan thought as he prepared himself for the next onslaught. The blows were barely a breath of time in coming. Duncan could not stop them all. His own blood poured down his chest as Nasiradeen's blade sliced, cutting through cloth and skin.

Duncan staggered but did not fall. The wound would heal; he had not time to let the pain of it penetrate his concentration as he strove to find the weaknesses that might bring him victory— that meant his life.

There . . . he saw again the drop of the left shoulder before a slice or lunge and the slight shifting of balance before a diagonal cut. They were so subtle, so quickly covered by attack, that a few years ago Duncan would not have seen them. It was only his training in the martial arts of Japan and China that alerted him. Silently, MacLeod thanked Hideo Koto and May-Ling Shen for all they had taught him.

Duncan knew he would have to bring all their training to bear if he was to prevail.

Still the fight went on. Lunge, slice, parry cut, high, low—entries sought, barely blocked. Nasiradeen had size and strength, and though he was quick, he was a fraction slower than MacLeod. And he was too confident. That, most of all, MacLeod could exploit.

He gave a calculated stumble and watched the arrogance, the certainty of success, flash across the Gurkha's face. With it came the opening Duncan had been waiting to find. Nasiradeen's sword swung wide; Duncan spun inside and drove his elbow into the Gurkha's face. With a half turn, the razor edge of his *katana* laid open the Gurkha's arm and slid into his side.

Nasiradeen was not stopped. His sword flashed again, bit deeply into Duncan's thigh. Duncan fell, but used the fall to turn. He sent all the strength of desperation and survival through his good leg, out into his foot. The bones of Nasiradeen's knee shattered beneath his heel. The leg bent backward, and the Gurkha screamed with agony as his leg went out from under him.

Duncan rolled again and was up again in an instant, ignoring the blood and pain in his thigh. His blade whipped to Nasiradeen's neck. "If I let you live, will you take your army and go—leave this land in peace?" he asked one last time.

"No," Nasiradeen growled. "If I live, this land is mine."

"Then you leave me no choice," Duncan said.

"Shiva will welcome my soul."

"Then go to Shiva," Duncan said as his *katana* swung, sliced—and was free.

The first mist of the Quickening swirled around Duncan's feet before the body hit the ground, thick as fog on a winter night. Mist became fire, bathing his body with elemental heat. Power gathered, struck, swept through him like lightning from a cloudless sky; the lightning from Shiva's hand.

Of their own accord, Duncan's arms lifted. His *katana* pointed to the sky, balancing him, keeping him on his feet as Immortal energy surged. And in the light and thunder, the fire and mist, came Nasiradeen. All he had been flooded Duncan in an unstoppable wave of knowledge and power. Duncan saw each twist and turn that had blackened the Gurkha's soul; felt the disdain that he now knew had covered a heart too long without love.

Sorrow piled upon sorrow, loss upon loss. Duncan's own soul shattered with the pain of it and fell back in ill-fitting pieces.

Then it came to him, soft as laughter carried on the wind, gentle and cleansing as the early-spring rain. A voice, more felt than heard, whispered his name as invisible arms wrapped around him.

We are one, the voice said; beloved, it saved him.

Now and forever; he was not alone.

And for all the lives to come; Xiao-nan was with him. She would always be with him.

The lightning ended. Duncan fell, spent, to his knees. He felt the ground solid beneath him and knew the chasm had closed, the blackness had receded.

He had survived.

The body of Nasiradeen lay in a crumpled mass a few feet away, and his head was not far from his body. As Duncan waited for the effects of the Quickening to pass, for his strength to return and his wounds to complete their healing, he knew what he must do next.

Slowly he stood and crossed the distance. He bent and picked up the Gurkha's head, ignoring the expression of shock and surprise that was now Nasiradeen's death mask. Then he turned toward the Gurkha camp and the waiting army.

The massive cluster of men were waiting as Duncan crested the rise. Five hundred or a thousand strong—Duncan did not know their number, but they were an ocean of armored warriors staring at him in wide-eyed terror; they had seen the lightning that was their leader's death. Duncan smiled in a grim, unrelenting expression. He wanted their fear. It was, perhaps, Lhasa's best hope of survival.

Blood-covered, his hand wound into the hair of Nasiradeen's severed head, Duncan marched forward. He changed his face into a wild and savage snarl. He looked like a demon from the darkest depths of Hell as he neared the camp. The men nearest him struggled and stumbled into one another as they scrambled to back away.

Duncan raised his arm and swung. He let loose the head he carried and watched it arch upward, a hideous missile against the brilliant blue sky. Within the mass of men before him, an opening cleared as, pushing and shoving, they moved away from where the head must fall.

It landed with a sickening thud and lay there, sightless eyes staring upward, all arrogance gone.

Now Duncan raised his sword. He brandished it before him like a bright flame of victory.

"The way into Lhasa lies through me," he shouted. His voice sliced through the morning, sharp as any sword. "Who will fight me now?"

No one answered. Duncan waited a moment more, then he continued, "This invasion is over," he shouted. "You will trouble this land no more. Take the bodies of your dead and *GO*. I will be watching. I stand ready to do battle with anyone who defies these words."

With that, Duncan turned back toward the city. He kept his head high, his body tense and erect as he walked. He would not—could not, for the sake of the city below—let the army see his weariness. Although the battle was over for now, shock and fear would soon fade, and there was still the chance that someone among Nasiradeen's troops might find the strength to rally the army for one last attack.

Duncan knew he must be ready to fight again.

Chapter Thirty-two

Brother Michael and Father Jacques were there when he pounded on the gate. They asked him no questions, though the look in their eyes said they, too, had seen the fire of the Quickening, even if they had not understood. Together, they climbed the ladders to the top of the wall and watched.

It was not long before they saw riders from the army come retrieve their leader's body. Soon a long plume of black smoke rose from the funeral pyre. When Duncan made no move to turn away from the sight, the others stayed with him, waiting.

Throughout the city, people began to creep from their homes, looking for news. They needed either direction or reassurance. When Duncan gave them neither, would not turn from his contemplation of the distant pillar of smoke, Brother Michael descended the ladder and took over the job himself. Soon the news was spreading throughout the city that Duncan had won the challenge and was now waiting to see that the army was departing. The ordeal was not over yet, but most of the people of Lhasa faced the morning with more hope than they had known throughout the night.

Up on the wall, while Duncan watched the distance, Father Jacques watched him. The priest did not know the meaning of the wild pyrotechnics that had risen out of the little hollow where Duncan fought, nor would he try to guess. Father Jacques had long ago accepted the existence of Mysteries.

What he did know, as he looked at the man next to him, was that Duncan MacLeod had battled with demons this day, demons that had nothing to do with swords and armies.

The eternal battle, Father Jacques thought. *Good versus evil, darkness or light. We all tread the narrow precipice between them, making our way warily through this life. But I think for this man the edge is much closer, the threat of falling a much more continuous danger.*

Off in the distance came the sound of men's voices shouting indistinct orders; horses snorted and whickered, carts creaked. Father Jacques saw Duncan's shoulders stiffen. The priest could feel the tension radiating from the man as he readied himself for whatever was to come.

Father Jacques nodded silently. He saw the path this man walked, understood it clearly as he understood his own—perhaps more clearly than Duncan did himself.

Always at the forefront of the war for what is right—one foot in Heaven and one foot, perhaps, in Hell. I do not envy you the road.

The army folded as the wind swept away the smoke of its dead leader. Father Jacques did not have to watch the road to know; MacLeod's posture told him everything. As the threat diminished, tension was replaced by release, and then by weariness, as if a bowstring had been unhooked and the weapon set to rest.

"Monsieur MacLeod," Father Jacques said softly as Duncan turned away from the view and headed toward the ladder. "What will you do now?"

Duncan looked at the priest, and Father Jacques saw that he understood the question was not about the next few hours, but the years to come. There was a sad irony in his eyes as a brief, wan smile barely twitched the corners of his lips.

"Go on living," he replied as he swung himself onto the ladder and began to descend.

When Duncan reached the Potala, he did not go to his room, though his body cried out for rest. There was no rest in this place anymore. He went to the audience chamber where he knew the Dalai Lama would be waiting. He knocked once, then entered without waiting for a reply.

The young man was not sitting on his usual cushion. He stood contemplating a tapestry on the far wall. Duncan saw that his own belongings had been packed in his travel bundles and were piled at the Dalai Lama's feet.

Duncan sighed as he came into the room. The Dalai Lama did not turn, did not speak until Duncan was by his side.

"It is done then," the Dalai Lama stated flatly. "You have killed—willingly, despite my words."

"Yes, Your Holiness," Duncan replied. He would give no further explanations, no excuses; he had made his choices as clearly as Nasiradeen had made his on the hills outside the city. And all that could be said between himself and the religious leader had been said last night.

The Dalai Lama said nothing, but Duncan saw the tightening around his lips, the slight clenching of the hands behind his back. The young man continued to stare at the tapestry. Finally, Duncan also turned to look at it.

He had seen it countless times as he sat in this chamber and though its vivid colors and designs had been beautiful, they had had no meaning to him. Now Duncan saw it for what it was; the great Kalachakra Mandala. The sight of it flooded him with the memory of days in the sun and Xiao-nan by his side.

Xiao-nan . . .

Though her love was still with him, so was the grief. In an odd way he now welcomed the pain of it, but he held it as a thing apart from this scene he knew must be played. For a moment he felt like a spectator to his own life, watching a half-remembered play where lines are heard with the dichotomy of recognition and surprise.

"I have spent most of the night in this room," the Dalai Lama said at last, "thinking of your words. Many things I sought to understand about you have now become clear. I will keep your secret, as I promised you last night, but you must leave Tibet and not return. Your path does not lie among my people, Duncan MacLeod. There is no place for a life of violence in the palace of Enlightenment."

"Perhaps not," Duncan answered as he, too, stared at the tapestry, at the elemental circles of time enclosing the gardens and palace of the way to eternal peace.

"Perhaps all I can do," Duncan added softly, "is to guard the gates."

The Dalai Lama turned to look at him. In the young man's eyes, Duncan saw the disappointment and the flashing anger of a teacher who knew his words had been abandoned, and of friendship strained perhaps beyond endurance. The look did not surprise Duncan, but it did sadden him.

"You must go," the Dalai Lama said.

Duncan nodded. It had all been like a dream, living here, hoping for a different life than the one he lived. It was now time to wake up.

Duncan looked for a moment longer into the Dalai Lama's face. He knew that whatever the young man might think at this moment, his words and the memory of his friendship would stay with MacLeod for a long, long time, changing him in ways he had only begun to understand.

Duncan bowed to the religious leader. Then he picked up the bundles at his feet and turned away.

Chapter Thirty-three

Two hundred years older and, he hoped, a little wiser, Duncan MacLeod knew the Dalai Lama had been right to send him away. Part of him had known it at the time, though he had been too heartsore to realize it.

The long, overland trip back to Europe had been a dark tunnel of grief. He returned to a world on the brink of madness. The American War for Independence was over, but its repercussions were only beginning to be felt.

In England, King George III teetered on the edge of insanity while his son played at being Regent. The British Parliament was tightening its hold on its other conquered lands, particularly India, afraid of losing them as they had lost the colonies in the West. But as their grip tightened, the seeds of future insurrections were sown.

In France, the taxation had become so oppressive, the people were starving, and, with the success of the American Revolution, they saw a way to throw off their own bondage. Civil unrest had begun the slow boil that would soon lead to their own war for independence, but one that quickly disintegrated into an era of terror and blood.

The French Revolution opened the way for the Napoleonic era. Looking back, it seemed to Duncan as if the whole century had been filled with war. He had fought for the causes he found just and, in doing so, had locked the memory of his time in Tibet away into a secret corner of his heart visited only in the safety of half-remembered dreams.

The sound of the door opening banished past thoughts. It was the present he must deal with now.

Duncan turned; the fourteenth Dalai Lama, exiled ruler of Tibet, stood in the doorway. Duncan kept his face carefully neutral though once more he felt his stomach tighten. Facing the past was never easy, even when you have four hundred years experience doing so.

The Dalai Lama said nothing for a moment. His eyes remained as dark and unreadable as they had been all evening. Duncan made the first move; he bowed slightly to the Tibetan leader and waited for whatever words—whether of friendship or recrimination—were to come.

The Dalai Lama returned the gesture. He turned to the two attendant monks that stood behind him and spoke in rapid Tibetan. Duncan almost smiled to hear the language again. The monks bowed and stepped away, closing the door and leaving Duncan and the Dalai Lama alone together.

"Now, Duncan MacLeod of the Clan MacLeod," the Dalai Lama said, "we may speak freely with each other, without worry about what others might hear or say. I have kept your secret through many lifetimes, as the holy Jam-dpal Rgya-mtsho, the eighth of my line, promised so long ago. I will not break that promise now."

"Thank you, Your Holiness," Duncan said. The Dalai Lama crossed to a cushion and dropped easily into a seated position. He motioned to the place next to him, inviting Duncan to sit.

The action brought a strong wave of déjà vu for Duncan. Standing in this room, half a world and two centuries away, he was for an instant transported back to the many weeks he had spent in the holy city of Lhasa.

The current Dalai Lama was watching him, dark eyes now twinkling, and in his eyes Duncan saw none of the hurt, the anger, or the disappointment that had been in the eyes of the eighth Dalai Lama the last time they met.

"Well, Duncan MacLeod of the Clan MacLeod," the Dalai Lama said, "You are unchanged, as you said you would be. Through each of my lifetimes, the memory of you has remained clear, and I have wondered if we would ever meet again."

The Dalai Lama stopped and stared at him for a moment. Another wave of déjà vu swept through Duncan. As with his predecessor, Duncan felt in the Dalai Lama's gaze as if his soul were somehow opened and read.

"But you are also not as unchanged as your face would tell me," the Dalai Lama said, cocking his head to one side in the old familiar gesture. "It has been a difficult life you have lived. Darkness and light have both touched you, I think. Yes?"

Darkness and light, joy and sorrow, hope and despair; Duncan knew these forces shaped him now as they had two hundred years ago. Somewhere between them he walked the narrow path that was his truth.

"It has been two centuries, Your Holiness," he replied. "What man is immune to such things? If he does not know them, is he truly alive?"

The Dalai Lama nodded. "Ah, Duncan MacLeod, always did you ask such questions. It is good, this seeking for answers, but it does not make the living any easier."

"No, Your Holiness, it does not."

Duncan looked around the room at the many tapestries that lined the walls. Once more his eyes came to rest on the Great Mandala.

"Yes, Duncan MacLeod," the Dalai Lama said. "It is the same tapestry. I took it from the Potala when I fled into exile. When we looked at it last together it was an unhappy time."

That one day, yes, there had been sorrow—but before that, sunlight and joy. It was these Duncan thought of as he looked at the tapestry.

"What happened after I left Tibet?" he asked softly. There were many people he had cared about—Mingxia and her parents, Father Jacques, the Capuchin monks; he hoped they had lived good, happy lives.

The Dalai Lama shook his head. "I am sorry, Duncan MacLeod," he said. "My memories are not as yours. Some things I remember the whole of, others only pieces."

Duncan nodded a little sadly. *The Great Wheel has spun*, he thought, still not turning his eyes from the tapestry. *What is it the* Rubaiyat *says? "The Moving Finger writes; and, having writ, moves on . . ." Words from a different land and a different time, yet the same truth. I accept it, but it still would have been good to know that all had been well.*

"And you, Duncan MacLeod," the Dalai Lama said. "What have you done these many years?"

Duncan's thoughts slid quickly over the centuries. Memories of faces and places swirled before him like a vast kaleidoscope of loves and hates, successes and failures, journeys and battles and longings.

"I have gone on living," Duncan replied.

The Dalai Lama nodded once more, slowly, his gentle middle-aged face filled with compassion. "Once I would not have understood the cost of those words," he said. "But now—tell me, Duncan MacLeod, have you found peace in the path you walk?"

Duncan did not answer right away; there were no easy words for such a question. No, he admitted to himself, it was not peace he had found. It was, perhaps, something more important.

"I found myself," he said at last, hoping the man next to him would understand.

The dark eyes that met his twinkled gently in a timeless face. But these eyes possessed a knowledge of the world his predecessor's had lacked. They had seen Tibet fall to invasion and his people suffer all the atrocities Duncan had fought to prevent two hundred years earlier.

Yes—this Dalai Lama knew the meaning of the words Duncan had just uttered.

"And do you still guard the gates?" he asked softly.

Duncan smiled. "Someone still must, Your Holiness."

The Dalai Lama nodded very slowly. "And will you never find a way to put down your sword and enter the gate?"

"Perhaps in time, Your Holiness. When the Great Wheel spins again."

"And when that day comes, Duncan MacLeod, I hope that we will sit together once more in the beauty and sunlight of the Potala gardens."

The Dalai Lama's words sent a flood of warmth through Duncan. The thought of returning to Tibet, of walking again down the streets of the holy city, of sitting again in the hills among the blue orchids, brought a joy that was like the gentle caress of love and laughter. Even after two hundred years, he knew he was not alone; Xiao-nan was still with him. She lived in his soul.

For all the lives to come, they had promised. He thought about the other great loves he had known; he thought about

Tessa. Perhaps Xiao-nan had been part of each of them, as she was and would always be part of Duncan MacLeod.

He looked at the Dalai Lama and smiled. "So do I, Your Holiness," he said. "So do I."